Parker's
Island

Parker's Island

JOAN THOMPSON

ST. MARTIN'S PRESS • NEW YORK

Library of Congress Cataloging in Publication Data

Thompson, Joan, 1943–
    Parker's Island.

    I. Title
PZ4.T47Par   [PS3570.B63]   813'.5'4   78–21413
ISBN 0–312–59669–3

To Penny, who listened and cared
and to those other dear friends who
know who they are.

❧ *1* ❧

Forty feet below her perch the waves crashed against jagged rocks. From far out at sea they began in orderly swells, but arriving on shore they erupted into white frothing chaos. In the distance stark blue sky outlined the peaks and plateaus of the coast. Only the occasional shriek of a gull and the pounding surf interrupted the warm June calm.

To Gwyn Connell, wedged between two outcroppings of shale that comprised the crest of this particular cliff, the view was of her private prison. In eighteen years she had left the island fewer than a dozen times, the last time to hear the reading of her father's will. That her island in the Atlantic seemed paradise to others struck her as preposterous. Perversely she pulled at a loose thread on her skirt, knowing as she wound it around her finger that she was unraveling the entire hem of her work skirt.

"I just bet they'd love it if they had to spend one winter here," she muttered. "I'd love it too if I could be waited on all summer and then merrily pack my trunk and sail back to Boston." She spoke with the soft burr of the native islanders. There was a hint of the Gaelic and also of the French in the *r*'s which rolled out of her mouth.

Parker's Island had been settled more than one hundred and fifty years before by fishermen from the Channel Islands. These hardy souls had been joined by a small colony of Scots and a smaller group of Welshmen trying to escape the mines. By 1892, the three elements had blurred around the edges until only the old-timers could recall the three accents which had blended into the delightful sound which issued from Gwyn.

The island was situated six miles off the coast of Buckley, Massachusetts. Actually, it could be said to be off the coast of any number of north shore towns from Marblehead to Rockport, but Buckley was closest as the crow flies. Also, the town of Buckley was the port which supplied the island with goods from the mainland. Three times a week Ethan MacNeil made the round trip from Buckley to Parker's Island carrying mail, drygoods, and liquor to the hardy islanders.

One section of the island was pasture, and along the edges of this pasture were closely tended vegetable gardens which were the sustenance of the island. There were few cows; sheep were more practical on the rocky terrain; besides, the sheep gave the wool for the heavy fisherman's sweaters which were each boy's pride and joy. Not until a lad had caught his first big fish would a mother start to knit the patterns of her ancestral village into the garment which marked him as a man of the sea.

Bordering the farm and pasture area was Parkertown. This village faced due northeast while the vegetable gardens lay to the south. As a protection against the fierce Nor'easters which blew across the island like a scourge, the houses were made of stone. Since there were few decent trees on the island (one couldn't count the scrub pine and sumac as real trees) this was a necessary wisdom. The houses were tidy with swept steps and driftwood fires in the hearth. The women who swept the steps also cleaned the fish and baked the scones and found a little piece of time to knit their bright shawls in defiance of the grey stone which surrounded them.

On the southwestern coast of the island, the sunny

side, were the twelve Victorian summer houses which surrounded the Spraycliffe Inn. These houses were connected by a series of boardwalks whose boards were constantly being replaced by the custodian of the Parker's Island Society. The Society made its headquarters in the rambling inn on whose verandas the gentlefolk of Boston would sip their lemonade and watch their adolescent sons and daughters amusing themselves on the lawn with games of croquet and badminton.

From her perch on the western slope Gwyn had seen these young people walking about the island exploring the native habitat, as it were. Dressed in their summer white they resembled clusters of swans as they floated along the paths which led away from the confines of their elegant hotel.

Many of the Parkertown residents served these people. Some resented this. Others, particularly the widows, were grateful for the work. And in a fishing village there are always widows.

The sun was descending from its noonday pinnacle as Gwyn pushed herself up, leaning lightly tanned forearms against the warm shale. Reluctantly, she got to her feet and, smoothing her apron over the blue of her homespun skirt, its hem now sagging miserably, she reached for her shoes, sitting down once again in order to lace them. It was time to go to work. She disliked cleaning the rooms at the Spraycliffe—the affluent residents were surprisingly untidy—but her mother was head housekeeper at the hotel, so the chambermaid job was as inevitable as the fog that rolled in every summer evening at eight o'clock.

It was Gwyn's habit to work steadily from seven in the morning until her lunch break at one o'clock. Taking her lunch with her, she would get as far away from the hotel as time would allow and eat in solitude, gazing out beyond her limits, trying to see something new. But as was usually the case, today brought no adventure.

Once when she was fourteen, she had seen a ship-wreck. The islanders had rallied around in their boats and rescued everyone except for one small boy. Gwyn would never forget the face of that young mother, standing on the pier, wrapped in grey woolen blankets and staring straight ahead while the fisherman searched the black sea, vainly trying to recover the child. From that night on, the sea had been Gwyn's enemy, for that same night it had claimed her father's life.

A gentle man, a teacher who had married an island girl, Gareth Connell must have been touched by some kind of divine madness to stay there teaching the island children in a rundown schoolhouse. Conscientious, he was the sort of man who would go out in violent weather to search for a small drowned boy. And he had found the lifeless child, only to catch a chill and die himself within a week.

"Madness!" thought Gwyn; and yet remembering that face on the pier three years past, she was unsure.

Were it not for her mother's widowhood, she would have left the island when she turned eighteen the past April, but Gwyn knew her mother would never leave. The strong Celtic blood of Enid Connell had held firm for forty-eight years of storms and work and loss. Gwyn knew that her mother would never force her to stay, but the same compassion that had killed the father held the daughter here.

The sun was warm this day, and wildflowers were overflowing onto the path as she made her way back to the hotel. On an impulse she bent and gathered up an armful of buttercups and marguerites and carried them back to her mother. As she approached the kitchen door, she encountered a young man of about twenty years, dressed in a white seersucker suit and a diagonally striped necktie.

"Hello. Wherever did you find the flowers? I've never seen such a lovely big bunch," he said pleasantly as if they were old friends.

"Up by the West Cliffs. Likely you've not been there," she added, wondering what he was doing there in the kitchen yard. Despite the cap which he held in his hand, his nose was sunburned, and he had a pleasant look in his clear blue eyes.

"Is it all right for me to be here? I just wanted to get away from my crowd for a while. Their games get tiresome; not physically—actually they could all use more exercise—but boring, do you understand?" he asked.

"I'm not sure I do," she replied. "I haven't played games since I was a child. You must mean the croquet and cards and all that."

"That and the endless jokes and gossip. But I'm so sorry. Here I'm rattling on and you've probably got a hundred better things to do than listen to the complaints of a spoiled fellow like me," he said.

"Are you spoiled?" she asked.

"Of course! All our crowd has too much money and time and nothing useful to do."

"They should try my job, they'd not be spoiled long," she answered smiling. She liked his frankness and was glad that he knew he was spoiled. Turning away, she opened the large kitchen door. He took its weight from her so that she could carry the flowers inside, and said, "May I ask your name?"

"It's Gwyn Connell," she replied and, fearing she had been too familiar with a guest, she stepped quickly into the kitchen, hearing "Mine's Tom Warner" as she shut the door.

"Who was that you were talking to?" asked Enid Connell. A slender woman, aproned and dressed in blue with a mobcap on her chestnut curls, she smiled when she saw the flowers.

"One of the guests, a young man. He was just passing the time," answered Gwyn.

"Well, I wouldn't encourage that sort of thing. It's the

best way I know for both of us to lose our jobs. These
flowers are lovely. I'll arrange them for the dining room.
What a pity that wildflowers don't last longer.

"Oh, you'd better do room twenty right away. Would
you believe that that woman just got out of bed and here
it is two o'clock? I'm glad we don't work evenings. Mrs.
Cole tells me they're up 'til all hours playing cards and
dancing. Sometimes even on Sundays!" Briskly she set to
work arranging the tangled mass of flowers.

How Gwyn loved this woman, so strong and cheerful
despite her cares! She seemed to be content. The job was
good by island standards, and Enid had many friends. Having a schoolmaster husband had given her a special status
among the islanders who, though poor, were not unap-
preciative of education. Her evenings were cheery enough,
with a good fire in the hearth and books sent over from the
mainland. And, her earlier disapproval notwithstanding,
Enid was not above a good game of cards herself. Add to
her creature comforts the companionship of a handsome
daughter and the occasional celebration, and her life could
be worse.

Gwyn climbed the stairs to room twenty. A lovely
dress lay in a heap on the floor, and messy pots of rouge and
lip color were scattered about. The disarray offended
Gwyn's orderly spirit, and she set to work with a ven-
geance. When she was through, she looked about, satisfied,
and then took one frivolous peek at herself in the long oval
mirror.

With a scarf tied around her black hair and a dirt
smudge on her cheek she was hardly the picture of ele-
gance, but her skin was flawless. Only the ocean mist can
produce a complexion like Gwyn Connell's. A tan had
darkened her; by summer's end she would be a gypsy, but
she was glowing, partly from the sweat of her own labor.
Her eyes were a strange color that changed hue much as

did the sea. On cloudy days they seemed grey, but under a clear sky they shone cornflower blue.

Sighing at her vanity, she picked up her dustmop and went downstairs, passing a lively group of young people in the lower hall. She scanned them for signs of Tom Warner, but he was not there. Returning through the long back corridor to the kitchen, she sat on a high stool to help her mother prepare the menus for the next week. Each Saturday they did this job together, describing dishes until their hunger drove them to hurry up and finish the job in order to rush home to supper and let the night crew worry about the guests for a while.

"How about asparagus and ham for tomorrow?" asked Enid.

"Yes and maybe blueberry pies for dessert?"

"All right, that's Sunday night," said Enid.

"And what about fish for Monday?" continued Gwyn.

"Fine, but don't forget that Ethan is bringing in lobsters for the bake on Wednesday, so we'll have to serve meat or chicken on Tuesday. Sometimes I wonder what would become of us all without Ethan. He asked for you yesterday when he was here; you've always been his favorite."

"I know."

"He's been a good friend to us, especially since your father passed on. You know, he hasn't changed much over the years; he still has that mischievous look he had when he was a boy. Do you know what he did to old Mrs. Beauville after church last week? Pinched her! Right you know where, and not ten steps from the chapel. She told me about it yesterday, but I could tell she liked it!" laughed Enid.

"Well, I imagine it's quite a compliment to be pinched when you're seventy-four," said Gwyn laughing.

"Seventy-five, and you'd best not forget it! She's very proud of her age."

Dusk fell and the two tired women went home for a

simple supper of chowder and shortcake. Tomorrow was
Sunday, their one free day, so they stayed awake reading
a bit late just on principle and at last went to bed, each
thinking her own thoughts.

❧ *2* ❧

In her narrow bed Gwyn fell to wondering. She had
always done a lot of wondering; and supposing. Suppose
someone left us a thousand dollars (her desires were moder-
ate, a million would have seemed presumptuous)? Suppose
Mamma married one of those white-suited rich men? Or,
better yet, suppose *she* did! Suppose just once something
different would happen, something wonderful to spin our
lives around like a top? Or, dread thought, suppose nothing
ever changes, suppose I spend my entire life stuck here on
this pile of rocks, turning grey as shale until my life just
flakes away and turns to sand.

At eighteen, she little realized that no change at all
would be the most extraordinary of her supposings.

Into her dreams that night intruded the fair face of one
Tom Warner. At first his image merely danced around the
edges of her sleep-alert mind, but soon the wildflowers of
the afternoon, even her mother's face, became a hazy frame
for the central focus of his blue eyes. So little had she to
stimulate her imagination that where she had fallen asleep
with a passing interest, she awoke at dawn with a full-
blown passion which lasted straight through Sunday.

Monday mornings, however, were no time for romantic fancies; there was hard work to do. And so she carried her dream hangover buzzing around inside her like a hive of sleepy bees waiting for the sun. She made her way from room to room, trying not to flinch at the feel of some stranger's sleep-damp sheets.

At noon she ate a hasty lunch with her mother and ran to her cliffs. Assuming her customary pose, she settled in for a few hours of unanswered anticipations. But she was too restless to sit idle, and so she began to weave a daisy chain. She became so engrossed in her charming task that she didn't see the party of five who were making their way onto her private cliff.

"Hello, Miss Connell," called Tom Warner in the friendliest possible fashion.

"Hello," she replied. She did not use his name for fear that he would attach too great an importance to her having remembered it. Behind him, three fashionable young women were whispering and glancing in her direction with an interest which Gwyn found unpleasant.

The other young man stepped up and Tom introduced the group calling out the names, "Susan, Mabel and Olive," as he gestured toward the girls and then saying "Ralph" as his friend tipped his boater. Tom looked as if he would have liked to pass a few minutes talking, but the girls hurried on scarcely acknowledging the introduction, and with a shrug and a wave he went on past until the group was again tightly knit as they disappeared over the incline.

Gwyn felt snubbed, but instantly recognized that Tom owed her nothing, not even a moment's conversation. After all, it was hardly his fault that she had dreamed about him last night. Who knows? While she was dreaming of Tom he might have been dreaming about one of the fair threesome, perhaps the redhead.

Standing up to stretch, Gwyn looked down at her shabby brown shoes. There was a salt line across each toe from where she often stood on the beach. Her dress was dark brown, perfectly suitable for a chambermaid, but she thought longingly of the billowing white skirts which had passed her by as if she were some drab marine creature and they the sails of three ships.

Something was coming to a boil inside her. She clenched a brown fist and shook it against the unfairness of it all. Her books had lied with their happy endings. Life wasn't like that at all. You were assigned your rung on the ladder, and you dared to climb only at the risk of having your hand stepped on by a prettily shod foot above you. Even as she railed against her lot she knew she was being unfair. After all, the three creatures who had ignored her were caught in their own rut. Even Tom had said that he found them tiresome. Small consolation. Their being tiresome didn't seem to prevent him from escorting them around the island. She hoped he wouldn't take them to Parkertown. Parkertown was her own, and she hated the thought of the condescending looks her home would inspire. Throwing aside her dark thoughts she placed the daisy chain around her neck. Rising, she whirled around in the sunshine until her brown skirt puffed up with an air petticoat and ballooned around her.

"Charming!" came a voice from behind her.

Dazed by embarrassment and the twirling, she had to shake her head to bring the face of Tom Warner into focus. "I thought I was alone," she said, stung into anger by her discomfort.

"Obviously. And do you often dance when you are alone?"

"No, well, sometimes. Actually it's none of your business." Her burr thickened as she forgot to ape the pretty Boston speech she heard in the hotel.

"You're quite right, Miss Connell, or may I call you 'Gwyn?' It's absolutely none of my business, and I was wrong to come up on you like that, but you must admit that

I could hardly be expected to know you were dancing around like a wood fairy."

"A wood fairy, indeed!" said Gwyn, smiling despite herself. "Mr. Warner, you may as well learn that pretty words don't catch many fish on this island."

"And what fish do you think I'd be trying to catch? One with daisies around it's neck?" he grinned, enjoying her outspokenness.

"Why are you here?" she asked, changing the subject.

"I wanted to apologize for the girls. They don't realize sometimes that they are being rude. I didn't want you to take it personally. You see, no one exists for them outside of their set. Everyone else is just there, like a table or chair. They feel no compunction to deal with them at all. It's quite pitiful, if you think about it, and I hope you won't hate us all for it."

"Mr. Warner, what those girls think or don't think is of no concern to me. Now if you'll excuse me, I have to get back to work." She took a strong stride away from him, but he matched it and walked back beside her.

"Would you mind awfully if I came up some day to have lunch with you?"

"I'm sure it's your parents who would mind awfully, Mr. Warner," replied Gwyn.

"Nonsense! I'm twenty-one, and besides, my parents aren't even here. They're in France. I came with my uncle this year, and all he cares about are his cards and his brandy."

"Why didn't you go to France with your parents? I'd never miss a chance like that!" asked Gwyn.

"They won't be back until October. I finished school this spring and have to go to work in September. Besides, I've been to France with my parents before. They're hardly fun company, bless their hearts."

"Where will you work? I didn't know that people like you had to go to work."

"But of course they do. You don't think all that money just goes on multiplying by itself, do you? Actually it does sometimes, but we spoiled fellows have to make some pretense of industry. I shall work in a bank. That will keep me surrounded by lovely money, so that I won't feel suddenly deprived of my natural fodder." He looked seriously into the blue eyes that warily turned up to him.

"You are teasing me, of course," she said, but his words disturbed her nonetheless. She had caught the note of self-mockery in his tone and wondered if he made fun of himself for her benefit or whether, perhaps, he had a surprisingly low opinion of himself. Gwyn did not approve of having a low opinion of oneself. Despite her occasional lapses into self-pity, she never despised herself. Deep inside, she had always felt as good as anyone else. It was only when they failed to notice this fact that the confusion started. This fellow, however, seemed to value her opinions. Perhaps he was a worthwhile dream after all.

Tom Warner left her by the kitchen yard, and it was not until he disappeared that she realized that nothing had been settled about their lunch together. That meant she would have to fix herself up every day just in case he came, and then he probably wouldn't. That night she repaired the hem on her blue skirt and started to embroider some daisies on another.

Monday evenings were generally dull. In fact, all evenings were dull except when someone unexpectedly dropped in or when the two women made a special effort to do something unusual. This particular Monday evening was settling in to be of the ordinary variety, but around nine o'clock there was a sharp rat-a-tat on the heavy door and soon Ethan MacNeil was sitting in front of the fire with a handsome woman on each side of him.

"It's good to see you, Ethan. We weren't expecting you 'til Wednesday," said Enid, picking up the knitting she had put down when she answered the door.

"There was a big package from Boston for the Crandall girl. She's been botherin' me about it for a week. Told me it was a new dress she was needing for some tea they're havin' tomorrow. Thought I'd best get it here; looks like weather tomorrow."

"Now don't you let those creatures be pushing you around. Why if they knew you were a property owner yourself, they'd never dare impose on you like that! How's the business going on anyhow?" asked Enid, happy to be sitting here, warm, with her old school chum.

She had launched Ethan off on his favorite topic, and the two women sat back to hear about the progress of his business enterprises.

Ethan MacNeil was fifty years old, and although he would never admit it, he was damned unhappy about it. Sitting on the old rocking chair he looked the very picture of an old salt, but he had the business sense for better things. When he had reached fifty he had realized with a jolt that he had left a good deal undone. No wife, no children, no responsibilities; he had avoided all the usual traps of civilization. But now he wanted it all. It was too late for the wife and children, but he had put down the foundations of a healthy mercantile business in Buckley and was fast cornering the market on the fancy Boston goods which the formerly simple-tasted women of Buckley were beginning to crave.

He stretched out a booted foot and scratched the still-sandy beard. He liked coming here to see Enid and Gwyn. There was a time when he had considered asking Enid to marry him. Two times, in fact; but he had missed both chances. Once was when he was twenty and Enid was eighteen. But there had been things he wanted to do, like traveling and visiting ports on the other side of the world, so he had delayed asking her, and when he came home after a year's run on a Merchant ship, she was married to that schoolmaster. The second chance was when Enid became a widow, but he had lost his enthusiasm by then. She had become too much the old friend to start all over thinking of her as a wife.

Besides, now there was Gwyn. There was a fetching creature for you! All good sense and bright eyes but with a strong taste for adventure that reminded him of himself. He had told her stories about Shanghai and the islands of the Far East since she was old enough to listen. Ethan was no fool, however, and could see plainly enough that Gwyn was grown up now. The very thought of setting her on his knee was disconcerting.

"Business is good," he stated. "I bought a couple parcels of land down near the end of Main Street. It's too far away to be a good location now, but I figure the way Buckley is growing, it'll be prime real estate in a few years. And would you believe it? They've asked me to run for the planning board next term. Told 'em they must be kidding, but they said, no, they meant it! Can you see this plain old fella sitting there with all those muckety mucks?"

"I can," said Gwyn. "I think you'd be perfect for the job. Why you're as sensible and wise a fellow as I know!"

"And how many would that be, lass?" asked Ethan with a twinkle in his eye.

"Oh, oh! Best not be teasing her Ethan. It happens I saw her with a good-looking young man just this afternoon!" said Enid.

"Mother! You never let on that you saw us," said Gwyn, blushing in the firelight.

"It's not my place to tell everything I know. You just be careful, that's all. I've seen those summer boys before. They sometimes get the idea that everything on the island is put here for their pleasure." She spoke easily enough, but she meant it just the same.

"Your mother's right, Gwyn," said Ethan, staring right at her, his usually merry eyes quite sober. "They're an odd lot. That Olive Crandall I was telling you about, the one with the package? Well, she's as tightly strung an instrument as I ever saw. Flies off the handle about any little thing. Pretty girl too, but spoiled rotten! They're all spoiled rotten, if you ask me. They just grab anything they want. If it was just for the summer folk, I'd have stopped making this run years ago! You know I just do it for the folks in Parkertown."

"Yes, I do, and we were saying just the other day that we don't know what the island would do without you," said Enid.

Ethan was always pleased to be appreciated. To hide his pleasure he rose to his full height and began to stir up the fire. He was a big man—over six feet—but not soft. He was broad-waisted with the trace of a belly—Ethan liked his ale—but he smelled of the sea and good tobacco, and in the dark of the cottage his presence filled the room with safety and warmth.

The threesome sat quietly for another hour, and then Ethan reluctantly rose and went back to sleep at his father's cottage. His parents had died many years before, but he kept the place as a home on the island. Trudging along in the moonlight he thought about Gwyn. He hoped she wasn't encouraging one of the summer boys. Ethan had been around long enough to know that those rich boys from Boston could ruin a girl like Gwyn without a twinge of conscience. He was angry at the nameless boy already. But what was Gwyn to do? He supposed it was a lonely life for a pretty girl. He'd keep a watch, just the same.

His cottage was less than three hundred feet from the Connells', but he prolonged his walk by slowing his lumbering steps. About twenty feet from his front door was the cliff. He stopped tonight and sat down in a concave spot which had been worn smooth by countless others. The night was cool, and occasionally the sea below would send a spray heavenward, misting his beard with tiny drops which glistened in the moonlight. Cupping his hand against the breeze, Ethan lighted his pipe. He loved his island but was honest enough to admit that the mainland controlled most of his thoughts nowadays. Still, it was nice to have a refuge to come home to, a safe haven in which to stretch out his work-wracked body. He had noticed that his mind played strange tricks on him here, took flights of fancy which would have been unthinkable in staid Buckley. Tonight, for example, the way the light from the fireplace had played on Gwyn's hair until she seemed like some Celtic princess, serene in her fiery element. For a moment he had felt cast back into the realm of his ancestors.

Yanking down the rolled-over tim of his woolen cap, he pulled hard on his pipe, feeling the smoke blown behind him by the sea air. It was past midnight when he went inside. He would be up at dawn to make a run to Salem, but Ethan had never needed much sleep. The long hours aboard his boat were rest enough.

❧3❧

At one o'clock the next day Gwyn waited on her flowery hill. She had packed a large lunch just in case. She was beginning to feel the first twinges of disappointment when Tom Warner plopped down beside her. He had come so silently that even her expectant ears had missed his arrival. And she would never have risked turning around to look for him. He must not think it mattered whether or not he came.

He turned to her and smiled. She was elated to see him, but cautious. In his hand was a leather-bound volume.

"What are you reading?" she asked.

"Hawthorne. I've always meant to read the *House of the Seven Gables* but never got around to it. It seemed blasphemous to be so near to Salem and never have read it."

"It's a good book but I've always preferred *The Scarlet Letter,*" said Gwyn, comfortable now that she was launched into her favorite topic.

"You don't say!" Why I thought young girls were not allowed to read *The Scarlet Letter,*" said Tom.

"My father was a schoolmaster. He believed that a child should read anything she wants," said Gwyn. "Do you honestly mean that Boston girls aren't allowed to read Hawthorne?" She was never sure when he was teasing.

"Oh they're allowed to read Hawthorne. But never *The Scarlet Letter!*" His teeth were white in the sunshine.

"And I suppose they've never heard of adultery either," said Gwyn, rather disapprovingly.

"You sound as if adultery should be taught in every school." He laughed softly, perhaps a bit surprised by the path this conversation was taking.

"Of course not. But you must admit it happens. It's always seemed stupid to me to deny what exists. It doesn't mean you have to approve of it."

"In Boston it is very easy to pretend that unpleasant things don't exist. Why my own parents are masters of the art. Do you know that my aunt ran away with a French count, leaving three children behind, and after twenty years my mother still says that Auntie is visiting friends abroad? She believes it too. Never mind that Uncle George has been remarried for ten years, Mother still expects Aunt Alice to reappear as if nothing had ever happened."

"How ridiculous! Oh, I'm sorry, I shouldn't say that about your mother." Gwyn colored to a lovely pink and looked away.

"Don't apologize. It is ridiculous, but she can't bear to think of Alice living in sin, so she has made up her own truth. Mother's a sweet duck. Actually, I adore her. We tease her about her ability to deny the obvious, but she doesn't mind a bit. I think she's rather proud of being able to create a whole new world for people when they don't behave. Rather creative of her if you think about it!"

"All very well unless she tries to create a make-believe life for you," said Gwyn, fascinated.

"But she has! Why ever since I was small, all I've ever really wanted to do is paint. I went persistently from pencil drawings straight through charcoal and watercolors to oils, and the only comment I ever got was 'Very sweet, dear.' She has been determined that I would be a banker ever since she saw me with some play money when I was three. The strange thing is that she's half-right. Money does interest me, there's a definite magic to it. So she was correct about that. You see, she's often half-right. She selects what she wants to see and tosses out the rest."

"Do you still paint?" asked Gwyn. She liked creative people.

"Sometimes. I've done a few decent things since I've been here."

"Would you let me see them sometime?" asked Gwyn.

"If you like." He stood up and peered over the cliff. "Let's go down there. I can see a little hollow that looks just right for a picnic." He picked up a small parcel which lay on the grass beside him and took her hand. His grip was firm, and she noticed the fine blond hairs which covered the back of his hand. She blushed slightly but he didn't notice, as he was carefully picking his way halfway down the cliff. She sat down in the hollow, and he sat very close to her—closer than necessary, if the truth be told. She could feel the gentle pressure of his leg and shoulder as he moved to pull his lunch from its wrappings. He had also brought enough lunch for both of them, and the two suddenly laughed at the array of fruit, sandwiches and sweets they saw on their laps. It was a curiously intimate moment, revealing as it did that they had been thinking of each other during the morning.

She found him an amusing luncheon companion and laughed heartily at his descriptions of the goings-on at the hotel. She told him of the same goings-on from the servants' side, and he enjoyed the fresh point of view.

"Look! There's Ethan!" she cried, as the familiar boat passed them. She waved but, getting no response, assumed that Ethan hadn't seen her. She described him to Tom, who seemed relieved to learn that Ethan was a middle-aged man.

After lunch she rested her head on the rock and closed her eyes. She felt an arm around her shoulders but didn't resist; it all seemed too peaceful and innocent. Suddenly she remembered the time. "Heavens! I've got to go back," she cried.

"Must you?" He sounded unhappy.

"Yes. I must."

"May I come again?" he asked. His eyes were the light blue of sailors' eyes, and the square jaw was firmly set.

"Yes, but now I really must run." She scampered up over the cliff, not seeing the smiling eyes which glanced over her trim ankles with obvious appreciation.

She was late getting back to the hotel. Her mother gave her an appraising look but kept silent.

She thought about him that evening, long and hard. She thought about his yellow hair and the blue of his eyes. Especially she thought about the feel of his arm around her shoulder. She thought about his obvious love of literature and his ability to make her laugh. She did not think about his station in life or about the mother who hated unpleasant truths.

Considering that most of this thinking was done while she readied the plates for the lobster bake, it was astonishing that only one butter dish was broken. Picking up the pieces, she cut her finger and thrust it into her mouth.

"You look just the way you did when you were four, standing there with a finger in your mouth!" said Ethan, coming onto the wide veranda with a stack of folding chairs under each brawny arm.

"I cut myself. No, please it's nothing!" she said as Ethan deposited the chairs and carefully examined the wound.

"You're right, it's just a scratch." He sat down on the veranda steps and looked across the lawn to where the keepers were busily hanging Japanese lanterns from tree to post along the boardwalk. "Sure as hell better not rain tomorrow!" he said. "Those hothouse flowers don't seem as if they'd take to eating lobsters in the rain. Bad enough that they won't go down on the beach. Who ever heard of a lobster bake on a front porch anyway?"

"Ah but don't forget that I'd end up lugging these great masses of food all the way down to the beach if they decided to be authentic!" said Gwyn. She sat down beside him and sighed with fatigue.

"Do they work you hard?" asked Ethan. His face was furrowed with concern as he examined Gwyn's face for signs of strain.

"No, not really. But it gets so monotonous here. Sometimes I wake up in the morning as tired as when I went to bed." She rested her chin on her fists.

"Your ma ought to've left this island soon as your father passed on. I told her the longer she stuck around, the harder it'd be." He scowled. "But there's no reason you couldn't leave. I'll bet I could fix you up with a respectable position in Buckley. Why there's two or three new ladies' shops just opened this year. They must need help."

"Oh Ethan! What do I know about ladies' clothes? I only own but one good dress, and that's five years out of fashion."

"But you've got style, a way of carrying yourself that's

very high class. Why there's dozens of highfalutin' ladies in
Buckley who'd consider themselves damned lucky to have
half your good looks."

"Do you really think so?" she asked.

"What do you mean, do I really think so? I've been
tellin' you so for eighteen years, haven't I?"

Gwyn colored faintly and fell silent. The Japanese
lanterns were being tested one by one and flickered in the
advancing night like fireflies on the lawn.

"Do you know? I think maybe I will pack up and leave
this place. Would you bring me back and forth to see Ma
if I moved to Buckley?" asked Gwyn.

" 'Course I would. Your mother could come and see
you whenever she likes once the season's over. It'd do her
as much good as you!"

"Naturally, I couldn't leave until fall, but that's all
right. It'd give me time to get ready, prepare myself," said
Gwyn, excitement rising in her voice.

"That's my girl! I'll talk to your mother myself, make
sure she knows you'll be looked after." He rose and
stretched out his burly arms. "C'mon, I'll help you finish
up here and walk you home."

The two worked fast, and before another half hour had
passed, they were on their way to Enid's cottage. They
were silent, but their silence was one of ease and familiarity. When they came within the limits of Parkertown,
Gwyn looked across the water at the lights of Buckley.
They looked to her like the welcoming beacon from some
enchanted land.

Turning his head slightly, Ethan observed Gwyn's
delicate profile as she stood motionless. The breeze had
blown her hair away from her face; and her brow, usually
partially covered by the shining black of her hair, shone
translucent white in the demilight. Her lashes were a jet
fringe and the blue of her eyes was transparent, giving her
a mystical beauty. The nose was small but strong, with

sharply defined nostrils. Her lips were reddened by the sea air and were now slightly parted, so lost was she in her reverie.

"Come along, lass, your mother will be waiting up."

"What?" said Gwyn, startled to remember that she was not alone. "Oh yes. We'd best get along."

Where had she been, just now? wondered Ethan. In Buckley, no doubt, dressed in a pretty dress. He'd see she had some decent clothes before she left the island. It was a crime to see her weighed down by the drab colors of a working maid. He'd see her fixed up all right, maybe even get her a silk petticoat, if Enid didn't object. And a bonnet. One of those little nothings that women seemed to fancy, a clump of feathers that sat on the hair. She'd have to put up her hair if she lived in Buckley.

Now it was Gwyn's turn to wonder what it was that had brought that half-smile to Ethan's face.

"Penny for your thoughts," said Gwyn.

"I fear my thoughts will cost a bit more than a penny." He chuckled at his private joke, and Gwyn was left to wonder why. They reached the cottage and he bade her goodnight.

⚜4⚜

The lobster bake was a huge success, but watching the goings-on from her respectable distance, Gwyn fought down a bilious anger that rose and fell somewhere in her chest. Although she was mature enough to despise a life of perpetual leisure, she still envied the young people their proximity to Tom.

She and Tom had agreed to separate their pleasure from her business. To his credit, he was embarrassed by this necessity, but Gwyn could not afford to lose her job and told him so. And now she had another reason for tending to business.

She had not had the opportunity to tell Tom about her anticipated move to the mainland. The more she thought about it, the more she thought that perhaps she would not tell him at all. After all, she had few enough secrets and she was vain enough to desire an air of mystery.

She moved swiftly down to the lawn, pulling a trash cart behind her. Every few steps she would stoop and pick up an empty lobster claw or a discarded red corpse.

"I suppose the girls here have never had the pleasure of inhaling the putrid stink of yesterday's lobster shells!" she thought. Why even one shell left behind was enough to poison the air around it for days.

Giving the lawn tables a wide-enough berth, she continued cleaning up. Several of the young ladies were standing under parasols, resting a while before the dancing began. In the center of the lawn a large dancing platform had been set up, and on the veranda above the platform a small dance band were readying their instruments.

Now finger bowls were offered on the table which covered a large section of the veranda. The men gathered round this table while the more fastidious ladies retired to their rooms to freshen up.

As for Gwyn, she made one last tour of the lawn, then handed her cart over to a groundsman and dashed to the kitchen. Smiling at her mother, she rolled up her sleeves over the old stone sink and began to scrub away at her wrists and hands with a fury.

"Not so roughly, dear, you'll ruin your hands," said Enid.

"My hands are about as ruined as they can get now; one more scrubbing won't matter. She gazed out the window above the sink and resolved to make herself some good hand lotion. Rich ladies might not care to have their silks snagged by rough-handed shopgirls.

The dancing continued far into the evening, but for Gwyn the party had been over the minute the last shell had been gathered up for dumping far out at sea. Resolutely she turned her back on the mirth makers, even on Tom; she would not permit herself to be covetous.

Gwyn had seen envy firsthand. There were women who had resented her mother for being married to the schoolmaster. "Why couldn't she have picked one of her own; no, she must have someone from the mainland, someone finer than us!" they mocked. And the daughters of these women, Gwyn's generation, were waiting for a flaw in the schoolteacher's daughter. Perhaps she would be uppity or (how delicious) stupid! Alas, no such luck! Gwyn was neither uppity nor stupid, and she was pretty besides. In the face of Gwyn's good nature the envy softened until it became a thin pocket, unopened, even forgotten, but lying there, flat against the hip in case of emergencies. Gwyn enjoyed her friends, many of whom were married now, but her awareness of the way envy twisted a face, and even more so the mind, made her shun it.

Gwyn was generally sensible notwithstanding her fantasies and dreams, for even these had the underpinnings of hope and hope is never entirely unreasonable. She thought about herself often during the next few days. Tom, a new job, a change in her life, became separate items, as if she were a paper doll and they the new paper fashions to be taken on and off to see how they became her.

And she was a more becoming Gwyn dressed in her new aspirations. When she met Tom for lunch he noticed immediately that she had assumed a new confidence. Once or even twice he was able to fix her gaze with his own, a formerly impossible task.

"I've never seen eyes your color before," he said.

"They're just blue!" she replied.

"But such a blue! They run the entire spectrum in their highlights. Do you know I have all shades of blue in my paint box, cerulean, azur, cobalt, ultramarine; but not one comes close at all. When I paint you, those eyes will be the most difficult part. You will let me paint you, won't you?" He seemed to be sincere, so she answered honestly.

"I don't know if I want you to. Once when I was ten or eleven Daddy took me to Salem to some museum there. They had a lot of old portraits. You know, the kind that people used to have done for their families, where the heads are all the same shape and the eyes are always staring straight ahead. There they all were in a museum, perhaps hanging across from someone they knew and hated in real life. Sometimes I believe the old Indian superstition was right, and a bit of your soul goes out into the painting and lives apart from you from then on.

"I imagine that some of those people were delighted to be hanging in a museum with everybody looking at them, but I'm also sure that others were miserable and embarrassed. I could hardly look at some of them, because I could see that they were private people. They made me feel guilty, as if I had broken into their bedrooms after their deaths. Can you understand?" she asked.

"I understand that some of those artists must have been pretty damned good to make you see all that in those faces."

"There you go, seeing it from the artist's point of view. I'm talking about the people."

"Well, they must have wanted the portraits done in the first place," said Tom, relaxed and smiling.

"Why that's not true at all. You know some husbands

can get their wives to do anything," said Gwyn.

"And vice versa. But don't forget that they had an effect on you and that's the very purpose of art, to stir you emotionally. Looking at it in that light, it doesn't really matter if they were willing subjects or not," said Tom.

"That's sounds cruel, although I'm sure you don't mean it to."

"But of course it's cruel!" said Tom. "In art the end result it supposed to transcend the human circumstance which brought artist and model together. Many of the great works of art were done for sheer financial gain. Money. Perhaps that's one of the reasons I find money so fascinating. It can create beauty and great literature as well as greed and snobbism."

They had so much to talk about. His conversation stimulated her like mugs of Ethan's ale. She felt her cheeks grow rosy and her eyes bright as they debated or agreed on art, music, government, all the topics her island friends found dull or more likely incomprehensible. There can be no greater joy than to find a new friend of similar intellectual abilities. To start a sentence and see the immediate gleam of comprehension in another eye. To share a sidelong look when someone passes by and to know that one other person is thinking precisely your thought.

This day, the day of the great discussion of art (to Gwyn they were all great discussions) was cloudy. Gwyn had a shawl around her shoulders but despite it she began to shiver as the sun went behind a cloud.

"Here, take my jacket!" said Tom.

"But then you'll be cold," said Gwyn.

"Then we must bundle up." Tom slid over next to her and put his arm around, rubbing it up and down her arm to warm her.

"That's nice," said Gwyn, and again she turned her eyes to meet his.

Naturally, he kissed her. Then he hugged her very

tightly and for a long time. When he released her she knew that they had reached a new point, past friendship. After a few more minutes they held hands and walked up the cliff to the special place out of sight of the hotel where they had agreed to part after their lunches.

After that day, Gwyn never again wondered whether Tom would be there for lunch. He always came and with each successive lunch they became dearer and dearer friends until the kisses became a regular part of their meetings and his scent became as homey and familiar as that of the sea. He was frail in ways which cried out to her and she brought him a freshness he found irresistible after the confines of his childhood.

It was their very innocence that eventually betrayed them. Their love when it finally threw off its disguise and showed itself, was the love of sweetest youth, the kind of love that sees nothing but purity and desire. Who knows what finally carried them into something more dangerous? Perhaps it was the damp golden curls on his neck, after he had sat discoursing on the rocks or the fierce bloom of her cheeks after his kisses. Maybe it was the way that, standing, she was just up to his nose, so that she had merely to tilt up her chin to capture his lips.

Even the trembling of his hand as he lowered her dress to caress her skin was reassuring to Gwyn, she so desperately wanted him to want her!

The first time they made love he took her into a cool cave in the rock. It was a shallow hollow but was almost shut off from the sea and completely invisible from above. He had brought a blanket for them to lie on. Hanging over his arm the blanket was a banner of his intent. Gwyn also knew what they were about to do and followed silently as they reached the cave and spread out the blanket. Swiftly, but in a way that suggested a small boy ridding himself of a Sunday shirt, Tom pulled his jersey over his head. She kissed the exposed shoulder, deeply inhaling the musky smell of sun-warmed flesh. He drew her to him and in a moment she took off her dress. He was stunned by her body. Her responses and movements were far more than he would have expected from an untouched eighteen-year-old girl. But then, Gwyn had always had a timelessness and that aura of having lived many lives before.

Tom was a considerate but eager lover, and Gwyn had no regrets at all. Later, climbing the hill, they exchanged conspiratorial looks, thoroughly delighted to have discovered that they were good at still another thing.

Once they had made love, they thought of little else. Gwyn's conscience may have tweaked her when she set out alone for an evening walk to meet Tom, but she was too engrossed in her own joy to allow the concerned face of Enid to keep her home.

Strangely enough they still found time to talk. Gwyn became bolder in her opinions, which Tom found charming; and he, feeling secure about her love, dared to introduce subjects which might have offended her before, subjects like agnosticism and the rights of women.

He was surprised to discover that she wanted less for her sex than he did. Where he saw women's rights as an absolute necessity, she saw them as a matter of personal choice by the women involved. Politically they were both liberal, but liberal in a way that might be considered conservative in later times. The one great source of agreement was on the rights of the individual to do and believe as he chose. After, and often before these conversations was the lovemaking, which was consistently satisfying and tender, with a freedom which more experienced lovers have often lost through years of cynicism and disappointment. Ways of expressing love which would have seemed shameless just weeks before were as natural as the flight of the gulls. Fortunate indeed was this young woman who made love for the first time in the sunshine with a partner as enchanted with the whole thing as a child in a candy shop. Like the heat of the summer sun, their love intensified with each new day until it seemed that she must either turn away or be consumed by it.

❧ 5 ❧

July was hot and dry.

Gwyn had become a sailor almost before she could read, and although she never completely lost her fear of the sea, she was handy on a boat. Because of her skill and amiability she was called upon to give sailing lessons to certain young people at the hotel.

For these lessons she wore a divided skirt which her mother found scandalous, the young ladies ludicrous, and Gwyn comfortable. She was amber brown now, which made her light eyes shine out like those of some exotic sea witch, and her body moved with a new womanly confidence.

This particular day she was to instruct young Olive Crandall in the rudiments of sailing but in less than fifteen minutes Gwyn learned that this would be impossible. Olive was a patrician beauty. Her long blond hair was twisted into a loose chignon at the back of her neck, but soft wisps escaped and shuddered in the breeze. She was shrewd and alert but absolutely devoid of any desire to learn. Somewhere, somehow, Olive had learned to swim, but this did nothing to reassure her. Her

mother had insisted on a set of four sailing lessons, however, so here they were acting out the charade.

"Good morning, Miss Crandall," cried Gwyn to the
elegant creature on the dock.

"Olive, please, and then I can call you 'Gwyn.' " They
went aboard, and Gwyn set out toward the coast, thinking that it would amuse Olive to come across some other
boats.

"Now at last I can find out all about you and Tom
Warner!" said Olive, clutching the side of the boat with
slender fingers. Was that a note of menace in her light
remark or was Gwyn becoming fretful over nothing?

"I don't know what you mean," said Gwyn evenly,
although her own knuckles went white on the tiller.

"Oh, pooh! Of course you do. Why he meets you somewhere for lunch every day and half the time we can't find
him at night for bridge. His uncle always says he's "off"
somewhere, but I'll bet you know where!"

Olive was poised for an attack. There was something
precisely threatening in her tone, a deliberate attempt to be
the grand inquisitor and to force Gwyn into the role of
hostile witness.

"I know him, if that's what you mean. Watch the
boom, we're coming about! You should really be handling
the jib sheets, you know." Gwyn scrambled to fasten the
sheet into the winch and then cast a glance at Olive, who
had done little more than shift into the opposite seat.

"I'll tell you what! I'll learn the names of all the silly
ropes if you'll just sail the stupid thing. Why they call a
rope a sheet I'll never understand anyway." Olive pouted
slightly and pushed her hair behind her perfect ears.

"It's not a rope it's a line, for starters," said Gwyn,
relieved to have escaped the subject of Tom at least momentarily.

"What do you and Tom do all that time alone together?
Oh I realize that's impertinent, but honestly you'd blush if
you could hear the girls gossip," said Olive.

For the first time that summer, the outside world set its heavy foot on Gwyn's happiness. The thinly veiled sneer on Olive's perfect features cut her happiness in two. So they were all guessing, making up smutty stories. She wondered if Tom were aware of his companions' speculations. She forced an easy laugh to her lips. "Why I could as easily ask you the same question, Olive. Heaven knows, you and your friends see much more of Mr. Warner than I do!"

"Oh Mr. Warner, indeed!" Olive smiled. "You certainly know how to keep your mouth shut, I'll say that for you!"

"Perhaps I should ask you why you are so interested in me and Tom Warner?" said Gwyn coldly. She realized as soon as the words were out of her mouth that she had made a grave miscalculation. Olive Crandall had a soft, almost pliable exterior, but there was a malignant curiosity in her eyes that suggested a more than passing interest in the affairs of Tom Warner. She would make a dangerous enemy, an enemy who would break the rules and worse, an enemy without either the brains or sensitivity to realize the damage she was capable of inflicting.

Olive did not respond. Instead she fixed green eyes on Gwyn and smiled a crooked smile which unnerved Gwyn completely.

Abruptly Gwyn tacked and headed for shore.

"Why did you do that?" asked Olive. "It seems to me the wind is coming more from the other direction."

How annoying! thought Gwyn. She's right; it was a poor maneuver. Wasn't it strange that she should be so aware of which way the wind was blowing?

Gwyn decided to set her course to go around the island. At least she could give Olive her money's worth of scenery. After all, her mother must expect something, and Gwyn was a girl who always lived up to a bargain.

As a rule, she never took an outsider near Parkertown, but today she had the thought that perhaps Miss Crandall needed to have her nose rubbed in a little honest poverty.

Edging the island was a low growing clump of scrub pine, and then the first tiny shack came into view. It was haphazardly painted a bright yellow and belonged to Augie MacLeod, who used the floor for cleaning fish and the hammock which hung from the rafters for sleeping. A good beginning.

Next were three cottages, all run-down, but being made of stone, somewhat presentable. These belonged to the Curran sisters. In reality their names were Mrs. Leary, Mrs. MacDougal and Mrs. LaBrecque, but as they were all three widows and as each had lost her husband at sea within three years of their respective marriages, folks had gone back to calling them by their common maiden name. They did not live together, the sensible solution to their poverty, because they simply couldn't get along with each other. It seemed that despite island custom they could not reconcile their husbands' different nationalities. And so each one sat by a one-log fire and ate her one-dish meals and got together with her sisters only on Sundays when Ethan brought the priest over from Buckley to say mass. In the tiny stone church they sat in a row, rosaries in hand, looking for all the world like peas in the pod. After mass they walked home and lived their separate lives until the next Sunday.

Next to the Curran sisters' homes was the MacNeil cottage. Gwyn remembered Ethan's parents; a jolly plump mother and a thin gnarled father who used to dance like the Bonnie Prince in his kilts at the community parties.

Next to Ethan's house was a short spread of rock and sea grass and then came the Community Hall. Not much of a hall really but big enough to hold the eighty or so people who used it for everything from sewing bees to dances.

In front of the hall was a rust-free bell, which alerted the islanders to all news good or bad. A call from the bell and you went to the hall, at three o'clock in the morning or at high noon. It might be a shipwreck, or maybe Colin Burke couldn't wait 'til morning to tell everybody that his wife had twin boys, and once in a while it was Eustis McComb (generally called "Useless") all liquored up; but no matter who rang it you went. It might be important, like the time John Cooley's roof caught fire or the time little Martha Horan fell into the well.

"How quaint!" cried Olive, without any trace of condescension in her voice.

"I suppose it must seem so to you," said Gwyn. "You might feel a bit differently if you lived there."

"Is it so very awful?" asked Olive, coloring and keeping her eyes away from Gwyn.

"No, it's not, not at all!" said Gwyn, determined not to be an object of pity.

"Where's your house?" asked Olive.

"Right over there past the running field."

"I don't see it. Which one?"

"The one made of stone, just seaward of the Catholic church."

"It's pretty. Your mother must take good care of it."

"It used to be a rectory when we had a live-in priest, but when my father came to teach they rented it to him because we've always used the church as a schoolhouse during the week and by then the priest was only coming over on Sundays. My father made them sell it to him when he earned enough money. Good thing, too!"

Why was she telling Olive all this? She didn't even like the girl.

"Tell me Gwyn, are you Roman Catholic? I've never known a Roman Catholic before." said Olive.

"No, we're not. I don't know why. Most of the people in Parkertown are though, with all the Irish and French blood. My mother's people were Scottish; I guess maybe that's the reason."

"What do you do about church?"

"My mother holds a service at home on Sundays, just reading from the Bible and prayers, nothing fancy. We're considered to be freethinkers around here, I guess, but no one seems to mind." Gwyn was mercifully not ashamed of herself or her mother.

"How odd," said Olive. "I've always thought everyone went to church." She sat perplexed but did not pursue the subject.

Now they were passing the last dozen cottages in Parkertown. Here and there towheaded children ran ragtag and barefoot while near water's edge women with hitched-up skirts were thrusting pitch-forks into the flats on the northeastern side and filling their clam buckets. Moorings were empty; everyone who owned or could work on a boat was out fishing.

"Look at that funny little place all alone there, the one with all the children!" cried Olive.

She pointed to Colleen Murphy's falling-down bungalow. The fair Colleen was sitting on the porch next to her elderly mother, who rocked rythmically in the summer sun. As far as Gwyn knew, no two of Colleen's five children had the same father.

It was a good thing for the men of Parkertown that Colleen went ashore from time to time or there'd be hell to pay. The story that Colleen gave out was that she had a husband on land. The town where he lived always changed with the telling. It was a handy enough alibi, especially since the natives were wary of stirring up that particular chowder. Too much risk involved. Gwyn chuckled as Colleen lazily scratched her ribs, but she made no comment to Olive. She was almost sure that Olive had been sent out to learn sailing, not the sexual habits of Colleen Murphy.

They lazily passed the pastures and gardens, and finally the large Spraycliffe Inn loomed into sight.

Once Gwyn had seen a doll with two heads. When you

looked at her one way, she was a shabby ugly doll with a long patched skirt, but when you flipped the skirt over, underneath was a beautiful bride's head and the reverse side of the patched skirt was white satin and lace. Two in one. The plain and the fancy. Parker's Island.

❦6❦

Olive Crandall was not the only person affected by the lovers. Like the concentric circles drifting outward from a pebble tossed into the sea, so the emanations went out from Gwyn and Tom toward those around them. Their very awareness of each other made them oblivious to the frown on Enid's face and the raised eyebrows of Olive and her friends.

Once Olive had spoken up, the outside world seemed to come crashing in around them. Gwyn told Tom of her conversation with Olive, and he became first angry, then protective and finally guilty.

For the first time he perceived himself as a predator. No matter that Gwyn was willing; custom called him seducer and Gwyn the victim. He knew enough of human nature, as well as biology, to know that Gwyn was an innocent. Strangely he felt that he had corrupted, no, not corrupted—exposed her. The new ideas which she seemed to devour had enlightened her to more than the good in man, they had also awakened her to the philosophical concepts of modern morality and to sin as a relative thing. He discovered that morally she was almost totally unaware of evil as a reality. She saw behavior as a practical thing, a reaction to circumstances. Astonishingly, she saw nothing wrong in their intimacy until Olive put her on the defensive.

Before the first sailing lesson, Gwyn had gone back to work each afternoon still warm from Tom's lovemaking, bathed in his approval. She had felt wanted, desired by someone who wasn't obliged to love her because of birth or long acquaintance. Tom had chosen her. From all others he had picked her out, chosen the seashell from among the swans.

Now she could no longer meet her mother's eyes. Nervously she fussed with her hair, fearful of a betraying lock, a too-rumpled skirt.

"This is probably wrong," said Tom one particularly beautiful day soon after. She noticed with humor that he had waited until after their lovemaking to discuss the morality.

"I know," she replied, damning Olive in her heart.

"Anyone who knew about us would say I was a wicked man of the world preying on a virtuous working girl." He attempted a joking manner, but his smile failed him and left him with a twisted grin.

"You know that's not true and I know it, so what do we care?" Her false bravado was touching. He stroked her firm jaw with the back of his hand and then sat back, crossing both hands around his knees, and looked out to sea.

"I think we should try to stop, go back to where we were before." His words were spoken clearly, as if he had rehearsed them.

"All right. Let's try." He didn't want her, didn't love her at all. She felt claws sinking into her chest.

"Oh Lord. I didn't mean just friends!" He paused and held her by the shoulders until she turned eyes brimming blue up to his. "Gwyn, I love you. I want you so badly it hurts, but it's not fair; there could be consequences."

She stared, uncomprehending.

"You could have a baby." It was out, the one thing the wise island girl had forgotten. Or had she? Perhaps she was tempting fate, forcing her own hand so that she would have to change her life.

"It all seems so wrong now. Oh no, no dearest, not you!" she cried, covering his hand with kisses. A tear fell on his hand. "I only meant now that we both know it's wrong we can't just go on doing it."

He held her close, resolute. They would be friends in love, soul mates, anything but lovers; but even as he thought it he felt her small arm around his neck and his body ached for hers.

"Go now Gwyn. You're right, we can't go on like this. As soon as my parents get back from France we'll get engaged, but until then it's my duty to protect you."

She wiped her eyes and left, then ran back to embrace him once more, hungrily, as if he were going off on a long journey.

That night she tossed in her bed. Engaged. He had said engaged. "But," said a little voice, "that's what they all promise. Say you'll marry her and she'll do anything you want." "No!" her heart cried. "He's good and decent and loves me!" She continued thus until a worse scenario presented itself. Her monthlies were a day late. Her breasts were hard the way they were each month before she flowed, but perhaps this time they were swollen because she was going to have a baby.

She thought of Colleen Murphy, surrounded by children and, worse, stuck forever on Parker's Island. Heart pounding she rolled onto her back, and clasping her hands together as she had when a child saying prayers with her father, she silently cried, "Oh, dear God! Let there be no baby and I'll never do anything wrong again. Just this once, let me get away with it."

How many young women have cried out the same pitiful prayer to God, and how many have forgotten the promise as soon as the favorable answer comes. But for now she had done all she could. She had worried and prayed and promised, and now she could sleep at last.

In the next room Enid heard the turnings in her daughter's bed and wondered. The girl knew the facts of life—they were hard to hide in Parkertown—but shouldn't Enid have another talk with her? She was not herself, that much was sure. Enid believed in her daughter's virtue but realized that she was probably a fool to do so. After all, it had very little to do with virtue. It had to do with being young and lonely and most likely bored to death.

Enid had seen Tom Warner and grudgingly admired his good looks and kind manner. He was never flippant to his Uncle as were most of the young people to their guardians, and he seemed a cut above the shenanigans of his peers. Ah, but it was his very virtues that made him dangerous. Naturally her Gwyn would not care for a lout! They would have a talk, soon, mother and daughter.

And, not far away, Ethan MacNeil lay in his big double bed savoring a private anguish. The bed had been his parents' wedding bed and he liked its size. Not many hammocks or holds could accommodate a man of Ethan's proportions.

Tonight he tried to sleep, tried to block out the afternoon.

He had been on his way over from Buckley and was coming in past the cliffs. Ordinarily he came straight across to the loading dock near the Inn, then took his time going around the pasture lands to Parkertown. He enjoyed watching the white silhouettes of the grazing sheep as they moved sluggishly from tuft to tuft. The rows of corn, already waist high, promised a decent winter for the islanders and consequently less work for Ethan.

For the last two years he had been considering giving up the island run, turning it over to a younger man; yet each time he thought of someone else unloading the fruit or handing out the mail to eager hands he felt possesive, unwilling to relinguish his seigneurial feelings of responsibility for this strange band of rock dwellers. Sometimes he felt torn in two by his loyalty to Parker's Island and his deepening attachment to the town of Buckley.

Buckley was like a child making the huge transition from mother's lap to schoolyard. The earth had held its denizens for over a hundred years, and now these same farmers and dairymen were being called upon to create an efficient town government and a modern economy. It was no easy task, but the brighter and braver amongst them were molding some sort of structure from their planning meetings. Of course, they would always be dependent on Salem for their larger banking needs, and a hometown newspaper was out of the question at this time, but still, it was exciting. Listening to his peers in Buckley, Ethan felt the same elation that he once had as a young man, high up in the rigging, looking for the first sighting of a new port.

He sailed past the fields and on past Parkertown, returning a friendly wave here and there. The day was hot, unusual for the island, and he decided to take a spin past the west cliffs before reversing and coming back to unload at the Parkertown pier.

He held the wheel loosely—there was little pull from the current—and gazed up at the hills. "Ho! What's that I see?" He chuckled to himself as he caught the flash of tumbling naked limbs from inside a small cave. Only one flash and then the cliff wall was as solid as before. He wondered, idly, how many young lovers had taken refuge in the coves and hollows of the West Cliffs during his lifetime. Probably Colleen Murphy and her latest beau. One of these years she'd find one that wasn't already married. She'd had her eye on Ethan for some time but "no thank you, ma'am. I get all of that I need from a certain house on the Buckley road and no six children to go with it!" thought Ethan.

Lazily, he turned the boat around and headed back to Parkertown. When he passed the spot in the cliffs where he had seen the lovers, he turned his head the other way. He was young once, and no hypocrite.

At the pier, Martha Horan, now eleven and quite recovered from her fall down the well the previous year, gave a little shriek and ran to tell the other villagers that Ethan was there. She enjoyed being the bearer of good news. Before her, it had always been Timmy Roberts who had been Ethan's herald, but Timmy was fourteen this year, sprouting hair on his upper lip and well beyond such lapses in his dignity.

"Three letters for the Curran sisters!" he cried. The Curran sisters had a niece in Boston who worked as a maid at the Parker House hotel. She always wrote to all three aunts at once to avoid hurting any feelings, and it was amusing to see how long the sisters could hold out before comparing letters. The niece told wonderful tales, of electric lights and theater parties and debutante balls where the girl being honored was always dressed in white just like a bride. Sometimes she enclosed clippings from the newspaper showing illustrations of a hat just like one she had seen in the lobby the preceding week. Her letters gave the Curran sisters a certain prestige on the island and were much appreciated by the local girls who were forever trying to make their homemade frocks into something sensational.

After the mail was handed out, Ethan unloaded the crates. This trip he had brought fresh produce of varieties not found on the island, and several bolts of cloth all the way from Darcy's Emporium in Salem. There were also some Boston newspapers for the more sophisticated and, as always, a carton of books from the brand new lending library in Buckley.

Lastly he cleaned up his deck and tied up his sails and

put his boat on its mooring. He intended to stay the night. Rowing in, in his dinghy, he was contented and looking forward to a nice cup of tea with Enid. It was two o'clock, the time she usually paused for her lunch at the hotel. Stopping to greet friends along the way took a few minutes, but it was time well spent. Ethan thrived on the affection of his fellow man and gave great attention to the words of his neighbors. He knew which baby had the colic and how Mrs. Lloyd's rheumatism was coming along, and he also knew which lad fancied which lass and vice versa.

Walking slowly along the narrow path which was the scenic route between the village and the Inn, he was surprised to see Gwyn rushing up from the cliffs. Her face was pale, but there were two bright spots of crimson on her cheeks. When she saw Ethan she did not greet him in her usual fashion, rather she half-whispered, "Hello, Ethan," and fell into place beside him. The path was not wide enough for two to walk abreast easily, and so he felt her uneven breathing and the heat from her arm.

"Is anything wrong, lass?" he asked.

"Wrong?" She looked frightened. "No, nothing's wrong; I'm just late, that's all. I'm sorry, I've really got to run!" She dashed of ahead of him.

In his mind he saw a brief picture of naked tangled arms and legs and painfully a realization came over him. The sudden knowledge of what he had seen hit him so fiercely that for a moment he lost his breath and had to rest on a driftwood log for several minutes before he continued on. "Not my Gwyn!" his heart cried, "not my sweet Gwyn." He was desolate, and for a short time kept taking deep breaths to keep from crying aloud. Then came anger. Terrible pounding anger that some scheming louse from Boston had spoiled his Gwyn and brought her down!

His head eventually cleared, and he went on down to the kitchen door from where he could already hear Enid's cheery voice humming a tune. He had lost his taste for company, but he knew that he must warn Enid about what was going on. During his years at sea he had learned to mind his own business in touchy matters, but this was different. He was like an uncle, or a brother, to Gwyn and he felt responsible for her. He couldn't tell Enid what he suspected, it would break her heart, but he must find a way to put her on her guard. Who knew who else might have seen them! Once again he felt an urge to strangle Tom Warner. He had no doubt that the boy involved was Warner. Gwyn had talked about him entirely too much for it to be anyone else.

❧ 7 ❧

"Hello, Ethan." Enid planted a friendly kiss on the ruddy cheek. "Sit yourself down, I'll make us a pot of tea." She got the tea things out and set the kettle on to boil. "Now," she said, smoothing her hands over her apron and sitting down, "tell me all the news."

"First, I've got to talk to you about something else." He paused. "It's about Gwyn."

"What about her? Ethan, what's the matter? She's all right, isn't she?" There was a barely controlled panic in Enid's voice. To an outsider it might have seemed unwarranted, but to any islander to whom drownings were a way of life, her reaction was understandable.

"She's fine, fine!" answered Ethan quickly, half rising to lay a reassuring hand on Enid's shoulder.

"Then what is it?" asked Enid, again, a trace of annoyance in her voice, directed mainly at herself for having overreacted.

"Well, I just saw her coming up from the West Cliffs and she acted mighty strange, if you ask me. She was much too quiet and she looked as if she'd been crying."

"It's that boy. Dear Lord! I've scarcely slept since she took up with him. Oh I don't mind her having a fellow. I don't even mind her meeting him as long as it's daytime and out of doors. But where can it go? Tom Warner's going back to Boston in another month or so, and where does that leave Gwyn?" Enid brought the teapot to the stove and rinsed it with the now-boiling water. She then filled the pot and left the tea to brew while she reclaimed her chair.

Looking intently at Ethan, she spoke quietly. "There's no hope for the child as long as she stays on the island. It would be a different thing if she were like the other girls, setting their caps for some fisherman, but Gwyn's not like that. I suppose I shouldn't say it, her being my own and all, but there's always been a special quality about Gwyn. Sometimes I feel she's been alive before in a beautiful house with a library full of books and nice carpets on the floor. That's nonsense, of course, but you know what I mean, don't you?"

"Yes I do. It's as if she were waiting to go back to her real life, almost as if she knew she didn't belong." Ethan sighed.

"Well she doesn't belong here, that's for sure, and I've been a selfish old woman to have kept her! The only reason I've held her so long is I don't know where to send her. My people are all gone." She got up again and brought the teapot to the table.

"Can you help us, Ethan? I've been thinking. You know that friend of yours, Maurice Darcy, the one with the big store in Salem? Do you think she could get a position working for him? I know a shopgirl's not much but at least she'd have a chance. You could find her a room somewhere, couldn't you?"

"Now just hold on a minute," said Ethan. "It so happens I can do better than that. Of course, I'm spoiling a big surprise by telling you this, but your daughter and I discussed this very subject a few weeks back. I told her I'd see if I could find her a position right in Buckley. That way you'd be able to come over anytime you liked."

"Ethan, that's wonderful! But why was it a surprise?" asked Enid.

"She wasn't sure how you'd take to it, but I encouraged her. I hope you don't mind me interfering." He took a gulp of his tea and involuntarily smiled in satisfaction as the brew hit his stomach. He felt a knot unwinding now that a solution had presented itself.

"Interfering? You've likely saved our lives. No, I'm not exaggerating. There's nothing but pain ahead for our Gwyn if she tries to take on Tom Warner and his crowd. Do you think she could find a decent position in Buckley?" Enid was heartened by the news and the tea.

"It's all but sure. There's a French woman who just married Simeon Blanchard. He's on the planning board with me. She's going to open a very stylish dress and hat shop in September. Her name's Lucille or Louise or something; anyway I asked her if she could use some help, and she said she could if the help was attractive. Guess she wants someone who'll dress up the place. I described Gwyn, and Madame Louise or whatever her name is said she sounded perfect. So there we are. And! The Blanchards have a spare room in their new townhouse which they would be willing to rent to her as long as I would be responsible." Ethan grinned proudly.

"And to think you've been plotting away behind my back all this time!" said Enid. "Does Gwyn know? About the dress shop and all?"

"No, I was going to tell her today, but she didn't give

me a chance. Did you notice anything wrong when she came in here a few minutes ago?" Ethan's happy mood of a moment ago had vanished in the wake of his memory of Gwyn and her tear-streaked face.

"No," answered Enid. "I was just finishing up in the dining room and only heard her rush up the back stairs. She didn't say hello; that's unusual."

Ethan pondered a moment and decided to keep his mouth shut about what he had seen that afternoon. After all, it could have been anyone at all. Just because he had seen Gwyn coming up from the cliffs didn't mean a thing. And it had been almost an hour between the time he had seen the lovers and the time he had seen Gwyn.

"Perhaps they had a quarrel. You know how young people are." His words were sensible, and he almost succeeded in convincing himself.

"Young people and perhaps us old-timers too. Don't forget we've been sitting here stewing about it for half an hour and she's probably forgotten all about it by now!" Enid laughed and stood up, relieved and ready to go back to work.

That had been the afternoon. Ethan had left the hotel and gone back to Parkertown to pick up the mail and have a cold mug of ale with his old boyhood pal Oakie Williams. Oakie had lost his leg when he was nine years old. He had crushed it between the pier and the float. Since then he had had a series of oak peg legs, hence the nickname. He ran a tavern. Actually it was called a restaurant but all it sold for food was homemade sausage on a stick and pickled eggs with crackers. Perhaps it was the extra pickled egg that kept Ethan awake later that night.

Whatever it was, Ethan was unable to get more than three or four hours' sleep. Even if all three could have left their sleepless beds and discussed their worries it would have done no good. The truth was so much worse than Enid or even Ethan suspected.

Ethan awoke tired and irritable. He dreaded the trip back to Buckley. The sky was overcast and although the islanders spoke of a heavy mist, rain is what it was.

Gwyn awoke at six o'clock with a familiar stain on her nightgown and fairly leaped from her bed in relief and gratitude to God.

Enid, seeing Gwyn's happy smile at breakfast, relaxed and decided she had made too much out of yesterday.

On the way to the hotel, Enid almost mentioned Ethan's good news about the dress shop but the day was wet and the path muddy, so she decided to wait until they were warm at home that evening.

Rainy days were twice the work at the hotel. Everyone but a few stalwarts stayed indoors. The card playing and restless wandering from meeting room to library and dining room left behind a debris of misplaced volumes, mixed-up cards and a scattering of crumbs. On dark days Enid generally put out small trays of light food for those who cared to nibble. On these days, people also tended to be edgy and querulous. Behind several doors, Gwyn could discern a raised voice or two.

At lunchtime, Gwyn ran to the window and seeing the now-heavy sheets of rain that were falling resigned herself to lunch in the kitchen. When she entered the room Enid was poking up a fire in the old stone fireplace. The hotel was not an informal establishment, but there were handsome stone fireplaces in all the main rooms for cold days. The groundsmen were kept busy replenishing the logs for these hearths and thus they also hated rain, much preferring the wholesome activity outdoors.

"Just pray that no one gets the grand idea of popping corn over the open hearth again," said Gwyn. The two women laughed aloud remembering the time during the past summer when a portly dowager had insisted on having an impromptu corn-popping party in the game room. Enid had searched the kitchen until she found four ancient popping baskets with long handles. Everything seemed to be shaping up nicely until Enid volunteered to supervise.

"Nonsense!" the grand dame had bellowed. "I've been popping corn since before you were born." Reluctantly Enid had left the group to their own devices only to hear, a few minutes later, what sounded like a Fourth of July celebration, followed by a veritable orchestra of screams and bellows. Fearing the worst Enid and Gwyn had raced into the game room, only to be greeted by what looked like a heavy snowfall surrounding the hearth. The stout lady was protesting loudly that how was she to know that the baskets could only hold half a cup of kernels before popping over. "Why, when I was a girl we used two cups at least!" she insisted, as another flurry of kernels flew past her nose from the abandoned baskets on the hearth.

"Do you know," said Enid, "that to this very day I'm still finding popcorn in the most unlikely places? Just last week, Mr. Wiltshire opened a chess set and found half a dozen kernels mixed in with the pawns." They laughed again, holding their sides with mirth.

It was good to be here with Ma again, thought Gwyn. She had given her mother so little attention since meeting Tom.

"While you're here, let's talk about the dance," said Enid.

"Which one?" asked Gwyn. There were two dances coming up in mid-August. One, at the hotel, was to be a costume ball. The hotel kept large trunks full of every imaginable kind of costume. Stuffed inside the antique trunk were pirate hats, powdered wigs, Indian headdresses, ornate gowns (very popular with the middle aged women), clown costumes from Harlequin to Punchinello and a staggering array of swords, cummerbunds and lorgnettes. Each guest drew a number from a hat. The holder of number one got first choice of costume and so on down the line until the last few needed incredible ingenuity to compete at all.

Twenty years ago, Mr. Hodges, owner of the Inn, had bought the entire wardrobe of a defunct traveling theatre company. Mr. Hodges always appeared on the scene for the ball, invariably dressed as Mephistopheles, an amusing affectation when one considered that he was both portly and bald.

It, nevertheless, pleased the guests to see their host in costume. Mr. Hodges came to the Inn only once every three weeks during the season to survey the books and to check the service and inventory. The fact was that he had become a wealthy man since he had bought and remodeled the Spraycliffe Inn twenty-eight years before and was now uncomfortable in the role of proprietor. He vastly preferred bringing his family to other luxury hotels and being treated as a guest. Still, he was a fair-minded man. The staff respected him and were grateful that he didn't interfere with them. Most of the help were islanders, and islanders didn't take very well to criticism.

The other dance, which strangely enough fell just one week after the Spraycliffe Masquerade, was held at the community hall in Parkertown. In their own original way the islanders celebrated harvest before the event. Rather than wait until the cold chill of October was upon them, they had their festival in mid-August. Everyone came and all quarrels were set aside for one evening. Even Colleen Murphy came and danced with all the men without raising one disapproving eyebrow. That is to say, unless she danced more than once with the same man.

The island boasted two of the finest fiddlers that ever stroked string, and as one was Irish and the other Scottish, the competition was fierce.

Add to the general chaos a healthy dose of Augie Mac-Pherson's bagpipes, and the din was dazzling to the ears of all concerned.

Of the two dances, Enid and Gwyn naturally preferred the latter. The masquerade represented drudgery

and the ironing of crumpled costumes and a vain attempt
to outlast the revelers in order to have a clean kitchen and
dining room by morning. The presence of Mr. Hodges also
added to the pressure Enid always felt at party time.

In past years Enid had kept Gwyn out of sight in the
kitchen. She had no desire to make a Cinderella of the girl,
but she felt, wisely, that the sight of the jewels and elegant
figures might make her dissatisfied with her lot. Worse, the
girl might lose confidence in herself if thrown too often
into comparison with the wealthy Boston socialites. Perhaps she also feared that some inappropriate male might
see the pretty child and try to exercise his eighteen-nineties
notion of *droit de seigneur*. Enid was worldly enough to
know that some men considered any social inferior to be
fair game.

And so Gwyn had remained out of sight during former masquerades. This year, however, after much consid-
eration Enid had decided to throw Gwyn into the fore-
front. It would do Gwyn good at this particular time in her
life to see the contrasts and face them boldly. It would be
a warning to that Tom Warner too, to see his chosen companion in her role of servant. There was no cruelty in
Enid's decision. In fact, somewhere in the recesses of her
mother's heart she hoped that Tom Warner would turn out
to be Prince Charming and would see Gwyn for the dear
girl she was. If not, then it was better that the girl face up
to it now before anything amiss occurred.

"I've found a costume for you for the masquerade!"
said Enid.

"Oh, so it is the masquerade we're discussing. Surely
I won't need a costume in the kitchen!" said Gwyn.

"Ah, but you'll not be in the kitchen this year," said
Enid. "It's time you took over from me with the carrying
of all those trays into the ballroom. I'm just not going to
run my feet off another year and that's that." She found it
difficult to meet Gwyn's astonished gaze.

"But, Ma! You've always loved mixing in with the people, and who'll help Mr. Hodges judge the costumes?"

"Oh I can manage that part all right, but you'll have to do the rest of the trotting to and fro. Besides, there's the costume I told you about. It's an old serving wench's dress with a laced up bodice and a blouse with puffy white sleeves. I found it in the back closet when I was cleaning up the attics for the onslaught. The neck's a bit low, you know how they wore 'em back then, but the skirt's a decent length if you wear high boots. The skirt's red and the lace-up vest is black with red and green embroidered flowers on it. You'll look a picture in it."

"I'd really rather not. There's Tom, you see."

"What's he got to do with it? A job's a job. He knows you're a working lass, so it'll be no shock to him."

She got up and carried her lunch plate to the sink. The conversation was over.

For two weeks Tom and Gwyn held fast to their vow of abstinence. It wasn't easy. Intimacy once experienced is difficult to foreswear, but Gwyn's preoccupation with the details of the masquerade and Tom's growing self-respect helped them resist the urgent call of their bodies. The lunches were shortened because of Gwyn's heavier work load, and then it rained for four days in a row which kept her in the kitchen. The secret

evening meetings were abandoned altogether, both parties agreeing that the temptations were too great.

At first Gwyn felt rejected, her young body protesting
its neglect, but when it became apparent that Tom loved
her as much as ever she relaxed and they dove into political
discourses. Tom had read *The Prince* by Machiavelli and
begged Gwyn to read his copy that they might discuss it.
So each evening until the light failed, Gwyn read in her
cottage. She was appalled at the cynicism in the book as
well as the total disregard for the well-being of the masses.
Tom found the book satirical and this led to argument and
a resumption of intellectual intimacy.

On the day of the masquerade, Gwyn did not see him
at all. She and her mother were assembling a large cake in
the general shape of the Inn. Enid had made the first one
three years before, and Mr. Hodges and the guests had
declared it such a wonder that she had been compelled to
repeat the feat each year.

"To think how much fun this was the first time,"
sighed Enid, trying to put on icing in neat vertical lines to
simulate the balusters in the wide veranda stairs.

"It's your own fault for doing it so well in the first
place," laughed Gwyn, licking icing off a finger.

"Maybe so, but you would think that with the punch
to make and the cold buffet, they could leave me a little time
to think."

"Cook has done a wonderful job of the supper. Three
kinds of seafood salad and a beef aspic thing that looks
beautiful. She's also done a turkey and two hams and it all
looks perfect," said Gwyn. She was fond of the cook, who
used to sneak her treats when Gwyn was younger.

"Oh I know, I shouldn't complain. Cookie has the hard
job. Well, that's about done it except for the lettering over
the roof. What do you think?"

"I think it's beautiful and you too!" cried Gwyn. "As
a matter of fact, I was wondering how long a good-looking

woman like you will be willing to live alone. Why don't you propose to Ethan?"

"Oh get on with you! Ethan and I know much too much about each other to ever be comfortable married. I'm not his type, nor is he mine. But he's a dear friend to me, and sometimes those are worth more than husbands! Now scoot and get dressed, they'll all be down in an hour. Did you iron Mrs. Waverley's dress? She was in here asking a while back."

"Yes, I hung it on her door. Are you sure you don't need me?"

"No, I'm fine. Your costume is in the second maid's room. Don't forget the cap!"

9

The sky was still bright with summer's sunset when the guests began coming downstairs in morale-supporting clusters of three and four. The first few archangels and Mexican bandidos wore a peculiar expression on their faces, as if they had been caught out in their underclothes, but after the initial shock of looking like jackasses in public had worn off they began to enjoy themselves immensely. In fact, the first arrivals appeared to have secured some sort of strategic advantage over the latecomers, rather like the first ones wet at a bathing party. Their guffaws were intended as much to embarrass as to amuse, although they were unaware of these darker motives.

The younger set, usually the most boisterous and forward of the guests, were curiously restrained. One young lady, known for her wit and daring, seemed to have been entirely overwhelmed by her costume of abbess.

Standing in the ballroom doorway, Gwyn was amused to note that only in a Boston Brahmin crowd could a Mother Superior be assumed to be in costume. Gwyn was hovering around the periphery of the room, passing the first of many trays of canapés, when she finally caught sight of a striking sea captain who was trying to catch her attention. How handsome Tom looked! He was wearing a blazer of navy blue, undoubtedly his own, judging from the fit. The only accessories he had added were a captain's hat and a spyglass. During the week past he had told Gwyn that he detested costume dances and would disguise himself as little as possible. He took a glass of champagne from a passing waiter and leaned against the fireplace wall, staring directly at Gwyn with open admiration.

Gwyn, with her usual discretion, realized the foolishness of their revealing any mutual affection in public, especially since a stout mountie, whom Gwyn immediately recognized as the card-playing uncle, was following his nephew's movements with interest. Perhaps after a summer of total immersion in whist he felt obliged to give at least perfunctory attention to his responsibilities. In truth, he felt a perfect fool, keeping an eye on a grown-up man. But Tom's mother was his dearest younger sister, and he would never have refused her urgent request to "keep an eye on Tommy."

When Gwyn became aware that she was receiving a certain amount of positive attention from the group of single men nearest her, she quickly turned and headed for the safety of the kitchen where Cook and Enid were frantically arranging canapés on large silver trays and supervising the pouring of champagne into long stemmed crystal glasses.

"It's all timing," declared Cook, whose real name—like her formerly trim figure—had been forgotten years ago. "You've got to time the canapés for the moment after they put down their glasses. Otherwise they turn 'em down, because they want to leave one hand free for talking. Never met a businessman yet who could talk without his hands."

"Here Gwyn. You'd better get back out there and pass these." Enid thrust a large tray into Gwyn's reluctant hands and gave her a gentle shove from behind to get her moving.

"And move around into the middle of the room. Some folks get trapped there!" called out Cook as Gwyn left the kitchen.

Gwyn began to enjoy the attention she was getting as she walked primly from group to group. With her rosy cheeks and soft exposed throat she was easily the prettiest girl in the room, thought Tom. He felt his blood rise at the sight of her. How cruel of chance to have left her here on this island like a princess in a tower.

Tom, no special snob, nevertheless subscribed to the theory of nature's aristocrats, believing with all his heart that in all classes of life were those who were born with a special quality which separated them from the ordinary run-of-the-mill folk around them. He saw this quality in Gwyn as clearly as if she were wearing a crown. Others could see it too, he was sure. Why, his own uncle was watching her; not with a leer but with the respectful admiration she deserved.

Her dark curls were caught up under a white cap, and shining tendrils fell down onto her back. Her teeth were white as she smilingly accepted a compliment, and her eyes would have turned ordinary men to weaklings had she dared to look directly at the guests.

Tom felt a private satisfaction that she was his and tried to imagine his uncle's expression when he learned that Tom was going to marry her. He really must sit Uncle

George down for a man-to-man talk soon—if he could only get him away from his damned cards. Reluctantly he began his round of obligatory dances. He decided to dance only with married women so as not to offend Gwyn.

Feeling eyes on his back, he turned to see Olive Crandall dressed as a wood nymph in pale green, which certainly did set off her blond coloring. He smiled and got as far away from her as possible. All summer he had been aware that she had singled him out, and he had been made increasingly uncomfortable by the knowledge. She was very good-looking. Money too. "A match made in heaven," his mother would declare. No thank you, thought Tom. Olive Crandall has an sharp tongue. He did admit however that she was bright enough and her criticisms of others, although sometimes cruel, were not only amusing but often uncannily correct.

The evening passed slowly for Gwyn. She was jealous of every woman Tom danced with, even though she knew they were all married. She carried food and smiled and didn't even lose her composure when Mr. Hodges grabbed her and gave her a fat buss on the cheek. He did it, after all, almost in front of his wife, so there could be no offense taken. She managed to talk with Tom only once when she caught him alone. Taking an unwanted cucumber slice adorned fancifully with ripe olive from Gwyn's tray, he whispered, "Tomorrow, please! Let there be sun but even if it pours, promise me we'll lunch together." He looked covetously at her, which made her shiver with delight and quickly retreat to her kitchen lair.

By midnight the party was well underway. Faces were flushed with dancing and wine, and old Mr. Werner of the Beacon Hill Werners was pressing the band for a polka. Gwyn decided she liked them all much better in this mood; they could be extremely dull on other occasions.

At two o'clock in the morning Miss Hortense Leighton, having surreptitiously consumed an unseemly amount

of liquor from the pocket flask of a certain Donald Prender-
gast, was most unattractively sick on the stairs, sending her
mother into a near faint despite her own rosy glow. This
incident sobered the party considerably and prompted several discourses on the declining morality of the young by
old gentlemen who seemed to be having a degree of difficulty in standing upright. Mr. Werner, polkaed-out, sat
heaving in a velvet chair, straining said article of furni-
ture to its limits. The skeletons of turkeys and cold rib
roasts stood like so many prehistoric remains on the buffet table.

Finally, all but a few determined brandy drinkers
retired, having declared the evening a grand success
(Miss Leighton's indiscretion notwithstanding), and
went to bed.

Gwyn managed a quick wave goodnight to Tom, who
retired early, and the entire staff began the cleanup opera-
tion. This tedious labor was completed at approximately
four thirty in the morning, and at last Gwyn and Enid
escaped home thanking the stars that shone above them
that tomorrow was Sunday.

৪*10*৪

"Good heavens Gwyn, it must be almost noon!" cried
Enid Connell as she hastily tied a wrapper around her trim
waist.

"Noon?" mumbled Gwyn. Oh no! she thought, Tom

will be waiting! "Ma, would you mind if I packed a picnic for Tom and me?"

"Did you two make plans?" asked Enid warily.

"Yes, that is, we mentioned lunch and it's such a nice day and, well, I wanted to ask him to take me to the Island Dance."

"Oh Gwyn, do you honestly think that's a good idea? He'd hardly fit in, and I do so hate to make our home friends uncomfortable. They don't get much of a chance to relax, you know."

"But I want him to see how I live. Don't you see that I'll never know if he cares for me unless I see how he gets along with the folks in Parkertown?"

"Why don't you bring him here for lunch if you really want him to see us as we are?" suggested Enid.

Gwyn was silent. She was not ashamed of her home, it was one of the nicest in Parkertown, but she was reluctant to expose so much of herself to Tom. She was so vulnerable already. If he were not sincere, it would add to her humiliation for him to be allowed into the bosom of her family.

She was, however, curious as to how her mother would react to him at close range, and her natural optimism rose up. "All right. I'll get dressed and go fetch him back. Are you sure it's all right?"

"Of course it's all right. It's high time he came here to your home; besides, I have some lovely roast beef from last night, and there's some leftover peach pie from the other evening."

Gwyn jumped into her clothes and raced off to the cliffs, her heart pounding.

That's right child, thought Enid. Go quickly before you change your mind.

Tom was standing on a high rock, looking down at the surf, when Gwyn came up behind him and put her arms around his waist.

"Hello! I thought you'd forgotten me," he said. They both had shadows under their eyes, the only evidence of last night's party.

"My mother wondered if you would like to come to lunch at our house," she said.

"Honestly? Well, that's a step in the right direction! I was beginning to wonder if you were ashamed of me."

"Of course not! But you know how mothers are; I wanted her to make the first move." She smiled and added, "I'm not sure she trusts you very much."

"Guess I can't blame her." He looked at Gwyn's concerned face and laughed. "C'mon, mustn't keep a good mother waiting. My own mother'd skin me alive if I were late to lunch."

"You mustn't think we islanders are as strict as that! Ma's very nice, you know. I'm sure she'll like you."

"I certainly hope so. Say! Do you think I ought to make a declaration of my honorable intentions?"

They were almost at the front door.

"Heavens, no!" cried Gwyn "You'd scare her to death."

"One step at a time eh? All right, love, we'll do it your way." He nervously adjusted his tie and together they entered the front room. Enid, aproned, came out from the kitchen and stretched out a hand. "Hello, Tom Warner. Of course I know you already, but we may as well make it official. Come on in and sit down."

Things went well. So well that Gwyn could scarcely contain her elation. Lunch was simple but delicious, and Gwyn realized with satisfaction that Tom was that rarest of people, one who could put others at ease. He had plenty to say but could listen as well. Gwyn was also very proud of her mother. Enid was gracious, without putting on airs. The three decided over tea that Tom would come to the dance on Friday night. The idea appealed to him, he was interested in the islanders but except for Gwyn he had had little opportunity to meet any of them. When he heard that there would be pipers he was delighted.

"My father went to an affair in Scotland once where there was Highland music and dancing, and he's never forgotten it."

"Oh it's a grand sight," said Enid. "All the kilts whirling around and don't ask me the next question that's on your mind because I won't tell you!" She laughed merrily.

The only negative note was sounded when Ethan came to the door. He often stopped by after his Sunday run to have a bite or a bit of tea.

"Hello, Ethan. Come on in and meet Tom Warner," said Enid.

Ethan's smile froze when he spotted Tom all comfortable in Ethan's favorite chair. "How do you do, Mr. Warner," he said. "I can't stay, I just came by to see if you girls wanted me to bring over anything special on Friday for the dance."

"You're coming, aren't you, Ethan?" asked Gwyn, content to have her three favorite people together all in one room.

"I'm not sure yet," replied Ethan stubbornly.

"But Ethan, you always come. Why who will dance the fling with Ma?" cried Gwyn, unaware of the angry set to Ethan's jaw. "She says no one can dance as well as you."

"I'll do my best, lass. Nice to meet you Mr. Warner," he said coldly, then turned heel and left.

"What's wrong with Ethan?" asked Gwyn.

"Oh he's most likely tired out from the run. He and I aren't as young as you two," said Enid.

"I'd best be running along myself," said Tom, rising. "Thank you for a delicious lunch, and I'll look forward to the dance."

"Don't dress up too much; we islanders aren't much for fancy clothes," warned Enid.

"Except for kilts, of course," teased Tom.

"Except for kilts," agreed Enid.

"I'll walk you out," said Gwyn. She scampered out

beside him in silence until they were out of earshot of the house.

"Well, how was I?" asked Tom. "Did I pass muster?"

"You were wonderful. I can't wait for Friday night. To tell the truth, I never thought Ma would let me bring you. She's very protective of her islanders."

"Ah yes, but who will protect me?" asked Tom. "I thought your friend Mr. MacNeil would eat me up in one bite. Is he always that frightening?"

"No. He must've had a hard day. He's usually very funny and nice."

"Perhaps, but I had the distinct impression that he'd have thrown me over the cliff for fifty cents."

"Oh, you!" said Gwyn, giving his arm a squeeze good-bye. She wanted to jump and kiss him, she was so happy, but neighbors' eyes were everywhere, especially on Sundays.

Friday night was hot and muggy. Gwyn despaired of her hair even though she had tied it in rags under her head scarf to curl it while she dusted the bedrooms at the hotel. She would wear her tartan skirt with the matching scarf across her chest. True Scottish women never wore kilts, and although Gwyn was Scottish only on her mother's side, she was a stickler for authenticity.

The extreme humidity had a wearying effect on both Enid and Gwyn. They had asked for, and received, permission to leave work early and a good thing this was, as both needed a bath before the party and bathing was time-consuming. First there was the water to be heated over the woodburning stove. If they put too much water in the heating cauldron, it became too heavy to pour, and if they used less, it cooled off too fast in the copper bathing tub. The soap was strong and made few bubbles and only the precious drops of rosewater which Enid poured into the tub saved the experience from being dreadful. Hair-washing was easier, done under the pump in summer and spring.

Leaning back in the steaming tub, her knees drawn up

in order to fit, Gwyn gave herself up to daydreams. She pictured Tom dancing, a highly improbable event even if he were Scottish, which he wasn't, but ah, this was only a daydream and as such exempt from ordinary logic.

"Gwyn!" called her mother, "wake up! A lovely way to drown, dear, and just think of me ringing the bell and all the young fellows running to pull you out of the tub." She laughed. "Why don't you take a nap and I'll wake you before it's time to go."

Gwyn staggered drowsily from the tub, the now luke-war water running in gleaming rivulets between her rounded breasts. She dried herself and went to lie down on her bed. The heat was intense and unusual for Parker's Island. She lay in slumber while her mother went out behind the cottage to empty the bathwater. Late-afternoon sunlight poured through the curtains and played on Gwyn's naked body as she drifted from dream to dream.

Ethan MacNeil, though still smarting from the encounter with Tom Warner at Enid's house, had come to his senses enough to go and apologize to the two women. He did not know why he had behaved like such a jackass. That business about not knowing if he would go to the dance or not, rubbish! He hadn't missed a dance since the year he took that last sail to the East Indies in 'eighty-six. Dammit, that Warner was not about to spoil his good time! Let Gwyn have her romance. Summer was nearing an end and that would finish it. Then she would come to Buckley where he could keep an eye on her until she met someone more suitable.

Gently he knocked at the cottage door. Ordinarily, seeing the door ajar, he would have walked straight in, but the sensitive nature of today's mission made him shy. When he received no answering call he decided to leave a note. He entered the front room and in his neat hand wrote that he would see them that evening. Mercifully, a light breeze had arisen and he searched for a paperweight to hold the paper down. As his eyes scanned the room, Gwyn's bedroom door slowly swung open and he rose to catch it before it hit the wall. Standing by the bedroom door, he saw Gwyn on the bed. She lay still, one slender arm raised above her head lifting the full breast below. Her hair, tied in childish rags, contradicted the sensuality of her womanly body. Feeling a rush to his groin, Ethan quickly turned and silently shut the door. Leaving the cottage he broke into a run until a sweat broke out on his brow. He reached his house in a state of total confusion. Surely his feeling when he saw Gwyn's nakedness was wrong, perverted. He was practically a father to the girl. Minutes later, he went inside and forced himself to attend to the kilt which was hanging sternly on the closet door. He busied himself with domestic chores until it was almost time for the dance. Even then he had to fight the image of her body from his guilt-laden mind.

✤*11*✤

The Island Dance began earlier than the masquerade at the Inn. It would also last longer, until the sun was almost up on Saturday. Already the groups were forming. The French were in one corner, the Breton women among them wearing stiff white caps and starched dress aprons while their men were ruddy-cheeked with a wine-induced glow. The Irish were all over the room, naturally sociable and eager to get things started. The Scottish women were clustered together in their long tartan skirts awaiting the

arrival of their men. Much to the annoyance of the Irishmen, the Scots insisted on arriving en masse with a piper
at the front.

"You'd think they were off to a battle instead of a
dance!" scoffed one fellow. "Aye," retorted a pretty young
mother who wore a MacArthur scarf across her bosom.
"But to a Scotsman there's not much difference between
the two!" This sally was greeted with appreciative guffaws
from the Irish and French, but their laughter was quickly
submerged in the din of the pipes.

"Good God!" cried Tom, forcing himself by sheer will
to keep his hands from covering his ears.

"You mean, Great Scot, don't you?" replied Gwyn, a
merry glint in her eye. The noise swelled as the pipers
entered the barely furnished hall. The lack of proper draperies in the windows lent an echoing effect to their music,
and the result was deafening.

Gwyn spotted the red plaid of the clan MacNeil and
waved as Ethan strode in. He was easily the manliest figure
in the procession, standing a good four inches above the
next-tallest man. Behind him flashed the yellow and black
of clan MacLeod, and so it went, birds in full plumage. The
pleated skirts of the kilts flared out behind the marchers,
and Gwyn's heart stirred as it always did at the sight and
sound of her beloved Scotsmen. Her mother was born a
MacIntosh, and Gwyn had always believed that even a
drop of Scottish blood was enough to make your blood rise
to the tune of the pipers.

To Tom the noise began as sheer cacaphony, but gradually his ear became accustomed to it and he began to
discern the melodies under the noise. He was fascinated by
the bagpipers themselves and way the brawny elbows kept
the air flowing through the pipes in a steady stream.

He felt drab as he looked around at the colorful attire
of the natives. To a Boston boy this party was more like a
masquerade than the one last week at the Spraycliffe. He

recognized some of the groundskeepers from the Inn. They were transformed by their good looks and self-esteem. Where yesterday they had bent low over the rakes and hedges, now they stood tall and dignified.

"Would you like to dance?" asked Gwyn.

"I'd rather watch for a while if you don't mind," said Tom. "I have the strangest feeling that they're not going to do one dance all evening that I'm familiar with."

"Then you'll just have to learn a few. Watch Ethan. He's a marvelous dancer," said Gwyn.

"And I also have a feeling that the last person Ethan MacNeil would want for a pupil is me!"

"So you're still scared of him because of the other day, are you? I'll be sure to tell him, he'll appreciate it!" Gwyn was at her mischievous best tonight. Comfortable with her own people she was lively and pert, one toe tapping to the pipers.

"Let's get a bit of supper, shall we?" she asked, taking Tom by the arm.

"On one condition," said Tom. "You'll have to identify some of those dishes for me.

"Oh you sheltered Bostonians," sighed Gwyn in mock despair.

The table was bowing under the weight of heavy pots and serving platters. There were corned briskets of beef, French ragouts, smoked finnan haddie and several other dishes, most of them unrecognizable to Tom.

"What are these?" he asked.

"Kippers. Little fish. We have them for breakfast on toast sometimes, but they're good anytime."

"What's this here?" continued Tom, heaping his plate with food and trying unsuccessfully to keep everything separate so that he could taste it all.

"That's haggis. Surely you've heard of haggis! Why it's practically the national dish of Scotland. You'll love it."

"Very well, lassie. Haggis it is," cried Tom gamely.

"But that will have to be all this trip; my plate's overflowing."

He seated Gwyn next to an empty chair and fetched two foaming mugs of ale.

"What? No Scotch whisky? Just because my mother's here doesn't mean you can't at least try some."

"Believe it or not I've had Scotch whisky and liked it very much, but if I'm correct, this will be a long evening and I can't guarantee my staying power if I drink Scotch tonight. Besides this ale is twice as strong as any I've had before."

They sat silently for several minutes until Gwyn said, "Enough. I can't eat another bite or I'll pop my waistband buttons."

"What wonderful food!" said Tom. "Do you know, I rather liked the haggis, honestly. What's in it, anyway?"

"Haggis? Oh it's just the heart, liver and lungs of a sheep, all chopped up with onions and oatmeal and fat. Did you truly like it?" asked Gwyn laughing out loud as a horrified look crept over Tom's face.

"Thank you so much for telling me," said Tom, fighting down queasiness.

"Of course, that's not what makes it taste so good," continued Gwyn. "It's the way they cook it that's special. They put all that nice filling into a sheep's stomach and cook it up. Would you like some more?" She put on a sweet insincere smile.

"You're joking, of course," said Tom.

"No. It's all true," said Gwyn, breaking out into giggles.

Swiftly Tom raised his ale mug and took three healthy swallows. He continued, in fact, to swallow long after the ale was gone, but eventually he regained his color and the two went closer to the dancers.

After most of the participants had eaten their suppers, the dancing began in earnest. The musicians were of all nationalities, and so the tunes played were varied. There was no doubt that although the French country airs were popular, they were only a warmup for the reels and flings. Irishmen and Scotsmen whirled alike as the music became faster and faster. Enid didn't lack partners, and once she and Ethan received applause for a particularly spirited Highland fling.

It occurred to Gwyn that Ethan had not asked her to dance, but she attributed this neglect to the fact that she had an official escort in Tom. Fortunately, few of the island boys had any such qualms, and she was pleased to show off her own dancing skills for Tom.

Tom watched her as a red-haired boy whirled her in his arms. Her dark curls flew out around the lovely face, and he could see her pretty legs as her skirt sailed out around her. He had drunk too much ale. He knew he should have been more careful, but everyone there had had his or her share, so he was untroubled. Even Gwyn was flushed with more than the heat. She fell, unsteadily against his side and murmured, "Let's go outside for some air. I feel a little tipsy." She laughed as he led her through the unseeing crowd and took her out the door and down over the hill to the sea.

"The air feels so good," said Gwyn, stretching in the moonlight. The cloth of her white blouse clung tightly across her breasts, and Tom began to unbutton the tiny buttons as she whispered, "Oh yes, oh yes." She leaned her head against his neck as he pulled the blouse away and began to caress her breasts. She kissed him hungrily, and in a moment or two they were making love with a passion which carried Gwyn completely out of herself and some-where into Tom where all was love and pleasure and summer breezes on the skin. When their passion was spent, she collapsed against him and they lay panting side by side in the heat. He was the first to recover.

"I love you," he said.

"I love you, too!" she cried and turned her head to see his eyes. He was looking at her with an intensity she had never seen before, and there were tears in his eyes as he brushed a stray lock from her brow with his gentle hand. For an instant she was frightened by his eyes but the instant passed and she said, "We'd better go back now. My mother will miss us."

Enid Connell had noticed her daughter leaving the room with Tom. For several moments she tried to put it from her mind, but when the couple failed to return within the half hour she became concerned. Everyone in the room had been drinking and dancing, the usual behavior for anyone over sixteen at an Island dance, but tonight the ale was one more thing for Enid to worry about. She returned to the food table, but had temporarily lost her appetite. The pipers were beginning to play their Coranachs and the plaintive melancholy of these dirgelike songs did little to alleviate her concern.

Then the two were back in the room, and Oakie Williams was spinning around on his peg leg as the musicians returned to their jollier melodies. The Irish were dancing next to Oakie and two of the younger women were stepdancing. All around was motion, and even Tom Warner had improvised some sort of ballroom dance to the lively music and was whirling Gwyn around in fine fashion.

"Gwyn's having a fine time, isn't she?" said Enid to Ethan, who was standing beside her, diplomatically munching on a wedge of soda bread.

Ethan brushed a crumb from his beard. "I don't like it," he said.

"But don't you think he's a nice boy?" asked Enid. "I'll admit I was worried before, but since we had a talk together I've begun to think he's all right, after all."

"It's not him. Oh, I know I was rude to him the other day, but it's Gwyn herself that has me worried. The way she looks at him as if he were her laird and master. It runs against my grain. This island was settled by men who swore they'd never be crofters again. No other man's land for them, they wanted a bit of their own even if it was on a godforsaken island. I just don't want to see her forgetting who she is or what she came from. That boy has nothing she needs, he'll only make her feel beholden, and for what, I ask you? A chance to ride around in some damned fancy carriage and kowtow to some snooty parents who'd never accept her? That's another thing. I've never heard the word marriage mentioned here yet!" Ethan's face was dark with some ancient rage.

Enid put a hand on his arm and said, "There's not a whole lot we can do about it, now. They care for each other and she's eighteen. My own mother had been married two years when she was eighteen. Besides, she stays home every evening now, so it couldn't be all that serious. She only sees him at lunch."

"Is that so?" Ethan grimaced. "Forgive me Enid, I'm half drunk and falling into one of my dark Celtic moods. She's a good lass, and she'll be out of this place in less than a month."

"That's right. Now give me a dance and let's forget it all." The two old friends took the floor and danced surprisingly well to a bright French song about a bridge. Hearing French music played on a bagpipe was an experience.

Tom and Gwyn, satiated and sobered, returned to the food table for pastries. Tom enjoyed the lemon bramble, a small variety of turnover, and Gwyn decided that there was no doubt whatever that lovemaking increased the appetite. She realized that by their spontaneous act of a half hour ago they had broken their vow of abstention, but she could not seem to muster up any guilt.

The hour was growing late. In the distance the rumble of thunder could be heard when the music paused, but the dancers showed no signs of stopping.

Already Tom regretted having taken Gwyn to the beach. Her lack of concern continued to amaze him. That she had a strong set of values he never doubted for an instant, but her complete trust in him was uncanny. In his heart he knew her confidence was not misplaced. Certainly he recognized that there would be problems with his parents, particularly his mother; but he was no weakling to be overridden by a demanding mother. He would have Gwyn, of that he was sure. And Gwyn was no obsequious servant. She was a high-spirited, intelligent girl. Educated too; far better, he suspected, than any of the girls at the hotel.

Feeling her warmth as he stood by her side he felt comfortable and, for the first time, completely at ease with a woman. He sensed more than knew that his strengths were intellectual rather than physical. He was attractive enough, he supposed, but lacked the size and temperment to be what so many women mistook for manliness. Athletic prowess always seemed just beyond him, and although he compensated with skill, he lacked the overwhelming lust to win that made heroes on the field of play. Only in his books and in his openness to new ideas was he totally secure. To have found a vibrant beauty who valued him for himself was a benediction.

Sexually he was not inexperienced, his way of life had brought him into contact with a good number of women, and he had been amused to discover that license was not the prerogative of the lower classes. Some very well-to-do ladies had behaved in ways that would have shocked the women at this island dance.

Despite the sexual side of their relationship, he recognized in Gwyn her complete fidelity. Promiscuity would have been alien to everything in her character. How lovely she was! He slipped his arm around her waist and scarcely protested as she pulled him once again onto the dance floor.

"Are you having fun?" she gasped between turns.

"Best time of my life," he answered truthfully. "I wish it could never end," he added.

"But it doesn't have to. We can dance on forever if we

like, year after year after year." Her laugh rippled across his soul and carried him with it. He felt like Prospero, king of his island.

But if Tom were feeling like Prospero, then Ethan was Caliban. His generous heart was weighty with unresolved confusion, and jealousy nibbled away at the edges of his composure.

Scotch whisky had failed to cloud his misery; perversely it had clarified his thinking. He watched Tom as a chained watchdog watches a trespasser, waiting for the one false move that will justify an attack. Such emotions were alien to his temperment and they ill became him. His face took on the temporary aspect of a lout, and all the blackness in his Scottish soul rose like bile in his stomach. The nagging twinge of pain which he had almost forgotten came back into his chest and he abruptly left the room to watch the approaching thunderstorm. "Let it rain," he thought. "Let the heavens drown their passion." Disgusted with himself he walked slowly to his cottage where he pulled off his boots and fell, still dressed, into a dreamless sleep.

Outside the community hall, the rain began to fall in heavy droplets. Carried on waves of thunder, the heavens opened and the dancers stopped to run to the windows and watch the glorious lightning over the water. The women reluctantly began to gather up crusted pans and discarded shawls. Several men in voices cracked with strain sang the last songs, and by three o'clock Enid, Tom and Gwyn were on their way home. Gwyn was exhausted and happy as was Tom, but Enid was feeling her years.

"Say goodnight now, love, and come on in; it's almost morning," she said.

"Good night, Tom. Thank you for coming," said Gwyn. The two women went inside. Enid was too tired to talk but Gwyn hummed to herself as she hung up her clothes, and in her dreams that night she danced on and on.

❧*12*❧

Months later, Gwyn would remember that night of the dance and realize in retrospect that it had been the very pinnacle of her joy. During the last few weeks of summer she and Tom made plans. He would return home at the end of August and start his job. By early October his parents would have returned from France and wedding plans could be made. During the intervening month Gwyn had promised her mother to reflect on Tom and what her life would be like if they married. The morning after the dance Enid and Gwyn had had the long-awaited talk.

"You say he is sure he can get around his parents?" asked Enid.

"Even if he can't, he has promised to marry me anyway," said Gwyn.

"Have you considered what it would be like if they disown him? There will be no money except for what he can earn at the bank. I know you don't care about money but can't you see how difficult it would be for him, who has had it all his life?"

"He won't care!" said Gwyn, defiance flushing her face.

"Not for a while he won't but what about later? Will he miss the life, the good clothes and dinners?

"Oh, Gwyn," she sighed. "I wasn't going to be like this. Please believe me, I don't want to discourage you, I just want you to think it through. Here he is, on an island, away from the influence of his family. Naturally he fell in love with you. Who wouldn't under the circumstances? But summer's over, dear, and people have a way of forgetting. I don't think for a minute that he's insincere, but once he's home, back with his own kind, he might not be strong enough to hold on to his love." Enid felt wretched having to voice these fears, but sooner or later they would have to be confronted.

"If you are so sure, will you make a bargain with me? When he goes back to Boston, leave him alone for a month. No letters, nothing. Then, when his parents get back let him decide. If he still wants you, I'll do everything I can to see that you can be married, but it has to come from him. If you were the man and he the woman, I'd say the same thing."

"You don't believe we can be faithful for even a month, do you?" Gwyn's eyes flashed furious blue. "Very well, I'll tell Tom not to write for a month. You'll see. You'll see that we could be apart for even a year and still love each other."

"Darling, I want to believe it. Do you think I don't want to see you have a life of your own? I love you Gwyn. I've never loved you as much as I do this minute. God willing, you shall have your Tom, but he must be sure!"

Tom, when Gwyn reported this conversation to him, reacted in an unexpected way. Rather than perceiving Enid's bargain as an insult, he saw it as a romantic challenge, one he was confident of meeting. He was disappointed at not being able to write to Gwyn, he imagined that their letters would have been wonderful exchanges full of insights and loving phrases, but he was just enough older than Gwyn to believe in the swift passage of time. In truth, he had wondered if Gwyn might not forget him once he had left the island. Of his own constancy, he had no doubts, but eighteen was an impressionable age and he, more than Gwyn, saw the wisdom of Enid's proposal.

Their last two weeks together were loving and fond, touched by the poignancy of imminent separation. After the episode on the beach there was no more lovemaking; with matters so close to resolution it seemed safer to abstain. The weather cooperated for them to resume their lunches on the cliffs.

On the day before Tom's departure they went walking. The Inn was closing in four days and already baggage covered the veranda, awaiting the large ferry which came once a day during the last week of the season. Ethan's boat was inadequate to the task of transporting more than sixty guests and their assorted maids, nurses, trunks and seaside collections. Little boys and girls took advantage of the confusion to escape the eyes of vigilant nannies. They scampered over the lawns and rocks like so many grasshoppers. The groundsmen made regular runs along the boardwalk between the Inn and the pier, pushing wheelbarrows full of unwieldy suitcases. Mr. Hodges stood by the veranda stairs exchanging goodbyes with the guests and looking, in his dark suit, like a solicitous undertaker. He was relieved to have the season end without major mishap. There had been the usual number of scrapes and bruises from the children, and Miss Leighton's behavior at the masquerade had left something to be desired. He had suspected a liaison between the very married Mr. Thornton and Mrs. Hasting's nursemaid but had been unable to prove it, so he hoped it had escaped Mrs. Thornton's eye. He depended on his regular clientele and would hate to see any unpleasant memories attached to the Spraycliffe Inn.

Pretty Olive Crandall was looking particularly fetching today; she seemed to have accepted Tom Warner's coolness with unusual good grace. Or perhaps, thought Mr. Hodges, she was merely biding her time. He, like all of his guests, was aware of the friendship between Mr. Warner and Gwyn Connell, but as they were never seen together at the Inn there was little Mr. Hodges could do about it. Ethan MacNeil had told him that Gwyn was leaving for Buckley in the fall so there was no reason to create a fuss, especially since he held Mrs. Connell in high regard. He could ill afford to offend her; she practically ran the Inn single-handed.

Tom's uncle was enjoying one last round of cards. He was delighted to discover that his winnings for the summer were more than his losses even though, as a gentleman, he had to feign a lack of interest in the pecuniary benefits of card playing.

Tom and Gwyn walked one last time to the cliffs. He held her hand and they were silent as they picked their way through the purple asters.

"See here Tom!" she suddenly cried. "We've worn a path here. There was never one before, I swear." She looked down at the winding path which seemed to lend a permanence to their summer. Gwyn put great store in little things and saw omens everywhere.

When they reached the edge of the cliff Tom put his arm around her waist. She leaned her dark head on his shoulder and gazed across to Buckley. "I suppose I shall never live in Buckley now," she said.

"No, I suppose not; no banks in Buckley," he said. "Don't worry, dearest, we shall come back to the island, perhaps we can even stay at the Spraycliffe."

"If your parents disapprove of me, there will be no money for vacations at the Spraycliffe."

"Then we shall stay with your mother," replied Tom. He had given up promising that his parents would accept the marriage. Gwyn seemed determined that they should be on their own despite her protestations to the contrary.

The sun had passed its noonday peak and had fallen halfway home before Gwyn was able to face her farewell.

The boat left early in the morning, and Tom's uncle had insisted on his nephew's presence at a farewell dinner that evening. Because of his card playing, Uncle George had made few demands, and Tom felt he must accede to the old fellow's request. He would need his allies in the family.

So this was goodbye for a month. It might have been a year to Gwyn, who was feeling the pressure of inevitable change. Strange that she had sat here for years praying for new worlds, a new life, and now that her wishes were materializing she felt an overwhelming attachment to her own patch of sea, to the very rock beneath her feet.

"Say you love me one more time and then go quickly. Please!" Her eyes were full, she tried not to blink and let the tears fall.

"I shall always love you, Gwyn, and this island forever. For the next month I will shut my eyes and see you standing here in the breeze with the sea around you and the flowers at your feet. But this is foolish. We'll be together forever in just a few short weeks, so give me a smile, dearest." He tipped her chin up and their lips met. He felt her mouth soft as petals and salty from the runaway tears. His heart contracted and he held her close, then abruptly released her and ran back toward the Inn.

For almost a half hour Gwyn stood frozen to the spot where he had left her. The sea was calm and the waves broke into gentle foam on the rocks below, but her eyes were clouded. Overhead the sun shone down on the forlorn figure, but in her heart was a chill as a premonition of disaster fell around her like a cloak.

Later, at home, she tried to read but her books failed her. Enid, returning from the hotel found her sitting, supperless, in front of the cold hearth, a look of doom on her face.

"Gwyn, darling. It will be all right. Don't look so low. All those worries I had were just a mother's foolishness, don't let me frighten you."

But Enid remembered another young girl who had

given her heart away to a handsome young schoolteacher. They were of a breed who loved with all their hearts and never forgot. Why even now, Enid felt as married to Gareth as she had twenty years ago. Death seemed irrelevant in the face of such devotion. Dear God, she thought, make him love her!

In the morning Gwyn stayed away from the Inn again. But at nine o'clock she could hold out no longer and ran to the hotel pier. She was too late; the ferry had pulled out and once again she was left standing alone, looking this time toward Boston. She watched the ferry until it was a mere speck nearing the coast of Marblehead. When she could see it no longer she gave way to great choking sobs. When she regained herself, she looked around, afraid she had been observed, but no one was there. She didn't see Ethan on the veranda, hidden by shade, watching her with sadness on his rugged face.

❧*13*❧

Now Gwyn's wait began in earnest. She established a routine of reading and working, allowing just so many hours for each task, so that the days might pass quickly.

Ethan had been shocked when Enid told him that Gwyn had decided to stay on the island until her month was up.

"But that's damned foolishness! How long do you think the Frenchwoman will keep the position open? And if the boy abandons her, what will she do then? She's only a lass, but I expected you, Enid, to have more sense."

"I did the best I could. He could have asked her to run off with him. At least this way she's safe until the whole matter is settled. She's not a child, Ethan. If I had forced her to choose, she would have chosen him. Don't think for a moment she wouldn't. We can't control her anymore. As a matter of fact, I was surprised that they agreed not to write." There was little more they could say. The facts were there and matters were out of their hands.

The days became shorter, and Gwyn and Enid were made busy laying in fuel and food for the inevitable harshness of winter.

For most of a week they harvested vegetables from the household garden and put up as much as they could. Enid was unable to put away as much as the other women on the island; her job allowed limited time for gardening. The supply boat brought her the necessities which she was fortunately able to purchase with her wages. The Connells also had a few sheep, cared for at a price by one of the full-time farm wives. They received their share of wool and were soon busy carding and winding yarn. The Inn was given a thorough cleaning, and lastly an inventory was made, so that Enid could order supplies well in advance for next summer.

Time passed more quickly than Gwyn would have imagined. After a week she was thoroughly exhausted and ready to take a few days off.

One day just five days after Tom's departure she realized that her monthlies were late. Impossible, she thought, but then she remembered the night of the dance. After a few more agonizing days had crept by, she was certain she must be pregnant. Still she kept her silence another week. It was probably the longest seven days of her short life. Again she prayed for deliverance; she wanted Tom but not this way. This time she received no answer. Or perhaps she received the strongest answer of all. How could it be? she asked herself and then laughed bitterly at herself. Why not? They had made love countless times, she should have realized the stupidity of her body's needs.

Two weeks after Tom's departure she told her mother. Enid paled. Unlike Gwyn she had been fearful of just such a catastrophe from the very beginning.

"Was it deliberate?" she asked. "Did you want a baby so you could keep him?"

"No!" cried Gwyn. "I wouldn't trap him. Why should I need to? He loves me. Oh, Mother!" She wept in shame. "What shall I do?"

"You will write him immediately, that's what," said Enid.

"But we promised."

"Never mind what you promised. You must write to him now, tonight." She stood and began to pace restlessly around the small room.

"How far gone are you; are you absolutely certain?"

"It must be almost a month. Yes, I'm sure." Again the tears, but this time the grief was mingled with relief at having shared her torment.

"Can you forgive me?" asked Gwyn.

"Oh, my dear child, there is nothing to forgive. It's all my fault, my fault. How could I have been so blind!" Enid's face was twisted with remorse. Her fine hands were clenching and unclenching her apron, leaving wrinkled patches scattered like blots on the starched white fabric.

She crossed the room and took Gwyn in her arms. Standing, she rocked her back and forth. In the firelight they stood embracing, heads bent with the burdens of their shared femininity. How I wish Gareth were here! thought Enid. He would know how to comfort her. Her own tears came later after she had helped Gwyn write a carefully worded letter to Tom in which she asked him to return immediately. She refrained from revealing her pregnancy, not trusting such information to the written word. Her tone, however, was urgent; she knew he would hasten back.

In the morning Gwyn ran to the island pier to catch Ethan before he left for Buckley.

"Ethan!" she cried. "Wait up! I have a letter!"

Ethan stood, puzzled, as the girl ran down the pier and thrust the letter into his outstretched hand. She did not stop to talk but merely said, "Post it immediately please! There should be an answer within a week."

She ran off again and Ethan looked down at the letter. Mr. Thomas Warner. But she promised! thought Ethan. For the first time he mistrusted her. Does Enid know? No, of course not, that's why she waited until the last minute to bring it to me. So she wants me to be her go-between does she? He angrily stuffed the letter into the flat water-proof pouch he kept for the mail. It lay next to only three other letters today, all addressed to the niece of the Curran sisters. A good breeze was coming up, and Ethan decided to stick to his job on the crossing. The letter had spoiled his sail. Usually he liked the fall runs the best, knowing that winter would soon be upon them all and fine days few.

Halfway across the channel between Buckley and the island he fixed his sail and pulled the letter from the pouch. Gwyn's delicate writing held his sight. Slowly he held the letter up to the sunlight and tried to make out the words within, but there were two pages or more and he could decipher nothing.

Just then, a strong puff of wind came up and the letter rustled in the air. His hand seemed detached from the rest of him and he watched in horror as it released the letter into the wind. He saw the white envelope flutter out onto the water where it lay for an instant before sinking under the waves, carrying with it Gwyn's hopes.

It occurred to Ethan that he had perhaps committed the most dishonorable act of his life. Why did his feelings for Gwyn constantly challange his morality? Still, she had promised not to write. He should have simply refused to post the letter, but it had happened too quickly for him to think it through. He would tell her what he had done when he returned next week. But even as he vowed to confess, he knew he would not. His motives had not been pure and he was man enough to admit that to himself. But not to Gwyn. She would suspect and then guess at his true feelings and be disgusted. He felt unclean and ashamed to be caught in this unseemly passion at his age. Things would have been all right, he rationalized, if she had not inadvertently aroused his slumbering blood. He set his jaw into the wind and took the line in a knotty fist. It was done. He must put it from his mind.

When he returned a week later, Gwyn was waiting on the pier. Her face was pinched and there were purple shadows under the feverishly bright eyes. He could not bring himself to speak; instead he shook his head and then quickly looked away in a vain attempt to avoid seeing the frightened disappointment on her face.

"Will you be coming over again this week?" she asked; there was supplication in her voice.

"Yes, lass, in three days and then again a week from today." By then she will know he will not answer, he thought. She'll probably assume that his blasted honor has kept him from writing. Damnation, he had probably elevated Tom in her opinion!

Ethan was prepared to accept the consequences of his act until he went to Enid's cottage for his cup of tea. "There was no letter?" asked Enid, in the tone of one who already knows the answer.

"You know about the letter?" asked Ethan, surprised.

"Of course I know. I made her write it," said Enid.

This was the second moment when he could have saved them all, but he let it pass, numbed by the force of his guilt. He could have asked why Enid had made her write the letter, but he knew deep within him that there could be only one reason. Still he kept silent, a wild unreasonable idea forming itself in his mind. He drank his tea and tried to talk of other things, of the house he had built in the center of Buckley and of his new dry goods store which he had tried to pattern after Darcy's emporium in Salem but on a smaller scale, of course. Enid half-listened, her mind far away, and Gwyn never came home at all.

Where was she? thought Ethan, grateful nevertheless to be spared the sight of the pain he had caused. Was she on her cliffs or perhaps down in the rocks recalling her lover? Never mind, he would make it up to her. She would never be happy with that frail aristocrat. He knew her, knew the passions that stirred her, and he knew her darker side, the island side that was stubborn and superstitious. They would scorn her in Boston. She belonged with someone who could love all of her, not just the bookish side.

Another week passed and it was almost the end of September. When Ethan came to the pier there was no one to greet him except a solitary gull, his eyes beady and accusing as Ethan made his way up the crossbars of the ramp. Gwyn must finally have given up, he hoped. Watching her these past times had been a misery, seeing her gradual acceptance of his empty mail pouch.

Tonight he had a glass of ale with Oakie Williams and then went on to the Connell cottage. On this way he stopped at his own place, washed his face and hands, and put on a clean shirt. He found the women at home by the fire. They both tensed with expectation as he entered, but when he shook his head again the life seemed to run out of them. He produced the bottles of ale he had brought along with him from Oakie's place and took his chair by the hearth. The fire glow hit the planes of Gwyn's face, setting her lovely features into relief.

"I've come to have a serious talk with both of you," he said, and waited for their attention.

"I want to marry Gwyn." There. It was out. The disbelief on Gwyn's face was only a little less wounding than the sudden look of gratitude from Enid. He went on, wanting to deliver his piece before they could protest.

"Now, I know I'm too old for you Gwyn but there's still life in me and I'd be good to you. You could live in Buckley in a nice house and be somebody. Enid, you could live with us if you want. I can afford it and although I'm not yet wealthy I will be someday soon."

"That's a very generous offer Ethan. What do you say Gwyn?" Ethan had not concealed his growing feelings from Enid as well as he had hoped.

"Mother, stop it! We can't do this to Ethan!" cried Gwyn, rising. "Ethan, I'm going to have a baby. That's what the letter was about. But there's been no answer and now there never will be. If Tom were coming, he'd have been here on the first available boat. You were both right and I was the fool." She began to weep and the other two were quiet, giving her time to compose herself.

"Lass. I guessed about the baby but that doesn't matter to me. If you're willing to let on it's mine, I'll be happy to have it. God knows I've wanted a babe of my own for a while now. Aw, don't cry, lass, it'll be all right." He took her in his arms and let her cry herself out like a child. All the while he stroked the dark hair and murmured comfort to her.

During this scene Enid sat, stunned by the passion she saw on Ethan's face. She had known that he cared for Gwyn, but she had not realized how much or in what way.

"Very well, Ethan," said Gwyn suddenly in control of herself and the situation. "I shall marry you but, please, as soon as possible. Can you take out the papers and bring the minister over?"

"I can and I will. As it happens, I've already made

some arrangements, hoping you'd say yes. We can be wed day after tomorrow if you're willing."

"Day after tomorrow?" said Gwyn dazedly. "That's fine, just fine. I'm very tired now. Goodnight, Mother, and thank you, Ethan." She turned and walked slowly into her bedroom and shut the door firmly but quietly behind her.

"You forgot something, Ethan," said Enid.

"What's that?" he asked.

"You forgot to tell her that you love her," said Enid. Her voice was scarcely a whisper but somehow it filled the room.

"Aye. That I do." he said. He found speech difficult, so strong was his emotion now that it had finally been unmasked.

Gwyn was oddly calm as she put on her long night-gown and tied back her hair. She crawled under the covers and lay staring at the ceiling. Her pain was too deep to have fully risen to the surface. She felt a minor relief at knowing her baby would have a name, but her heart was too full of Tom to see anything extraordinary in Ethan's proposal. Placing her hands on her still-flat stomach, she tried to understand her errors. That she should not have become sexually involved with Tom was obvious from practical as well as moral considerations, but it was the failure of her own instincts which troubled her most. If she had been wrong about Tom (with his candid eyes), then it was likely that she was wrong about many other things. Perhaps she should have written again or, better still, gone to Boston herself. The image of herself standing alone like a beggar on a doorstoop was unthinkable. No, the letter had arrived, Ethan would have seen that it went safely to its destination; and Tom had read it and done what? She could not imagine his putting it carelessly aside. Had his parents come home unexpectedly and prevailed upon him to abandon her? That was more likely. She should have known that his

family and the twenty-odd years he'd spent surrounded by
its values would ultimately be too much for one foolish girl
with her delusions of love. She had not seen her love as
presumptuous, she didn't now, but the old class-conscious-
ness was latent within her, threatening her self-esteem and
eliciting all the island pride. Ethan was good and, more
important, he was her kind. She knew him well enough to
believe that he would indeed love the child and keep them
all, Enid included, as a strong unit. Her mind drifted from
Tom to Ethan and, exhausted, she fell asleep.

❧14❧

Gwyn's wedding day was the antithesis of her dreams.
In the living room she stood, unadorned, beside her hulk-
ing husband-to-be as the inarticulate minister mumbled the
ancient words of marriage. The unfortunate Reverend
Plummer had been dragged most unceremoniously from
his bed late the evening before and been ordered to present
himself on the Buckley dock at nine o'clock the next morning. He had found Mr. MacNeil's haste unseemly. He
would have preferred to spend the day working on his
sermon, especially in view of the miserable weather, and
the trip across to Parker's Island had done nothing to alter
his unchristian mood. Rain fell like a shroud; he was ill-
dressed for a sea voyage.

When he arrived at the Connell house he mistook Enid
for the bride and was appalled when he was told that the

pale child with the sad eyes was Ethan's intended. The whole thing was wrong. Where were the guests? Only one witness besides the bride's mother was present, and a fine sight he was!

Oakie Williams was not his usual chipper self as he stood in the background, shifting uncomfortably from peg to leg. He shared the minister's dismay. Why, Ethan had shared his ale just two days before and never said a word! He was disappointed on a personal level also. Ethan had renounced his island run. Thereafter he and Gwyn would live in Buckley. Oakie would miss his friend. He would also miss the big island wedding with music and whisky that he had envisioned for Gwyn when her time came. Ah, well. He had lived long enough to leave things alone. When the proper moment came, he handed Ethan the ring that had belonged to the groom's mother for fifty years, and then he stepped back into the shadows as quickly as possible.

When he had declared the couple man and wife, the Reverend Plummer waited for the usual smiles and celebration which customarily followed the ceremony. When none came, he turned to gather up his things but Enid said, "Wait! We must toast the bride and groom!" She produced a bottle of wine and solemnly filled the glasses. Ordinarily Mr. Plummer eschewed spirits of any kind save communion wine, but the whole scene had become distasteful and he surprised himself (and Oakie Williams) by downing his wine in a single gulp and stretching out his still-cold hand for more.

Throughout the wedding Gwyn had stood silent, saying her words when called upon but volunteering no emotional response except when she was offered the wine. Then she smiled at her mother with her lips; her eyes remained passive. The minister began to wonder if the girl was all right in the head. Maybe he shouldn't have agreed to perform the ceremony without learning more about the bride. Still, Mr. MacNeil was an honorable man. Surely the

girl was merely nervous. She looked too young to be married, but there it was on her birth certificate, eighteen years
old.

Valiantly Enid chattered away as the couple walked to
the dock. Gwyn's clothes barely filled one valise, and Enid
fought down a lump in her throat as she noticed how thin
her daughter had become in a few short weeks. The
thought of returning alone to the cottage and sitting in the
gloom without her dear Gwyn was almost too much for
even her stoical spirit. She made her goodbyes brief and
promised to come for a long visit in November. It seemed
a century away. And would Gwyn take care of herself and
the baby? Ethan said he knew a good doctor, but Enid was
more concerned about her daughter's frame of mind than
about her health. When the boat bearing the newlyweds
and the slightly tipsy minister had gone off into the rain,
Oakie Williams shyly spoke. "I don't suppose you'd like to
come have a mug of ale with me, would yer?"

"As a matter of fact Oakie, that's just what I would
like, and bless you for asking!" She linked her arm in his,
and the unlikely twosome went down the road, each one
feeling all at sea.

After a stormy crossing, Ethan's boat finally reached
Buckley and not a moment too soon for the Reverend
Plummer, whose stomach was unaccustomed both to liquor and choppy seas. Gravely, he shook the hands of Mr.
and Mrs. MacNeil, and then hastened home hoping to find
a fire in the study. He also hoped that the weather would
suffice to account for his unusual pallor.

Buckley had changed since Gwyn had last been ashore.
Main Street had always been a local joke, its four buildings
hardly comprising a metropolis. Now, interspersed with
new shops were several large frame houses. Gwyn wondered which one was Ethan's but had still not found her
voice. Two farmers passed and scanned the newcomer with

stealthy glances. "Good day, Mr. MacNeil," they said. So
he was that well known, was he?

"Not much of a wedding was it lass?" said Ethan,
holding her arm.

"I suppose not, but it doesn't matter. We're married
just the same."

"Of course it matters. Just as soon as we get settled in,
we'll have a party." Seeing her alarmed look, he added,
"Not a wedding reception, of course. I guess it's better not
to advertise the wedding date, what with the baby and all.
I just meant a few friends to get you started here. You'll like
the Buckley folks, they're a straightforward bunch. All
these city ways are just as new to them as they are to us."

"Whatever you say, Ethan." Gwyn had decided to be
as agreeable as possible, but her heart was cold and pining
still for the other one.

They came to a great white house, and Ethan stopped
and said, "There it is, dearie. Not a finer house in Buckley
except for the mayor's, of course." He indicated a formal
brick residence a few doors away.

"I think I like yours better," she said. "It's made of
wood, and somehow it looks friendlier." They went inside
to see the large open hall with its winding stairs. Gwyn
found it incredible that she should be standing here amidst
this luxury. Oh, she had listened to Ethan's tales of his
house, but never had she envisioned a mansion house.

"Your house is beautiful, Ethan," she said.

"Our house, lass. Our house. Now c'mon and let's give
you a look around." How proud he was and rightly so,
thought Gwyn. Despite herself her mood lightened as they
went from one beautifully appointed room to the next.

The house was large, with high ceilings, and glistening
windows which seemed towering to Gwyn after the
clouded panes of her island home. There were five rooms
downstairs, the long parlor to the left of the wide hall and
the formal dining room to the right, and the library,

kitchen and sitting rooms to the rear. In the parlor were three rosewood sofas, one in blue, one in mauve, and one in palest rose. How extraordinary that Ethan should have selected such delicate shades! The draperies went from ceiling to floor and were of cream-colored brocade edged in blue. In one corner was a grand piano, over which had been carelessly tossed an Oriental shawl of intricate beauty. The walls were painted the same white as the draperies. It was a perfectly appointed room. Why, then, did Gwyn's heart ache for home and the tiny front room where she had read her books and sipped her tea? No, she must put those thoughts away. Forcing a smile to her lips she began to praise the rose medallion bowls and the ornate teakwood desk in the library.

All the bounty Ethan had brought back from the Orient was settled in the house in happy juxtaposition with Queen Anne chairs and Chippendale settees and tables. My husband must be very prosperous, thought Gwyn. How strange to think that our Ethan with his pipe and old boots has been living two lives. The idea enchanted her; but then, Ethan had always been a bit magical to her ever since she had listened at his knee to his wondrous tales. And now he was her husband.

A few minutes after the married couple left the dock, a train pulled into the Buckley station and out stepped a young man. He hurried to the town landing and hailed an old fellow who looked as if he knew what he was doing.

"Excuse me," he said. "Would you happen to know if a Mr. Ethan MacNeil is around? I want a ride out to the island and he usually goes out today."

"Ethan MacNeil? Why, sonny, he's not going anywhere today. Guess you haven't heard. He just got married. I saw him and his new wife just a half hour ago, coming back from the island."

"From the island? She's an islander then?" said Tom.

"Yup. Name's Gwyn Connell. A bit young for old Ethan, but he's probably still man enough to do the job." He laughed and his breath made mist in the chilly air.

"You must be mistaken. Did you say Gwyn Connell?"

"Aye. That's the one. No mistake neither. You don't forget a good looker like that with them blue eyes and all that curly dark hair. No, it's Miss Connell all right, or maybe I'd best say Mrs. MacNeil."

Tom's senses screamed denial. "Where are they now, do you know?" The calm sound of his own voice belied his panic.

"Most likely at Ethan's house. See down Main Street there? It's the big white one with the iron fence around it; but you don't want to be bothering them now. They're honeymooners!" He sat unruffled as the young man took off down the street at a run. "Young folks don't know when to butt out!" he called at the now distant figure.

Tom ran up the steps two at a time and banged the big brass door knocker. Ethan himself answered the door. Gwyn was nowhere in sight. The two men stood face to face for a long moment, then Tom spoke. "Where's Gwyn. I've got to talk to Gwyn."

"She doesn't want to talk to you. She and I are married now."

"But there must be some reason," said Tom. There was a desperate note in his voice.

"The reason is, she wanted to marry one of her own kind, so don't you come around worrying her now. It's done and there's nothing you can do to change it even if she wanted to, which she doesn't." All the guilt flooded over him as he saw the despair on Tom's face. "I'm sorry, lad, but that's what she wanted. You'll find someone else, just wait and see." There was tenderness now in Ethan's voice. All the old rage died in the presence of the younger man's misery. But Tom didn't hear the tenderness or even the exact words. He turned and walked back down the steps and headed back to the train station.

Nothing for me here, he thought. Suddenly the summer was like a half-forgotten dream, a dream that had never happened. But in the center of the dream was Gwyn. Beautiful Gwyn, who was brave and funny and who loved him! She was real enough. Not the Gwyn who hid behind Ethan and refused to face him, but his own Gwyn, and she would never fade away.

In the train station he noticed a shoeshine boy staring at him, and he realized with a start that he was weeping. His chin was wet with tears, and he reached inside his pocket for a handkerchief with which to dry them, but in a second his face was wet again with the silent tears steadily falling over the tightly clenched jaw. When the train to Boston arrived, he stepped aboard in a trance and took a seat in the last coach.

It was several weeks before Gwyn felt comfortable in her new house. For one thing it was too big. The long parlor which ran the depth of the first floor seemed immense in comparison to Enid's cramped front room. To be sure, there were fireplaces at either end, but with central heating they were more decorative than useful. Moreover, they were made of white marble with carved rosettes along the sides; there was no hearth with hanging pots to cry "Welcome."

The dining room was worse. The Chinese plates which a housegirl set before her were exquisite but foreign in a way that had nothing to do with their country of origin.

"They were my mother's. I gave 'em to her after the first trip I made where I got a partner's share. She wouldn't use them, though. Said they were too fancy for the island and that they'd make her friends nervous. As a matter of fact, I unpacked them just a week ago. We'll be needing them now that you're here. Folks are friendly hereabouts;

they'll expect to be invited to dinner."

Gwyn was already aware of their friendliness. The very day after the MacNeils came home, Mr. and Mrs. Simeon Blanchard had arrived laden with gifts. The Blanchards were, of course, unaware that the MacNeils were only a day married. Ethan had predated the wedding by two weeks.

Gwyn liked Louise Blanchard immediately. With her sharp features and modish clothes she was a new type for Gwyn. Outspoken and witty, she greeted Gwyn warmly and presented her with a loaf of bread which was at least two feet long.

"Americans simply do not know how to bake bread," she sighed. "Simeon bought me a decent oven last month, and so now I show off for you." Her English was excellent, a tribute to her quick mind. Simeon Blanchard was hand-some and quiet, and the two seemed to complement each other. The four had chatted amiably and drank tea from translucent cups, but as the Blanchards prepared to leave, Louise took Gwyn aside and asked her point-blank if she were feeling well.

"Yes, of course," said Gwyn.

"You look a bit white in the face. You call on me soon if you don't feel good. Is a promise?"

That evening at the dinner table Gwyn felt ill and for the next month she had regular intervals of nausea. The Frenchwoman's perception had been uncanny.

During this time Gwyn gradually familiarized herself with her surroundings. The house became more comforta-ble, and she even learned how to handle herself with the housemaid. This last task was the most difficult for one who had been a chambermaid just six weeks before. She won-dered what little Molly, the housemaid, would say if she knew about Gwyn's former life.

Sometimes in the mornings Gwyn would awake alone in the big double bed and gaze out the bay windows which overlooked the small harbor which was only a street away. From her vantage point, the main street tapered off toward the harbor. Ethan's store was several hundred yards away on the left. How imposing it looked, all right angles and Georgian brick! Next to it was Louise Blanchard's dress shop, and across from that was a small carpentry shop. The street was straight and wide. Some farsighted soul had planted rows of trees on either side. Gwyn was no horticulturist; the vegetation on the island was for consumption only, but she hoped these trees would be flower-laden come spring. No doubt about it, it was a nice little town. The big Congregational Church on her right was washed in pristine white and the dozen or so large houses were neatly maintained. It was a good place to grow, to put away the past and carry on.

There being no Presbyterian Church as yet; she found that she enjoyed the simplicity of the Congregational services and the straightforward old hymns. Still, there was a holding back in her, an underlying desire to shuck her new shoes and stays and run around once more with grass between her toes. She would think about the island as morning sickness overtook her and then she would fight back both illness and grief. But descending the stairs she would see the beauty of her house and the look in her husband's eyes, and she would think of her baby and of how good her daughter's life would be here in this happy town where her parent's friends would be the mayor and the businessmen, people who dined rather than ate, and people who dressed for dinner. She always thought of the child as a girl.

Ethan never touched her sexually, but continued to be charming. He introduced his friends gradually, fearing for her health, and after her nausea subsided he took her out calling. His friends were decent folk who were very kind to Gwyn. As new to this life as Ethan, they combined a sincere desire for self-improvement with an occasional lapse into earthy good humor.

It became apparent that Ethan was a favorite. She began to think of him proudly as "my Ethan." Her pregnancy was still not apparent when Enid came to visit.

"Darling. How well you look! From your letters I was afraid I'd find you quite wasted away!"

"I almost was, but two weeks ago, I suddenly felt well again, and now Ethan says he can't fill me up, I eat so much. It's lovely to have an appetite again. And you look well, too. Oh, Mother, I'm so glad to see you!"

The three were indeed happy to be reunited. On the first night of her visit Enid rearranged one corner of the parlor so that there was a sofa facing the fireplace less than five feet away. With this simple adjustment the room became home to Gwyn; in fact, her friends were to say in years to come that they loved to take tea with Gwyn Mac-Neil because her parlor was so warm and friendly.

Enid sensed that Gwyn had come to terms with her situation. Indeed, it would be an odd woman who could fail to appreciate the comforts which surrounded her daughter.

"Now. You must promise to stay the winter," said Ethan.

"Oh, I can't, really."

"But you must, Mother! The baby's due in May. Surely you'll stay at least 'til then?" cried Gwyn.

"I'll come back over in time. I promise," said Enid, but she looked amenable to persuasion and by the time Christmas came near she had succumbed to Ethan's arguments.

She had her own reasons for staying on. From the first night she had been aware that Gwyn and Ethan had separate bedrooms. She found this disheartening. Perhaps if she remained she could have a talk with Gwyn. After all, how could the two become close if they slept alone? It was not as if Gwyn were a virgin. Maybe it was the baby. Some men were shy with a pregnant woman. Considering that it was not his own child, it would not be surprising if Ethan were reluctant to approach Gwyn at this time. She decided to bide her time until after the holidays.

Buckley took Christmas to its heart. Ruddy-faced carolers began to appear on doorsteps two weeks in advance of the big day. The Reverend Plummer decided to shuck his usual Christmas sermon about the gift of life in favor of a new modern approach using the three kings as an example of wealth put to good use. Louise Blanchard went into an orgy of baking which necessitated her hiring an extra girl at the dress shop. The dress shop itself did a huge business as the new gentlewomen of the town prepared for Christmas parties.

Ethan and Gwyn were going to have a large party on the twenty-third. It was the first large gathering which Gwyn and Ethan were to host, and she was both nervous and exhilarated. She was beginning to show her condition, but fortunately the style in Buckley was still towards skirts with a lot of material and Gwyn had retained some sort of waist. She had confided her pregnancy to Louise (who was not at all surprised), and together they found the perfect gown in a shade of deep rose. The gown had an extra panel of white lace in front and unless one knew for sure, one would never guess that there were four months of child beneath.

In one corner of the parlor was a ten-foot Christmas tree. It was Gwyn's first tree. On the island there were no trees to spare, and they had had to content themselves with either decorating a bush outside or making one from branches and driftwood. But this tree was a glory to Gwyn. She was embarrassed to admit that she had never seen a real Christmas tree before. Her few trips to the mainland had been in the warm weather, and although she had seen pictures and read descriptions in her books, the reality was stunning. Like a child she pranced around and hung shiny new balls on the tree. Enid had the best surprise of all, for in her valise she had packed ten old ornaments that had belonged to her husband, Gareth, as a child. She had kept them packed away for years, fearful that the spirited young Gwyn would somehow break them and thereby destroy one more link between Gareth and his past. Gareth's parents had been unhappy with his marriage and his move to the island. When, after his parents had both died, he had been invited to take what he wanted from their estate, he had chosen only two things, the ornaments and a set of silver flatware for Enid. The remainder of the large estate had gone to charity according to his parents' wishes. Now, Enid held the ornaments up to the light, and they all exclaimed over the frail beauty of the tiny trumpets and lacy silver angels. How typical of Gareth to choose these treasures from his youth and how right that they should hang here on Gwyn's first tree, under which she stood entranced, Gareth's grandchild in her belly.

The dining room table was laden with sweets and puddings. Louise had designed a croquembouche, that most impressive of French creations, with its pyramid of cream puffs and caramel cocooned in spun sugar. Around this chef d'oeuvre were Enid's lemon brambles and tiny shortdough crescents rolled in powdered sugar. Ethan had concocted a punch which was comprised of so many different liquors that Gwyn preferred not to know the recipe. At least he had used red wine as a base, which gave it a proper color for Christmas.

The host was resplendent in his kilt. Ethan refused to abandon his favorite attire and seeing him in full dress, Gwyn was happy. In his plaid, he made her feel at home. He had promised to foreswear the bagpipes, however, which was just as well; Gwyn would have feared for the glass balls on the tree.

At nine o'clock the Blanchards arrived and the five lit the candles on the tree. Gwyn felt a catch in her throat as she saw these dear people in the candlelight of her very own tree. There was only one face missing, but Gwyn fought the image down and out of Ethan's house.

By ten the guests had assembled and were gaily admiring the house, the food and each other. Gwyn had engaged a group of carolers to come at midnight, and the choir, gathered around the new grand piano, led the entire party in song until almost two o'clock when the party, especially those members with small children, disbanded.

Outside, a light snow had fallen and when the last guests had departed, Ethan stood beside his pretty bride and watched the moonlight sparkle on the snow as the last voices trailed off down the street.

"It's a lovely night," said Gwyn.

"Aye, lass. That it is. And you were a lovely hostess. They all had a fine time."

"They did, didn't they? It was the carols that did it. Christmas isn't the same without music." Then, "Where's Mum?"

"Gone to bed. We'd best too. Let Molly clean up in the morning. You sleep in, I don't want you getting tired out." Ethan closed the door and the two went up the stairs.

"Would you help me with my dress. It's got buttons down the back, and I hate to bother Molly so late at night."

Ethan followed her into her room, watching her carefully as she removed her long gloves. Her hair was dressed with curls at her nape and she lifted them, inviting him to undo her dress. The provocation was not intentional, but the effect on Ethan was profound. He carefully undid the buttons one by one, and then as Gwyn slipped her arms out of the sleeves he slid his hands around her waist and turned her around. She looked up at him, at first surprised and then acquiescent. He carried her to the bed as easily as if she were nothing at all. As they passed the dresser, she saw them both reflected in the mirror for an instant and her body was stirred by the glimpse of the brawny man with the curling sandy hair who held her so lightly in his arms.

Ethan was a skilled lover, and although at first Gwyn

fought her responses her body betrayed her. She had had no physical love in the last months and was powerless to resist this man with his knowing hands and his passionately murmured phrases. When she awoke in the morning to find him slumbering beside her, his kilt in a heap on the floor, she sighed a little sigh in respect for her lost love for Tom. Then, glancing at the kilt once more, she laughed aloud and woke up her husband.

"What is it, lass?" he mumbled from under his beard.

"Nothing at all." She knew better than to take a man's kilt lightly. "It's just a lovely day, that's all."

He was fully awake now and pulled her tousled head down to his mouth. Once again she had the pleasure of his passion as the sunlight bounced off the new snow and washed the room in light.

That afternoon Gwyn insisted on walking alone to the harbor. Ethan was reluctant to have her go; he feared for her safety with the new snow on the streets. Luckily, he had to leave on a secret errand himself, so it was eventually decided that he should take her in the carriage to the town landing and retrieve her in half an hour's time.

In the carriage he placed a bare hand over her mittened one and gazed at her with such frank adoration that she had to look away. Watching him go off she marvelled at her duplicity. If she had run away with a salesman, she could not feel more cheapened. Tom was with her still. She could spend whole days without allowing herself to think of him and then, without warning, she would feel him with her and be weak with longing. Somewhere deep inside, she had known that she would enjoy sleeping with Ethan. Pregnancy had made her aware of her body, and this awareness had reawakened the old desires. If only she and Tom could have had it out. Yelled and screamed, if need be, and thrown objects around the room! At least it would have been official; "They quarrelled and parted," people would say. It happened every day. Instead, she was stuck somewhere between her past and her present. And the present was swallowing her up just as Ethan had known it would. Still she clung stubbornly to her pain, nursing it like a dying child that she wanted to see out of its misery but was loathe to lose.

Worse was the fear that she was shallow and wanton to have enjoyed Ethan's passion so totally. Each week as the pregnancy advanced she would say to herself "So many weeks" and into her mind would spring "Since he made love to you that hot night on the beach." She should be grateful that she was finally healing but she couldn't be, and she refused to give up the image of her baby's father.

Ethan bounded down from the carriage and walked into the carpenter's shop. For several weeks he had been sneaking away on pretext of business to use the shop of his friend, Mac Spinosi. Mac was the product of a seafaring father who had somehow found himself far from his sunny Italian home and succumbing to a blond Scottish girl from Buckley, Massachusetts. With tight blond curls and dark eyes, Mac was a delightful mixture of his parents. Behind his shop was a storage room, and it was here that Ethan had been working in secret on a cradle. But not just a cradle; rather, a work of art with carved roses and perfectly balanced runners. He knew the fashion was for high-legged bassinets these days, but he also felt certain that Gwyn would prefer the old way.

Today he was happy—no, ecstatic. Not only had he finally possessed Gwyn (such indescribable joy), but in doing so he had at last laid down his burden of guilt. He had vowed to make her happy and he knew that he had satisfied her as a lover. She could never have given herself so completely if she still cared for Tom Warner. So it was settled and it had come out for the best. She was his own now and in a strange way so was the babe. Holding her body, ripe with life within, had made him part of the child at last. He sang out to Mac, who showed him the crated cradle, and then the two men gingerly hoisted it into the back of the carriage where they covered it with a blanket.

$\S 15 \S$

Christmas eve was calm and bright just as in the song. But there was little silence. All the time Ethan had been preparing his surprise for Gwyn, she had been working on one of her own. As soon as they returned from the candle-light service at church, Gwyn took Ethan's arm.

"Come into the parlor Ethan," she ordered. "Now, cover your eyes and don't move. Mother and I have a surprise for you."

"But it's not morning! Presents should come in the morning," he protested. He nevertheless obediently covered his eyes and stood beside the tree.

"This present had no intention of staying in a box until Christmas day," laughed Gwyn. "Ready? All right, open your eyes."

Ethan obeyed and saw standing before him the totally embarrassed face of Oakie Williams.

"Oakie, you old bastard! Oh, forgive me, ladies," cried Ethan as he embraced his old friend. The two grinned and giggled like the schoolboys they had been together.

"How in the devil did these women of mine talk you off the island? Why the only other time I can remember you leaving was when that girl from the distillery talked you into taking her to that dance in Salem. Do you remember how drunk you got? No, of course you don't. It was me that had to put you on the boat home."

"Shut yer trap, Ethan, there's ladies present," said Oakie, red as a boiled lobster.

"Tell me, Gwyn. How'd you do it?" asked Ethan.

"Our Oakie is going to open a restaurant right here in Buckley."

"No! Why that's amazing! Plum amazing."

"And what's so amazing I'd like to know?" asked Oakie. "I'm one damn fine cook if I do say so, and why should I miss out on the bonanza. You sure have done well enough for yourself."

Now that Oakie had found his tongue, they all discussed his plans and made merry long into the evening. Gwyn felt right at home, as if she had brought the island to her own doorstep. She was also pleased to see that Oakie was enjoying himself. It had taken no little amount of persuasion by Enid and Gwyn to convince him to invest his small nest egg and abandon his island womb for the perils of the mainland. Despite Ethan's jocularity, Oakie remembered all too well his evening with the distillery maid.

"Perhaps Louise would help you with the baking?" said Gwyn.

"I hear she's bringing her cousin over from France to open a bakery. Most likely Pierre will be delighted to have a famous restaurant serving his bread and pastries," said Ethan.

"Pierre? Is that his name?" asked Gwyn.

"Haven't the faintest idea," replied Ethan. "It just sounded good." He guffawed at his own joke, and they all groaned in mock horror at his island sense of humor.

After Oakie had gone off to enjoy a night's sleep in an elegant four-poster bed, and after Enid had suggested that they all sleep a bit late even if it was Christmas morning

("After next year there will be the baby," she said), Ethan and Gwyn went to bed. He followed her into her room as easily as if they had been sleeping together all along. This night his lovemaking was at once demanding and tender; demanding because he no longer feared offending her and tender because he wanted to explore the depth of her responses at leisure now that he had her at last.

Gwyn was surprised by the extent of his knowledge, although she knew he had not been celibate these many years. What surprised her more was his insistence on her pleasure. It was a nice trait in a husband.

In the morning they went downstairs in their wrappers. Gwyn knew that they should have dressed, but this year was a transitional one and it had always been wrappers on the island.

Waiting under the tree was the cradle, filled with smaller presents for Gwyn.

"Oh, Ethan. It's beautiful. Look Mamma! See the little roses all along the side!" The two women admired the cradle, rocking it this way and that to show how beautifully it balanced.

"Wherever did you find such a work of art?" asked Enid.

"Made it myself," said Ethan proudly.

"Honestly? Why, I had no idea you were so clever at woodworking." Gwyn was suitably impressed.

"Well, you know how it is on board ship. Some of the fellows did scrimshaw to pass the time and some of them did knitting, believe it or not; but I also used to carve driftwood. Got pretty good at it, too, after all the years out."

"I should say so!" cried Gwyn. "And now our baby will have the loveliest crib in Massachusetts."

Ethan had never heard her say "our baby" before. Usually it was "when the baby comes" or "this baby of mine." "What do you mean 'Massachusetts'?" he said. "It

was my intention to make it the best cradle in America."
Ethan at this moment was a completely happy man.

They opened presents for almost an hour, savoring
each gift in a way that only adults can understand. There
was a little fur cape for Enid which completely bowled her
over. "It's too grand, you two. Wherever will I wear it?"

"Why not to meeting with the Curran sisters? They'll
be sure you have a gentleman friend on the mainland," said
Ethan.

"Yes. Just like Colleen Murphy," hooted Oakie.

"Oh go on, you two!" said Gwyn. Her hand rested
lightly on her abdomen, and a peculiar look came into her
eyes. Fearing they had offended her with their talk of Colleen and her fatherless children, Ethan quickly thrust a
present into her hands.

In the afternoon they all took a walk. Enid walked
proudly ahead with her cape on her shoulders and Oakie
on her arm. It was difficult to say which item attracted the
most attention. Gwyn had also received a fur jacket and had
presented Ethan with a top hat which he carried off splen-
didly. Only Oakie was unable to wear his present, a volumi-
nous checked apron which Gwyn had presented to him
amidst much laughter. Ethan had written him a note for a
tidy sum of money to help get him started in his business.
Altogether it was a wonderful day.

When they returned home, Oakie remained outside,
needing a few minutes alone after all the excitement. Enid
went upstairs to rest before dinner, and Ethan and Gwyn
sat down side by side next to the fire.

"Your mother surely has a hand with a needle. Those
baby things are downright heavenly," sighed Ethan.

"You seem to have taken to words like 'heavenly' recently," said Gwyn, smiling.

"That's your fault lassie. With you in my bed at night
and all my best friends around it's about as near to heaven
as I expect to get."

"Can you stand a wee bit more happiness?" asked Gwyn.

"Try me," said Ethan stretching his arm around her shoulder.

"All right. I felt the baby move this morning. Just after I saw the cradle. Do you think that's a sign?" She looked up at him, trusting and young in the firelight. "Of course it is, lass. He knew you were happy just then. Babies sense things, I think." Ethan took her seriously. He too believed in omens. "He was probably trying to let us know that we were a family at last."

"You said 'he.' Why do you think it's a boy? I'm positive it's a girl, and you know I've always been able to guess about other people's babies."

"Maybe other people's, but not this one. No, I feel it in my bones, he's a boy. Not that I wouldn't just as soon have a lass with her mother's big eyes and dancing curls."

"Flatterer," she said and rested her head on his shoulder. She was at peace and for the first time since summer she was able to think of Tom without feeling her heart break. Oh, there was still a twinge, but she could live with a twinge. At least the terrible pain of the fall had subsided. She felt considerably older than her almost nineteen years. Oddly enough, Ethan seemed to have dropped ten years at least.

❧*16*❧

It was a hard winter in Buckley. After the Christmas Eve snowfall, the weather settled into a pattern of snow and freezing rain. With the sea so close, the snow melted quickly, but then the frost would come leaving every twig and walkway slick and shining with ice. In the harbor, masts were frozen into glorious shafts of silver like the weapons of an arctic god.

Gwyn found herself almost housebound as her girth increased. She had expected to feel less and less attractive as time went on, but Ethan's adoration made ugliness unthinkable, so she settled for a sigh now and then as she turned her profile to the full-length mirror in the upstairs hall.

In February Gwyn turned nineteen. The family decided not to hold a large celebration (no point calling attention to her extreme youth), but there was candlelight and champagne and six of winter's scarce lobsters to enjoy. Savoring the white flesh, Gwyn recalled the lobsterbake on the island, and her feeling of separateness from the Boston crowd. Whatever would they all think to see her now, eating delicacies while surrounded by comfort and approval? Some small inner voice insisted on reminding her that Tom had loved her despite her relative poverty, but a stronger voice said "No, it is not love that forgets so easily."

By the time spring had begun to make its presence felt, Gwyn was tired of waiting for this squirming, tumbling child to be born. At the same time, she hoped the birth would be late. With any luck at all the child could arrive almost nine months after the wedding date. She congratulated herself on having married Ethan so promptly. At the time, she had done it mostly for pride's sake, but now she felt an intense affection for her unborn child and already she recognized in herself a maternally protective urge.

Finally the ground bared itself, leaving mud and dappled pools on the lawns. Before the last patches of snow melted, the snowdrops sprang up, followed by tiny crocuses and then the long-awaited burst of blossoms from the trees on Main Street. Ethan and Gwyn began their walks again, and sometimes, when he was at the store, the two women would stroll carefully down the Main Street to see how Oakie's resturant was progressing. He had decided to offer continental food, wines and fancy desserts. Occasionally he came to the MacNeil house for the expressed purpose of trying out a new recipe on his friends.

Already Buckley was eagerly awaiting the grand opening in June, and no one more than Gwyn and Enid. Walking past the door of the restaurant, they admired the new blue and white striped awnings, and then they pressed their noses to the wide front window to see how the interior work was progressing.

Inside was a massive mahogany bar with a gilded rococo mirror above it. Overhead were crystal chandeliers but below, the floor was as yet unfinished.

"It's really coming along!" said Enid. "Who would have thought Oakie would fancy such a formal place?"

"Buckley needs a good restaurant; somewhere to go on special occasions and a place for businessmen to entertain. It's wonderful to see the town growing so. I'm especially happy about the plans for the new library. If I do say so,

our Ethan was a good choice for chairman of the planning
board," said Gwyn.

"You love him, don't you?" It was more a statement
than a question.

"Yes I do," replied Gwyn. "But sometimes I still wonder how it would have been if . . ." Her voice trailed off but
it didn't matter. Enid knew what her daughter meant.

"I want so to put it all in the past, but with the baby
I'm afraid it'll always be there."

"But surely after the child is born you will see that it's
Ethan's in every way that counts," said Enid.

"Oh, I know that. Already it seems like his child. Most
of the time anyway." They continued down the street and
then reversed themselves.

"Won't it be nice when they put in the sidewalks next
summer?" said Enid, stepping gingerly over the muddiest
spots.

Gwyn's baby was due in mid-May but her date came
and went without a sign. As the days passed, she ceased
being grateful for the delay and became frustrated and
jumpy. Added to her impatience was the fact that her
mother and her doctor were not seeing eye-to-eye on the
way things should be done.

"Whoever heard of bathing a new baby once a day.
Why the poor thing will freeze to death before it's a year
old," said Enid. There was a contempt in her voice.

"Now, mother. You know Dr. Rogers said that you did
the right thing to keep me especially warm on the island, but
it's different here! With central heating we can bathe the
baby safely." Gwyn could scarcely contain her amusement.
Dr. Rogers and her mother both considered themselves
experts on childbirth and babies. Even though Enid had
only one child herself, she had assisted at many island
births.

Dr. Rogers was a bit modern in his ways, thought

Gwyn, but she admired him for it. After all, if Buckley was to make something of itself, it must be up-to-date.

"If you ask me, that baby will be as dried out as a prune with all that water," said Enid, unconvinced.

"Well, perhaps we can skip a bath here or there," said Gwyn. "He doesn't need to know." The two women laughed and went back to sorting the piles of little baby things that they had been stitching all fall and winter.

As is generally the case, the baby waited until everyone had given up hoping and then announced its impending arrival at the most inconvenient time. After three weeks of hovering close to home, Ethan had finally succumbed to Gwyn's blandishments and gone to Salem for his newest shipment of imported goods.

Gwyn had not slept well the night before (no unusual event these days) and was feeling particularly crotchety. Only Enid was prepared, perhaps in fear that the newfangled doctor would somehow manage the whole thing alone if she were not ever-vigilant.

In any case, Ethan had just left Salem on his way home when Gwyn sent out a hurried call for the doctor. By the time Ethan arrived home, Gwyn was sequestered behind closed doors, and he was left in the parlor with only Oakie and a bottle of rum for comfort.

"Good God, Oakie," he said. "Do you know that I'm scared out of my wits?" He took hold of the bottle but thought twice and put it down. An hour passed. Oakie, who knew absolutely nothing about childbirth, began to feel he ought to do something, so he pulled a Jew's harp from his pocket and began to twang out a fair imitation of a bagpipe.

"Aye, that's the spirit!" said Ethan. His collar was damp with sweat and his hair was curled more tightly than ever as he mopped his brow. On the table the bottle stood a quarter empty.

Another hour passed and it was five o'clock.

The bottle was now half-empty (or half-full, as Ethan chose to see it!), and the melodies were sprightlier and louder until Enid appeared on the stairs.

"For mercy's sakes, will you two be quiet? How do you think Gwyn feels up there struggling away while you two are singing at the top of your lungs down here?"

"Is she all right? Is everything going all right?" cried Ethan, chastened.

"Everything's fine, but it'll be a while yet." Having issued her bulletin, Enid remounted the stairs.

"Oh my God, Oakie! What if she's not all right? What if something happens to the baby?" The bottle had scarcely an inch in it and Ethan was beginning to act like a man in mortal peril. His fear was contagious, and when Enid came down the stairs an hour and a half later she found Ethan weeping in Oakie's arms while the bottle stood empty, a silent witness to his panic.

"Shut up your blubbering, you damned fool!" she cried. "It's a boy! Almost eight pounds. Gwyn's fine. She had an easy time of it."

Easy? thought Oakie. She calls that easy?

"A boy!" cried Ethan. "I knew it! I knew it was a boy. Can I see her now?"

"Just for a minute. She's tired out. You men have no idea how exhausting it is to give birth to a child."

"The hell you say!" shouted Ethan as he ran up the stairs, covering two at a time despite his age and size.

In the bedroom he saw his son for the first time. The little face was bunched up with incipient hunger. He kissed the radiant face of the mother and timidly touched the tiny fingers that flailed away at nothing in particular.

"Ah, lass, he's beautiful." Tears filled his eyes as he pushed the damp locks away from Gwyn's brow.

"Yes," she said, "and he's ours." They remained thus, discussing the wonder of the babe until Gwyn fell asleep in midsentence, and Ethan hastily called in the nursemaid who had been engaged weeks before. The nurse took the baby, relieved to have something to do at last.

Downstairs Enid and Dr. Rogers had opened a bottle of champagne and were toasting each other and the baby.

"I guess you do know something about delivering babies, after all," she said. "I've never seen a birth go so smoothly."

"That's because I had such a good helper," returned the the doctor gallantly. "But don't get any notions. That baby is going to be fed, and bathed," he added pointedly, "according to instructions."

"We shall see," said Enid confidently, a trace of the old antagonism in her voice.

"Truce," said Dr. Rogers. "And a toast to the pretty grandmother." Enid did not know whether to be flattered by the "pretty" or taken aback at being called a grandmother for the first time. She chose to be complimented on all counts as she accepted the toast.

Oakie was out cold on the sofa, and for a moment Enid's eyes met the doctor's and she noticed for the first time that his eyes were a lovely shade of green.

❦ *17* ❦

Gareth Jeremy MacNeil (called Jeremy from the first time he clutched Ethan's finger in his clammy fist) lived up to all expectations. He rolled from front to back at three months and from back to front at four.

More important, he smiled at the age of four weeks and, once started, rarely stopped. He had good lungs at feeding time and showed a healthy contempt for his elders from time to time, but his general disposition was sunny and his blue eyes bright. From the day of his discreet late arrival into the world, he set a pattern of accommodation and excellent taste.

Gwyn adored him. Her naturally loving nature was able, at last, to give itself wholeheartedly to another human being. In the private room of her thoughts she granted him the best of his three parents. He had his mother's Celtic eyes and his natural father's fair hair and pleasant expression, but somewhere along the way he had also absorbed Ethan's extroversion and lust for living. He would chortle when stroked and croon over his milk. And sometimes he would fix his mother with a knowing look that would cause her to roar with laughter at its premature sagacity.

Before he was a year old he could say several words, and he talked before he could walk. Ethan was a bit disappointed that the child was over a year old when he walked; he had come to expect precocity in all things, but Gwyn assured him that speech was just as important and as was usual Ethan acquiesced to her wisdom.

When summer turned to fall, Jeremy was dressed in his little navy blue jacket and cap and propped up in the carriage for all to admire. Ethan made an ass out of himself over the child, but he was forgiven. After all, a man who manages fatherhood for the first time at his age was due all congratulations.

Oakie's restaurant, The Williams House, opened to public acclaim, and Gwyn made the opening her first public appearance after Jeremy's birth. How wonderful it felt to be in clothes with waistlines again!

She was a beauty now. The womanly curve of her full bosom and the glow of contentment which motherhood brought had banished the last vestige of youthful awkwardness, and men's heads turned when she took her place at the best table in the restaurant. Ethan was so full of joy that he sometimes feared for the future. The old island suspicion of too much happiness occasionally rose to haunt him, but he brushed it aside, unwilling to let his darker side rise up to overshadow his new life.

On Jeremy's first birthday they had a party, inviting just the Blanchards, Dr. Rogers, a few of their close friends and of course Oakie, the boy's godfather. Oakie had long since become Mr. Williams when in public. He was quite the dandy these days, with continental clothing enhancing his role as Buckley's first restauranteur. Enid had summered on the island, doing her usual competent job at the Inn, but she had returned in the fall and was even listening a wee bit more attentively to suggestions that she retire to the mainland.

"When do you have to return to the island, Mrs. Connell?" said Oakie. He could not yet bring himself to call her by her first name despite the hours they had spent together.

"I should have been there last week, the season starts June first, but of course I couldn't miss Jeremy's first birthday, now could I?"

"Ethan!" cried Gwyn, "I have a wonderful idea! Let's all go over to the island for a few weeks. Jeremy's old enough to see his heritage, and since the weather warmed up I've had a call to go back."

Ethan had also missed the island but had been worried that a trip home might stir up painful memories. With his son on his knee, however, he felt secure and responded enthusiastically to her suggestion.

"Why not indeed, lass. You too, Oakie. Surely you can spare a few days. Louise would just love a chance to take over for a while wouldn't you, Louise?"

"But of course I would," said Louise brightly.

"That's just what I'm afraid of," said Oakie, half in jest. "She's been itching to run the place ever since she saw what a success Pierre's pastries were!"

Louise's brother had turned up one day the preceding year, and when she had introduced him as "Pierre" the entire MacNeil family had burst out laughing, causing the bewildered man to think that Americans were very nice if "un peu fou."

And so, two days after Jeremy's party the entire clan set sail for Parker's Island. At the last minute Ethan steered toward the village landing, avoiding the West Cliffs as much as possible. The air was clean with a pleasant nip of salt in it, and they all inhaled deeply, taking in as much nostalgia as air. With a rush, all the old love of the place engulfed Gwyn as she sat in the stern of the boat, holding Jeremy tightly for fear that he might fall overboard. As they disembarked, Buckley might have been a thousand miles away, so much did the island cry "Home!"

Old friends came out of cottages as they went along the lane. Even the Curran sisters came out of their respective houses at the same moment to greet the prodigals. Someone rang the meeting bell and within an instant they were surrounded. Jeremy was made much of and the city clothes came a close second, but the most laughter was provoked by the new Oakie Williams.

"Will ya look at that? What is it? It looks like Old Oakie, but if it weren't for the peg leg, I'd swear it was one of them French actors!"

"Hell no! That's no actor, that's one of them fancy riverboat gamblers; I'd know one of them anywhere!"

"All right, all right!" said Oakie, blushing. "If you're through making a display of your jealousy, will one of you tell me where a man can get a decent mug of ale on this island now that Mr. Williams' famous establishment has closed its doors?"

"You're not going to believe this, but do you know who's running the barroom now? And making a heap of money too?"

"Colleen Murphy, that's who! Why the place is full all the time."

"I'm not surprised!" said Ethan, laughing heartily. "Offhand, Oakie, I'd say she has a lot more to offer than you ever did!" The crowd guffawed merrily and Gwyn's heart cried, "It's good to be home; it's good to be home."

Ethan had let his cottage for the summer to a young artist from Chicago. The first time that Gwyn saw the young man perched on the West Cliffs with his easel her heart skipped and her breath caught in her throat. From a distance he could have been Tom. Of course, when he turned around you could see the beard and the fact that his eyes were brown. Still, the damage had been done.

With Jeremy staggering along beside her holding tightly to her hand she walked the old path to the cliffs and gave herself up to remembering. She let go of Jeremy's hand and he promptly sat down, unable as yet to walk alone. She sat down beside him and pulled him into her arms. How could she ever have thought that it would be all right? Why, sitting here with the fair child on her lap she could almost feel the sweet touch of her lover again. And to see his eyes staring guilelessly out from this tiny lad was a torment. It was a mistake to have come here. In Buckley she was fine, in control, but here on the island her defenses were blown away and she was as vulnerable as she had been two summers ago.

"Mummy cry?" whispered sweet Jeremy.

"No, no, darling. It's just the sun in my eyes," she said, burying her face in the soft golden curls.

Enid had given up her double bed to Ethan and Gwyn and was sharing Gwyn's old room with her grandson.

In the dark, Ethan's lovemaking was furtive but insistent. He too felt the lure of the island and was determined to call Gwyn back from wherever her memories had carried her. As usual, she responded to him but in his heart the old jealousy stirred. Did she ever compare him to the other?

Had Tom loved her so well? The fact that his questions were unanswerable and his fears unassuagable only made him cling all the more tightly.

By day there were picnics and boat rides. Enid went back to work and was momentarily alarmed when she saw the name George Eggleston, Tom's uncle, on the guest list. Sure enough, there he was, sitting at the card table, a bottle of porter at his elbow, looking for all the world as if he had never left. There was no sign of Tom, but Enid could not resist a subtle interrogation.

"So you came up alone this time, Mr. Eggleston?" she said, trying to speak easily.

"Couldn't get a one of them to come up with me," he replied. "They've all gone off to Bar Harbor. Don't see that place myself, but my nephew's wife is such a one for going where the crowd is. You remember my nephew Tom, don't you, Mrs. Connell? He came up with me a few years ago."

"Yes, I remember Tom." She fought back a quaver as she ploughed on. "So he's married now, is he?"

"He married a Boston girl this spring. Perhaps you remember her; seems to me she spent some time here too. Her name was Olive Crandall. Nice girl but nervous, if you know what I mean. Always flying around. Not the sort I'd imagine Tom would marry, but they seem happy enough."

"Then that's all that matters," said Enid.

Dear God, she thought, Gwyn mustn't find out, it would break her heart to think he had married that spoiled brat after walking out on her!

So Enid kept Gwyn away from the hotel, and when the vacation was over she kissed the suntanned faces and saw them sail off for Buckley. The island was not a healthy place for Gwyn just now, not when her new life was going on so well. Maybe later, when Jeremy was older, things would be different. She hoped but was not sure.

❧ *18* ❧

In Buckley things went on peacefully. Oakie's business thrived and Simeon Blanchard became mayor. Louise adored being the mayor's wife and entertained in high style whenever she got the chance; and high style for Louise was high style indeed! She even gave up the dress shop so enthralled was she with concocting parties and receptions.

Most startling to Gwyn and Ethan was the fact that before fall was over they found themselves expecting another child. Oakie could not comprehend the exaggerated elation this produced in Ethan. After all, "the old goat already knew he had it in him!" At first Gwyn was ambivalent but, inside, she wanted another child and when the new baby, a girl, was born the next July, they called her Ellen after Ethan's mother. Ellen was bonnie and healthy and sported a cap of golden curls that were so much like her father's that people laughed to see them. She was a moody baby, given to unexplained fits of crying. Gwyn would rock her daughter endlessly when these spells came, disregarding strict orders from Dr. Rogers to let her cry it out. Many an afternoon Ethan would return home to find his wife asleep in the rocking chair, Ellen snoring on her breast. But her sunny moods soon began to win out, and by the time she was a year old she was a delight, amusing everyone with her antics and driving her three-year-old brother almost to distraction. She walked early, and while her brother puzzled over the letters of his alphabet she was constantly out of doors and, if not watched, headed for the sea. Jeremy seemed so gentle and wise beside her. He loved books and stories and constantly asked questions of one and all who entered the house. Ethan and Gwyn were justifiably proud of their two children. Louise had given birth to a daughter, Aimée, right after Ellen's birth, so the two women had enjoyed their pregnancies together. Perhaps "enjoyed" was too strong a word to describe Louise's attitude.

One summer evening in 1896 Ethan came into the front hall with a bottle of champagne under his arm. His face was flushed with excitement.

"Get Enid," he cried "I have some good news for our one-horse town. Hurry up, Enid!" he called, as she bustled down the stairs.

"Now you two know how hard we've been trying to get a bank started here in Buckley? Well, there's a group of young men from Boston who have all been in the banking business and want to go out on their own. They decided to start up in a town where there was no competition and we're it, so let's drink a toast! This means there'll be capital available for new business and, besides that, it'll give us a position of sorts on the North Shore. What d'ya think of that?"

"Why, that's wonderful, Ethan," said Gwyn. "My goodness, a bank of our own. We're really coming up in the world, aren't we? When can they open?"

"By late fall if we can get the building up. It's going to be made of brick with a slate roof. Very posh. They're sending the new manager out next week, and Louise and Simeon are going to have a reception for him."

"What's his name?" asked Gwyn, a wild conjecture rising in her mind.

"Forgot to ask, but Louise'll tell you." He left the room to get wine glasses. Gwyn looked at Enid, her face dark.

"No, no, dear!" said Enid. "It couldn't be."

"But what if it is?"

"Ethan would know enough to find out," insisted Enid.

"But he didn't know that Tom was going into banking. There'd be no reason for him to ask."

"Hush now, here he comes."

At breakfast the next morning Gwyn picked at her toast and swallowed barely a half cup of tea. She thought that Ethan would never stop eating. His jovial mood of the last evening had carried over and indeed been enhanced by a good night's rest.

"It's getting on to eight–thirty, dear. You don't want to be late. Isn't it today that you are offering the Chinese lamps for sale?"

"Right you are. Seems that you've developed quite a taste for profit in your old age," he jested.

"Quite right. I've had my sights on a new big bed for Jeremy. He's far outgrown his little cot and Ellen will be ready for it soon." Would he never go? she thought.

After a prolonged goodbye he went down the broad outside steps and headed down the road toward MacNeil and Son, Co. The name had been over the door of the ever-growing establishment since the week following Jeremy's birth.

Waiting until he was completely out of sight, Gwyn put on a flowered hat and stepped into the warm sunshine. It was only half a block to Louise's house; still, she appreciated the new brick sidewalks. She made a charming picture in her morning dress of pale blue. The new fitted styles suited her figure, and she had the bearing which testifies to early good health.

Probably Louise will still be asleep, she fretted. But she couldn't wait another minute to know. She knocked loudly on the door, not caring whom she roused.

Louise's new maid answered and led Gwyn into the sunny conservatory, where Louise sat sipping coffee from a blue-edged Limoges cup.

"Enter, dear one. Where are the children? Aimée will be devastated if you have left them at home."

"They were up late last night, I'm afraid. Ethan was so happy about the news of the bank that he let them stay up far past their bedtime."

"A pity, but maybe this afternoon. But now! Is it not too wonderful about our new bank? Simeon is near to exploding with pride. And you, dear Gwyn, who are so good at making people comfortable, you must help me plan my little reception for the new manager and his wife. Simeon has not met him but has investigated him quite thoroughly and is most assured that he will be perfect for the job. He's very young, I understand, only twenty-seven I believe Simeon said, but is respectably married. A pity that; the young ladies would have had such fun scratching each other's eyes out over such an eligible fellow." She trilled a little laugh and handed Gwyn a cup.

"What's his name?" asked Gwyn, unable to contain herself another second longer.

"Thomas something. Hand me that yellow piece of paper on the table beside you. It's written down there. Ah, yes. Mr. Thomas Warner. And his wife's name is Olive. Ugly name, Olive! It makes me think that she will maybe have a green complexion." Again she laughed and started to lay out her plans for the reception. She didn't look up from her notes long enough to notice Gwyn's consternation.

"I really must go, Louise," said Gwyn, rising unsteadily.

"My dear girl, whatever is the matter?" cried Louise, taking her arm and helping her back into the chintz-covered wicker chair.

"It's nothing," said Gwyn. "I knew a boy named Tom

Warner. It's probably the same man; he said he was going into banking."

"He must have been a very terrible man to make you look so ill!" exclaimed Louise. "Now set down and tell me all about it."

"Terrible? No, I hardly knew him," she lied. "I met him one summer long ago on the island. His wife too, I believe, only she wasn't his wife then."

"You are quite sure you are not again enceinte?" asked Louise.

"No, no, I just stood up too fast. Your coffee is very strong, Louise."

"That's the only way to drink coffee, but if it makes you ill, I shall prepare it weaker next time just for you. By the way, what do you think of my new maid? Is she plain enough? The last one kept giving Simeon the most suggestive glances. It was all right until I caught him looking back at her one day. From now on they must either be elderly, overweight or bald. This one is far too young, but delightfully ugly."

"Honestly, Louise, you are too wicked! But now I must be home. Mother went out early this morning. Retirement is not coming easily to her, I'm afraid, and I don't like to leave Jeremy and Ellen alone with just the nurse. Come over later when you've had a chance to make your plans." She scurried from the room and out the door. Heading down Main Street toward the landing she saw nothing and felt nothing except the pounding of her own heart. Once at the landing she sat down too hard on a bench and tried to gather up her thoughts. Whatever would she do? To have him here in the same town, perhaps forever? And there would be no way to avoid him; Ethan was already a town father and had his responsibilities to the bank.

She was wretched, but it was several minutes before she pinpointed the core of her misery. Olive Crandall. He had married Olive Crandall! And now they would all be in

Buckley together, seeing each other at receptions, teas, everywhere. And all the time the sly eyes of Olive Crandall would be on her, wondering.

There was only one answer. She and Ethan must move out of Buckley! Even as she thought it, she knew it was absurd. Ethan's business was here, his friends and his happiness. Tom would gain nothing by admitting the truth about Jeremy. After all, it would only make him look like a cad. Surely Olive didn't know! She could not bear it if Olive knew about Jeremy.

Gwyn was as frightened as a human being can be and still live. The fear was so strong that she could scarcely move her fingers or even breathe. The fear was not for herself or even Ethan. It was for Jeremy. She knew that she would do anything to protect him, even if it meant taking him away against Ethan's wishes. Ethan! He would know what to do; he would reassure her and make it all right again. She stood up, feeling lightheaded once more and walked to the store. She looked up at the gilded letters above the door and, giving a little shudder, she went inside.

Ethan was sitting behind a massive oak desk. He was obviously very busy, but he stood up to kiss her cheek, and the clerk who had been attending him discreetly left the office.

"Ethan, something terrible has happened!" she said.

"The children? Are they all right?"

"Yes, yes, they're fine. Everyone's all right physically. Ethan? Did you know that the new banker is Tom Warner?" It was the second time today that she had said his name aloud. Already he was surrounding her again, taking her over.

"Oh, God, no, lass." He paled and began to breathe heavily. Gwyn handed him the glass of water which was on his desk. She had spoken too abruptly, forgetting that excitement of the wrong kind often brought these spells of shortness of breath on her husband.

When he had regained himself he grasped her hands. "I didn't know. I swear to God, Gwyn, I didn't know."

"Of course I believe you, but what are we to do?"

"Nothing to do but brazen it out, I guess."

"But what if anyone else finds out about, you know, about Jeremy?" It pained her to speak of it.

"No, no, lass. He'd not have told anyone!" He did not add that Tom couldn't tell what he did not know. How he wished his breath would stop coming in spurts!

"Don't you worry, love. We'll hold our heads high and rise above it all. My mother always said you must carry your head high no matter what."

"I told Louise that we knew him before."

"Was that wise?" asked Ethan.

"I thought it would all come out anyway, so there was no point in hiding it. Besides he's married to Olive Crandall. She'll not let me forget that summer even if he'd prefer it."

"Not that stuck-up blond? Why who'd have thought it?" Ethan was genuinely surprised.

"She's his own kind. You said it yourself, that sort always sticks together."

"Aye, and you're my kind. So let's just take it one day at a time. If we act like everything is all right, then it'll all pass over."

"Do you truly think so?" she asked, feeling a bit easier inside.

"Yes, but make me one promise?"

"Yes?"

"That you'll never talk to him about what happened or admit out loud to him or anyone else that anything ever went on between the two of you?"

"Of course I won't! Oh, Ethan, how terrible this is for you! And all my fault."

"Don't say that! Not ever! You and Jeremy and Ellen are the best things that ever happened to me in my life, and

I don't give a damn how it all came about as long as you
love me. You do love me, don't you, lass?"

"I do," said Gwyn, and looking into the worried eyes
she knew that whatever else she felt, this at least was true.

⸎*19*⸎

On August first, 1896, Gwyn Connell MacNeil kissed
her children goodnight, went into her bedroom, and shut
the door behind her. The ormolu clock over the striated
marble of her fireplace read eleven minutes after eight o'-
clock.

Sitting down at her dressing table, she looked at the
face before her. There was nothing in her mirror to offend;
indeed, even the most envious eye would not begrudge her
beauty. The hair was still as black as the irises of the sea-
blue eyes and the complexion was flawless. Still it was not
a face at peace with itself. Under the soft composure of line
and curve lurked the fire and longing of an island girl, a girl
quick to take offense, slow to forget. With agile fingers she
brought the curling hair forward and caught it in a loose
knot on the top of her head. The upswept hair made her
look more matronly, but the little curls which escaped the
tortoise-shell combs betrayed her once again. There were
two stubborn spots of high color on her cheekbones, super-
imposing a false image of gaiety over the unusual pallor of
her neck and throat. When she leaned forward, she could
discern a delicate scattering of freckles across her nose giv-

ing evidence of summer's spell, but she left them alone; it
was too warm for powder. The sultry heat carried her back
across the water to another party night, four years ago. It
was a lifetime ago and yet this very instant she could shut
her eyes and feel his lips on her throat and the soft abrasion
of her tartan spread out beneath their passion. Would it
never cease? To have one week without the sickening longing in her heart. She stared at the stranger in the mirror as
her eyes grew bright and spilled their pain onto the soft
down of her cheeks. The tears intensified the blue of her
eyes against the black lashes, and she saw again the child,
raging with the frustrated desires of a lifetime, a lifetime
of odd-man-out, and now having everything and nothing at
the same time. One summer. Throughout the compromises
of her adult life she had had one summer, one inviolate
piece of the universe locked forever inside her to be
brought out in secrecy and examined again and again, until
like sea glass, it shone deeper and brighter with the buffet-
ing of time.

And tonight they would take this too away, her one
modest treasure, and she would have nothing left in her
heart's deepest vault but the emptiness of what might have
been.

She rose and stepped into a summer gown of pale blue
silk embroidered with tiny silver fleurs-de-lis, the design of
her dear friend Louise. Necklines were low this year, and
she noted with grim pride the swell of her breasts against
the blue piping of her gown.

"We must rise above it," Ethan had said. And rise
above it she should. Here on her own ground surrounded
by friends and bouyed by the respect of her fellow towns-
folk she would indeed rise above them all. Them. Such a
big sound for Tom and Olive. Olive Crandall; never would
she be Olive Warner to Gwyn.

She fastened lacy earrings of carved ivory onto her ear
lobes and in one last act of bravado hung a locket contain-

ing the likenesses of Jeremy and Ellen around the elegant
throat.

As she stepped into silver evening slippers, she suddenly remembered the old brown work shoes she had worn
on the island, and a bitter laugh broke from her lips.

Outside her door Ethan heard her laugh and rapped
twice to bring her out. His own distress was of a different
nature. Guilt and fear ill-became him, he who was the life
and soul of any gathering. Lacking Gwyn's subtlety he had
decided to ignore the unpleasant possibilities. She was his.
Jeremy and Ellen were his, and despite his good nature he
would not give them up. And so they must go now to
Louise's and smile and drink (but not too much) and launch
the new banker and his wife into Buckley society. He
doubted if Buckley society in any way resembled what
Olive Crandall was used to, but so be it. The boy with
pained eyes who had stood on his doorstep four years ago
must be buried, walled away forever like a murdered man.

The Blanchard home was made of brick, and although
the architectural connoisseur would have deemed it Feder-
alist from the outside, once inside all resemblance ended.
Everywhere were pieces of the Empire, and the heavy Victorian of those American times had been cursorily dis-
missed as vulgar affection by the light touch of Louise. The
deep wood of settees was offset by the most fragile of wa-
tered silks, and where most of the Buckley residents fa-
vored heavy draperies, Louise had installed valances which
overhung curtains of thinnest silk in the most alluring
pastels imaginable. When the MacNeils arrived at nine
o'clock, Louise Blanchard was standing near the doorway
of her house, effusively offering up a cheek for kisses from
her friends and extending slim fingers to acquaintances.
Simeon was elegant in summer white as he looked to the
comfort of his guests. Gwyn and Ethan stepped into the
broad hall and took turns embracing Louise, who gave

Gwyn an extra squeeze of the hand, suspecting that this meeting with Mr. and Mrs. Warner was of some import.

Gwyn turned her head to look into the pale yellow salon to her left. From a point halfway across the room Mr. Thomas Warner turned as if magnetized. His blue eyes locked into hers, and in that instant all her carefully prepared defenses fell away. Once again they were alone together on the West Cliffs, their lunches on their laps. They were facing each other, and his lips were murmuring sweet, sweet words of love. It was a moment like death, irrevocable.

Later she would try to reconstruct the scene around them, the happy crowd dressed in summer pastels, the sudden smell of salt in the air as the wind turned back from the sea and puffed up the thin gray silk of the curtains until they billowed like phantom ships.

Tom stood vulnerable, a slender man in a fawn-colored evening suit. To the uninvolved he was handsome in a understated way. The years had etched a fine line here and there and the hairstyle was slightly changed but he was still her Tom. Intelligence and pain shone from the light eyes. How could these candid eyes ever mislead? Dishonor should have been a stranger to this face, and yet Gwyn's heart thought it knew better. Women would be attracted to Tom for all the wrong reasons and in doing so would fail to catch the very essence of his strength.

He turned away suddenly, unable to sustain this agonizing confrontation, and his abrupt movement broke the spell. Other faces came into focus; other voices claimed her, and once swallowed up by the crowd it was several minutes before she found herself being led to meet the new banker.

At his side was a woman who was certainly Olive, but she was so altered that for one second Gwyn was convinced that she was looking at a stranger. Yes, of course it was Olive, but she was so thin that even the soft folds of her green dress could not conceal the sharp shoulder blades,

and the heavy emerald necklace around her throat could
not distract the eye from the angular collarbones. Her neck
was so frail that the jewels which hung there appeared to
be a painful burden to the thin tissue of her skin. Her
bosom seemed unnaturally full on her slim frame and the
face, though still lovely, had taken on the aspect of the
vixen. Gwyn had prayed to hate her, to wash away her hurt
in angry loathing, but this creature with the high-pitched
voice was a caricature of the nymphlike Olive of four years
ago.

Ethan took Gwyn's elbow firmly in hand and made the
overture.

"Mr. Warner, how nice to see you again. Gwyn and I
were surprised to find out that you were our new banker."
His voice was falsely hearty; still, Gwyn had to admire his
fortitude.

"Hello, Mr. MacNeil, Gwyn," said Tom. His eyes
never left Gwyn's as he spoke. "You remember Gwyn, of
course?" He spoke to Olive but still looked at Gwyn.

"Why, how could I ever forget your little friend from
the hotel, Thomas darling? My! How pretty you look, dear.
So very chic. And Mr. MacNeil! Do you still run that
funny old boat back and forth to Parker's Island?"

"Mr. MacNeil now owns Buckley's largest emporium,
Olive." Was that an edge in Tom's voice? "Surely you remember I pointed it out to you when we arrived this morning?" Olive said nothing. She stared at a spot ten inches
behind Gwyn's head and then walked away toward the
table where Louise's man was dispensing champagne.

"You'll have to excuse Olive. She's had an exhausting
day; I'm afraid it's unnerved her. She's rather shy with
strangers. I think I should attend to her if you'll excuse
me." He walked quickly to where Olive was making short
work of a glass of the bubbling wine.

"Shy, is she?" growled Ethan. "Rude is more what I'd
call it."

"It must be just as difficult for her as it is for me. Odd, I had never stopped to think of it that way before."

"Well, I can tell you right now that you're four times the lady she ever thought of being! The nerve of her, walking off like that. She'll not do well in this town with that attitude, that's for damn sure!"

Ethan soon found himself surrounded by friends, and Gwyn stuck close to his side. Ordinarily, she was the farthest thing from a clinging vine but tonight was exceptional. She gave herself up, a willing audience, to his droll stories and found herself laughing even at those she had heard a dozen times before. He was making an incredible effort on her behalf, and she would rot in Hell before she'd let him down. Once, she caught Tom looking at her as she sipped her champagne and for a moment she was unable to swallow, but she braved it out, thinking that this was the worst and that each successive meeting would be easier. During the evening Olive drank too much champagne, although she certainly never became drunk; but her color was high and her laugh shrill by the time Tom and she bade their farewells.

After the Warner's departure, Louise almost flew to Gwyn's side.

"My dear! What a perfectly bizarre woman. And you knew her before, she says? The way she talked, one would think you had spent your summer licking her boots."

"That's not too far off the mark, unfortunately. One could scarcely have a more menial job than I did that year. But let her say what she will! I've never been ashamed of having worked hard. Lord knows, I've never made a secret of it," said Gwyn.

"Right you are, my dear, and that's why we all love you so. You really are the most charmingly frank person I know, not at all like sly, devious little me." Louise gave a little shrug. "Well, I can see that you are positively going to refuse to say anything nasty about her so I suppose it's

up to me to put her in her place. Really, being the wife of
the mayor does have its privileges! Now don't look so worried. I shan't eat her up, merely nibble a bit around the
edges. Have some more champagne and let's cool off on the
piazza. Such an odd word to find in America, 'piazza.' "

She floated on ahead and Gwyn followed her, grateful
for the friendship of one whose sharp tongue belied the
kind heart beneath.

"Now I must tell you something," said Louise after the
two were seated on the settee which swayed gently to and
fro as the women let the cooling sea air wash over them.

"This Thomas Warner," continued Louise, "is not just
a passing acquaintance of yours. Never mind," she went
on, as Gwyn opened her lips to protest, "I see what I see."
The settee creaked rhythmically in the dark. "Tell me
something. Are you fierce enough to hold on to your happy
life if this Tom and his peculiar wife make troubles for
you?"

"Fierce?" said Gwyn. "That's an odd word to use. If
you mean strong, then of course I am strong. You of all
people know how much I love Ethan and the children.
What possible harm could the Warners do unless I let
them?"

"I know that I sometimes choose the wrong word, but
this time I know what I mean to say. Fierce, like a mother
lioness protecting her cubs or a nobleman protecting his
castle. And," she added, "when you say 'unless I let them'
that tells me that you do not tell me everything, or even
anything. No, no. I am not offended. I also have my secrets.
Still, please know that I am watching over you. Your friend
Louise can also be fierce if her friend is threatened." She
made a terrible face and showed pretty claws and then
stood up laughing into the night air. Gwyn stretched up a
hand to her friend, and together they went back inside.

From across the salon, Ethan saw them enter, both
dark of hair and mysterious of expression. The blue of

Gwyn's eyes seemed softer as she smiled up at her friend, while under the slanted lids the dark chocolate brown of Louise's eyes glinted bright under the luminescence of her chandeliers. Thank God, Gwyn had a friend to lean on. Ethan feared they would all be needing their friends shortly. He had always had Oakie and countless others, less intimate, but nevertheless friends, but Gwyn had never had one special girl friend, a rare condition in an era where intense friendships between women were commonplace. Louise was worldly and loyal. She would look after Gwyn's interests in society. Still, he knew Gwyn well enough to know that she would never betray the truth about Jeremy. The thought of his son made him want to get out of here, to go home and kiss the little brow. He also wanted Gwyn with a ferocious desire that was never far submerged when she was near.

She surprised him that night in bed. She was aggressive and shamelessly abandoned. He was so excited by her frenzy that he failed to sense the desperation which lay beneath it.

❧20❧

If Gwyn had thought that the clocks would stop and the ground shift away under her feet, she was mistaken. Tom was civil, even cordial when next they met on the street, and if her heart twisted awry in her chest whenever she saw him, he was courteous enough to be either unaware or forebearing. In fact, had it not been for Olive the whole situation might have settled down into something resembling normalcy.

The first odd occurrence (if one did not count her rudeness at Louise's party) was a week later at The Williams House, where Ethan and Gwyn had taken Simeon and Louise to dine in honor of Louise's birthday. The friends were teasing Louise unmercifully because she refused to reveal her age. "And no wonder!" said Gwyn, rushing to her friend's defense. "If you two looked as young as Louise you'd be crazy to admit to a year over eighteen. So there!" She speared a delectable morsel of veal in emphasis. "Eighteen is it?" said Simeon, who was not so very much younger than Ethan. "Do you know I honestly can't remember what it was like to be eighteen. Guess we codgers will have to ask Gwyn about that."

Discussions about her youth always unnerved Gwyn, and as she was searching for a witty reply to set them off course, she felt a kiss on her cheek and a heavy cloud of scent falling over her shoulders.

"Gwyn darling! How enchanting to see you again. And Mr. and Mrs. Blanchard. How festive you all look. Are you having a party? I adore parties!"

Olive was flushed and smiling, but there was that same erratic rhythm to her speech and Tom, standing just behind her and to one side, was noticeably uncomfortable.

"Hello everyone," he said.

Oh, Lord, how handsome he is! If her knees had not been safely tucked under the table, Gwyn would have collapsed under the pressure of his presence. Would Louise ask them to join the table? Please no! Yes, yes, please yes! Gwyn had had three glasses of wine and was feeling reckless.

They remained chatting until finally, Simeon, perplexed by Louise's failure to extend the invitation, insisted that they all eat together.

"Gwyn how perfectly beautiful you have become! Hasn't she, Tom?" Gwyn froze waiting for his reply which was, of course, a quick agreement. "Tom tells me you have two children, Mr. MacNeil?"

"Yes," replied Ethan evenly. "A boy and a girl."

"How wonderful for you! And you Mrs. Blanchard?"

"We have a daughter, Aimée. She's just a little bit younger than Ellen MacNeil. They are such good friends. 'Pals,' I think you say here."

"Ah yes, pals. Just like my Tom and Gwyn used to be so long ago. Could I have just a bit more of that lovely wine? It must be French. The French make the best wine, but of course I don't need to tell you that, do I, Mrs. Blanchard?"

"Louise, if you like," said Louise, stealing a glance around the table to see how the others were holding up under this veritable assault of friendliness.

"So you all have lovely children? We have none but perhaps later on." Her face drooped and she reached again for her wine glass.

Ethan signaled for the waiter, fearing she had had too much to drink, and for several moments they were busy selecting their meals from the remarkably sophisticated menu. Moments after they had placed their orders, the celebrated Mr. Williams came to the table and in the finest continental fashion inquired after their comfort.

"Oakie. If I live to be a hundred, I'll never get over seeing you in that damned monkey suit!"

Oakie looked properly offended, but his eyes danced as he walked away limping only imperceptibly on his new artificial leg.

"I've just had the most splendid idea," said Olive. "Seeing Mr. Williams reminded me of the fun we used to have on the island. Why don't we all plan to spend a week together at the Spraycliffe Inn during the first week in September. Surely, Gwyn, your mother would love to go back as a guest, and it would be just like old times!

Why was she doing this? thought Gwyn. Olive was like a child picking at a wound, refusing to let it heal.

"Say! That sounds like fun," said Simeon.

Louise kicked him under the table, and he turned a look of pained surprise on her.

"Then it's all settled! The first week in September. We can have picnics and games."

"I'm not at all sure we can go," said Ethan firmly.

"Nonsense! I saw the sign on your store door saying it was closed then. That's why I picked that week!" cried Olive.

"But did you not say the idea just came over you?" asked Louise darkly.

Another blank stare from Olive. "No, Olive, I'm sure we can't go," said Gwyn. "My mother would feel most uncomfortable as a guest at the Inn."

"Then you will stay at her house, and we others shall stay at the Inn. There! You see? All objections settled. Now let us have some champagne to celebrate our plans."

Furious at Ethan for not having squelched Olive, Gwyn refused more wine but the idea titillated her. Tom's abandonment of her had been more than a humiliation; it had been a mystery, a mystery she knew she should leave alone. Still, her soul was deep, deeper than her hurt and willing to suffer again in order to know for sure what dark thing had driven her lover away. How melodramatic it all sounded, even to her Celtic ears. Almost like returning to the scene of the crime. She accepted Ethan's decision not to go; she knew that he had appeared to acquiesce in order to avoid setting off the ticking bomb that was Olive. Gwyn did not consider herself braver than Ethan but there was a probing side to her nature that, like Olive, could not let the matter rest. Then the face of Jeremy came before her and all fantasy vanished. Ethan was right, it was unthinkable that they should return to Parker's Island with Mr. and Mrs. Warner. Resolved to resist Olive's demands, the

MacNeils went home, the matter seemingly decided.

The next day, however, brought an unexpected twist. Enid answered the door at tea time and was momentarily flustered to see Dr. Rogers standing, hat in hand, on the porch.

"Well, sir, to what do we owe the honor of this visit? The children are fine as far as I know. Come on in." She brought him into the parlor. "Now what's the matter; you don't look a bit like yourself." She rang for tea.

"Is Gwyn here? I'd like to discuss something with you both."

"Yes, she's in the yard with the children. Our Gwyn has taken up gardening. Flowers. Nothing useful, but they do look pretty in the house. We had no room for flowers in our island garden. I'll get her." She hurried off, suddenly alarmed by Dr. Rogers's solemn demeanor.

When the three were finally seated with glasses of iced tea and lemon bread, Dr. Rogers spoke up. "This is a matter which has troubled me, concerning professional confidence and all. It's about the Warners. Mr. Warner—Tom—called me this morning to say that his wife is dreadfully upset about your refusal to accompany them to the island."

"Well that's just too bad, isn't it!" huffed Enid. "Does she need to call in a doctor every time she doesn't get her own way, because if that's why you've come, you may as well forget it?"

"Before you misunderstand me, let me say that you are not far from wrong. Mrs. Warner is a severly disturbed woman, and her upsets often necessitate calling in a doctor. I shouldn't be discussing this with you at all, but her husband asked me to see if I couldn't persuade you to make the trip. He feels it would be beneficial to his wife. You see, she has just begun to recover from a serious mental collapse. That's why they came here, to give her a complete change of scene. She has lost three children in the last two years; two early miscarriages and one at five months. It seems pretty clear now from what all her doctors say that she will never be able to bear a child. Gwyn? Surely you can see how terrible that would be for someone of her temperament. After the death of their last child she simply fell apart. Only recently has she been able to go out in company at all. Tom Warner has been wonderful through it all and, believe me, she can be very difficult. She won't accept the fact that she can't have a child, and she refuses to consider adoption. And," he paused for emphasis, "for some reason she wants this island house party desperately. Couldn't you all just come out for a few days? I wouldn't have told you all this if I didn't honestly believe that her sanity was at stake." He looked embarrassed to have said so much.

"Why didn't Mr. Warner tell us this himself?" asked Enid, the belligerent note still in her voice.

"Mother!" cried Gwyn. They exchanged glances and Enid looked abashed.

"Please," said Dr. Rogers, "just think it over, I beg you. It would only be for a few days, and she was making such progress."

"You sound as if you've known them for years," said Enid.

"I know her Boston doctor very well. It's an interesting case, almost classic." Aware that he had perhaps gotten a bit carried away, he rose.

"As I said before, think on it again."

Ill at ease, he crossed the room and left.

"Mental collapse my eye!" said Enid after he was safely out of earshot.

"Mother, just think of it! Jeremy is mine and she has nothing and never will have. Doesn't that strike you as unfair? I mean it's not her fault about Tom and me. We did it and we're the ones that should suffer, not Olive. Don't you see? I owe her something for having Tom's child. I'll explain it to Ethan, he'll understand."

"Of course he won't understand! It's too late to make

it up to her now. You'll just get more trouble by stirring
up old coals."

"Maybe you're right, but it will be good for her to go
back to a nicer time and place." Gwyn suddenly dropped
her head in her hands.

"Oh, Mother. I'm not trying to fool myself. I still don't
like her! I never will, but I owe her this. Otherwise I'll feel
beholden to her all the time. Just let me do this one thing
and then I'll feel better. After that she can go to Hell in a
bucket for all I care!" She stood and ran from the room,
leaving Enid sitting with three half-filled tea glasses and a
plate of untouched lemon bread.

Ethan most adamantly did not understand, but Gwyn
worked away at him until he realized that she was in earnest about her debt to Olive. He gave in against his better
judgement, more aware than anyone else of the potential
danger in the game they were playing. But then he never
could refuse to grant Gwyn what she wanted, especially
since she rarely asked for anything. Seeing her in the garden, the straw hat tied on over her upswept curls with a
mauve ribbon and her pretty hands enveloped in dirty
gardening gloves, he marvelled at her adaptability. From
chambermaid to mother and wife, and now hostess and
gardener. He chuckled as Ellen toddled up and pulled at
the bow of her mother's apron to get her attention.

Gwyn turned and at a distance of less than six inches
confronted a fat earthworm which was dangling from
Ellen's chubby fingers. She gave a little shriek of surprise
and Ellen threw back her head and chortled aloud with joy
at having made Mommy's eyes grow wide. "Ellen! Don't
ever startle Mommy like that again!" cried Gwyn, but she
was smiling. Surely she was happy here among her children and flowers, thought Ethan. And had he not provided
the setting for her contentment? Why then did he fear so
for her fidelity? Olive had changed and so had Tom. It was

as if their old personalities were characters in a book; a
book which had been read and then put back away on the
highest shelf to gather dust. They had all gleaned from it
what they needed to know, but someday, some boring,
heavy day, might not a pretty hand reach up and try to read
the old story once again?

Nonsense! He knew her through and through. She
would never let go of their life. Then he saw again the girl
with the shining dark hair running over the path toward
the cliffs, and he was afraid.

❧ *21* ❧

Enid had no particular objections to staying at the
Spraycliffe Inn. She had, after all, wondered often enough
what it would be like to be on the receiving end of the Inn's
good service. Gwyn was mildly surprised by her mother's
attitude until she learned from Ethan that Dr. Rogers
would be part of the entourage. Ostensibly on vacation, he
was going at least as much to keep an eye on Olive Warner
as to enjoy himself. The thought of lazy evenings, of cards
and books in the company of the MacNeils and the attractive Enid Connell was rather pleasant once he had made his
decision. Enid still occasionally shocked him with her out-
spokeness, and she did have an annoying habit of not treating his pronouncements as gospel; still, she was a fine-
looking woman with her chestnut curls and trim figure.
His first wife had been soft-spoken (rather timid, now that

he thought of it), but until her death ten years before she had been sweet and loyal and kind to his self-esteem. At the age of fifty-seven, however, he needed no such bolstering. The thought of a strong-minded woman was more appealing now that he had lost some of his swagger. His only daughter had moved to the Oklahoma territory (he shuddered to think of the living conditions) and he was lonely. This would be his first vacation in fifteen years. In addition to these musings, he was interested in the Warner woman; the whole subject of mental illness had caught his fancy.

He felt sincerely sorry for young Tom. The boy was too young to be saddled with a shrew. Despite his euphemisms to Gwyn and Enid, the prevailing manifestation of Olive's illness was a biting tongue. One day she would be soaring, drunk on some unfathomable psychic elixir, and the next day she would be withdrawn, suspicious and poised to lash out at anyone who tried to cheer her. He had discussed her at some length with Tom.

"You mustn't feel obliged to give in to her all the time, you know. In many ways she's like a child, and you're not helping a whit encouraging her tantrums."

"That's just it," said Tom wearily, "she's like a child. Not only in the tantrums but in the good ways. Sometimes she looks at things with such a fresh viewpoint that I find myself reevaluating things I've believed all my life. Just the other night she asked me if I didn't think that the thirteenth verse of Corinthians, the part about putting away childish things, didn't mean that we should all learn to stop hating our parents. I must admit I was stunned to think she had such perception. Straight out, like a child. You know the way children say things without seeming to have thought them through, still they ring absolutely true?" He looked into Dr. Rogers's eyes, and not for the first time Dr. Rogers thought, How young he is! Just a boy. What could have happened to make him marry Olive? Oh, of course, the sex thing was probably behind it, but Olive was not a

truly sexual woman. Her kind was often voracious, probably aggressive in the bedroom, but it was a false appetite
fed by the need for power and attention, not the easy volup-
tuousness of a truly sensual nature. Overbred, demanding
too much of herself and at the same time not enough. Tom
Warner was not going to have a pleasant life.

"Dr. Rogers? Can you help her?"

Never before had the good doctor felt so impotent.
For, to face facts, there was no way out for Tom. Divorce
was not legally possible, and even if Olive worsened considerably, it would be a cruel abandonment, not to mention a
social stigma never erased. Other men would let her illness
run its course and seek consolation elsewhere, but he knew
that Tom Warner was not one of these.

"No one can promise anything in cases of this kind,"
he replied. "She could very well improve. Who knows?
Sunshine and a vacation might make all the difference. Tell
me, why were you so reluctant to go to the island when she
first mentioned it?"

Tom eyes grew veiled. He turned away from the doctor and walked to the tall window beside his desk. "We
were not intimate the last time I was on Parker's Island. It
surprised me to learn that she had such an attachment to
the place. Also, I have some memories of my own which
might be better left alone, but of course Olive's health
comes first."

How complicated people were, thought Dr. Rogers as
he walked from the bank to his house near the southern end
of Main Street. That fresh-faced boy was hiding something,
and that something was tied up in some way with Parker's
Island. Being a doctor was like being an eavesdropper. You
were thrust into brief interludes of intimacy with people,
but you never learned the whole story. And a good thing,
too, he thought. If you had to hold all those tragic stories
inside you, you might well go mad, as mad as Olive Warner.

❧22❧

Jeremy MacNeil looked up at the veranda of the Spraycliffe Inn where his mother and father were talking with their friends. He liked Aimée's mummy very much. She always smelled so nice, and she laughed a lot and gave him sweet things covered with sugar to eat. Aimée's father was all right too, but he made Jeremy feel shy sometimes, because he was the mayor and Daddy said that the mayor was someone very important. Dr. Rogers was nice, but of course he was an old friend. The new man was nice too, but the new lady wasn't. She stared at him and she had pinched his cheek too hard. And he hated her laugh; it was too loud and sounded like the noise the weathervane made when the wind blew too hard. They were all busy laughing now. The new man wasn't there, he had gone off somewhere after lunch with a wooden thing that Daddy said was an easel. Perhaps, thought Jeremy, this would be a good time to go away myself and look around for a while. Ellen was asleep in her room with Nurse and nobody would see if he just went off to see the pretty water. He went around the strong smelling orange flowers at the corner of the hotel and took a big breath, impressed by his own daring. It was hard to be a good boy all the time.

Tom sat on a ledge of the West Cliffs, his easel braced in front of him. His canvas had scarcely been touched. Four years ago he had vowed never to set foot on this island

again. The sea seemed bluer than before; he had thought
that perhaps its stark beauty had existed this vividly only
in his imagination. The others doubtless thought him rude.
No matter. He could not have tolerated the two women
another moment. Olive, with her bright eyes, seeing things
everywhere, looking into him and seeing distorted images
of her own febrile imaginings. And Gwyn. The glory that
she had become! The chiseled lines of her fine face and the
luster of her heavy hair. She drove him to despair with her
presence. When he had first seen her four years ago he had
known that she was special but even in his love's deepest
projection he had never imagined that her hold on him
could be absolute. He had tried to go on without her—a
man must go on. His marriage to Olive had not been cold-
blooded; still, he should have known that his inability to
love her enough would not escape her finely tuned perception. Ah, Gwyn! Beautiful flower in bloom. Cruel island
enchantress who had forgotten him almost before his boat
had left the dock. Did she ever think of him and the way
they had been? He had stolen a hundred glances, trying to
discern a spark of remembrance, but on the few occasions
when her eyes met his she had looked away quickly, as if
he were a stranger. And so he needed these times alone to
bolster himself against the moments of agony when he
would be seated across from her at dinner or cards longing
to grab her by the pale shoulders and shake her until the
piled-up curls fell down her back and he could cry out,
"Why? Why have you done this? Married this old man and
turned into a statue that mocks us all?" He wanted her so
and hated her all at once. No one had the right to elicit such
love and longing only to turn it away, or worse, pretend
that it had never existed at all.

He sensed her all around him, in every aster along
their special path, a path almost grown over now. She was
in the gulls and the rock and in the sea around him. Everywhere.

On the first day back he had resisted her call, feeling exhausted at day's end from the effort, but the island won out and before twenty-four hours had passed he felt himself succumbing. It was not an altogether unpleasant sensation; rather, he imagined, like accepting the fact of one's inevitable death. Once he had let his defenses down, the feelings washed over him in a flood of passion and pain. He let the sensations have their way. It had been so long since he had felt anything but disappointment and resignation. He heard a noise behind him and saw Jeremy MacNeil watching him through Gwyn's eyes.

"Hello there, Jeremy," said Tom. The small figure stood silhouetted against the grassy slope of the cliff. Jeremy regarded him solemnly, then said, "Hello, mister man."

"You may call me 'Tom' if you like." The boy made him shy. "Does your mother know where you are?"

Jeremy shook his head. "Then we'd best go tell her or she'll worry about you." Jeremy held his ground. The blue eyes held Tom's. "Are you making a picture?" asked Jeremy. "Yes," replied Tom, "but it's not very good, I'm afraid. Do you like to make pictures?"

"Yes. I like to make trains and fishes. My daddy can catch fish anytime he wants. He has a boat. Sometimes he takes me too."

"That must be fun to go out fishing. Your father knows a lot about boats doesn't he?" said Tom, eager to keep the conversation going. He tried to put approval of Ethan into his question and must have succeeded, because Jeremy took a few steps closer and said, "My daddy knows lots of things."

"I'm sure he does. Tell me, do you like the island?"

"It's nice. Will you show me some more?"

"I'd like that very much. Let's go now and find your mother, and we'll see if she'll let us take a walk all around tomorrow." He was as unable to resist the son as the mother.

"All right," said Jeremy, and he reached out to take Tom's hand as they headed back toward the Inn.

Ethan had gone upstairs with the others to change for dinner when Gwyn realized that Jeremy was no longer playing on the veranda steps. She tried to calm herself as she called his name, but when there was no answer the old fear of the sea returned. She raced to the front dock and then turned toward the West Cliffs. Almost immediately she heard a voice cry: "Here we are! All safe and sound." Then the two figures emerged over the crest of the hill. One of Tom's arms held his easel, but the other hand held Jeremy's. She caught her breath and stared at them, wondering how he could so casually touch his own flesh and blood and not know it. She had been terrified of their first meeting but try as she might had been unable to detect any glimmer of recognition in Tom's eyes when he had first been introduced to Jeremy. And now they were approaching her and absurdly her eyes were filled with tears at the beauty of the two of them together.

"Mummy, Mummy! Tom wants to take me for a walk tomorrow. Can I go? Please?" He was flushed with anticipation.

"May I go," she corrected him. "I don't see why not. Daddy is going to take Grandma and Dr. Rogers and me for a sail. Perhaps you could go for your walk then." She knew she should never allow the two to become intimate. Tom's proximity was dazzling, however, and she could scarcely stop from reaching out to touch him, to touch again the softness of his hair and the firm leanness of his arms.

Jeremy set up a little dance of pleasure while the two grownups stared and stared at each other. The threesome went back to the hotel, Jeremy claiming a hand from each of them. Enid, looking down from an upstairs window, saw them approaching and saw also the rightness of them together. Into her heart crept a sadness, a profound sense of pity for them all; for her dear girl who had done no wrong except to love too much, even for Tom who had been young and weak and was now paying dearly for it, and for Ethan and Olive, condemned to be left forever outside the enchanted circle which the trio on the lawn represented. She could see no happy endings for any of them except perhaps Jeremy who would be the beneficiary of their love. She turned away from the window, not wanting to be involved in something over which her island sense told her she had no control. She should have let them marry. Then, before Tom went back to Boston. She had interfered once and would never step in again.

"Go in now, darling. Nurse is waiting." Gwyn kissed the suntanned cheek and Jeremy scampered up the steps, stopping at the top to turn around and call, "You won't forget?"

"I won't forget," cried Tom. Jeremy vanished inside and then they were alone. The sun was dropping in the sky, shining on the curls of the waves behind them and illuminating their young faces as they both stood there, knowing they should part. "He's a fine boy, Gwyn," said Tom. "He looks like you."

"Thank you," she murmured; then, afraid he would hear her heart pounding in the silence, she turned and started up the stairs.

"Gwyn?" he called.

"Yes?" she answered, not daring to look at him.

"Oh, nothing. I'll see you at dinner." He heard her go inside. It was another ten minutes before he could bring himself to go in and face Olive and her undeserved misery.

Olive sat alone in her bed-sitting room. She was comletely dressed for dinner, even to the ornate sapphire earbobs which hung almost to her shoulders. She stood and walked to the cheval glass and stared at the emaciated woman reflected there. Inhaling deeply, she watched in satisfaction as her still-full bosom rose to round out the otherwise flat expanse of her lower throat. Sliding her hands sinuously over her breast and narrow hips she gave an almost imperceptible moan as desire overtook her. It had been weeks since Tom had made love to her, long empty weeks of debilitating solitary passion. Even the term "made love" was ridiculous. He didn't love her, never had. He still loved Gwyn Connell. Ah, but Gwyn was married now to Ethan MacNeil. Lusty, muscular Mr. MacNeil.

As a girl she had observed his brutish arms handling the lines of his sails. Even then she had appreciated his physical prowess. How she would love to have him over her, driving her torment away with his lust. Lust was all that was left to her now. They all thought she was mad, driven out of her mind with disappointment because of the lost children. Little lost souls, tiny pieces of her shattered marriage to Tom, they danced around in her dreams taunting her with reminders of her emptiness. But they were all wrong, she was not mad, merely biding her time before accepting her loss. Surely they should be able to see that it was too much, losing the babies and Tom all at once. She missed him in her bed. The only time she was alive was in the heat of a man's arms. And that avenue was closing down. Why? Even if he didn't love her, he had never rejected her body. She pinched her cheeks. All those poor creatures waiting downstairs, envying her her inherited wealth were mere parodies of her Boston friends. Sows' ears, all of them, with their vulgar jokes and foolish sentimentality. Tom seemed to like them. She had fooled him there! She had convinced him that she found them all charming. That's why she had planned this ridiculous vacation. They would not be allowed to team up against her. She had broken their tacky little knot and placed herself in their dead center. If these were the sort Tom admired, then she would pretend to join them. Ah, no fool was she!

Strange how her body was becoming so thin, all but her breasts, of course. They were still magnificent. She deliberately stood away from the mirror so that the tiny lines and prominent bones which seemed to have appeared overnight would disappear. Time to go down now. Time to smile and chatter with her enemies. She would see if she could tempt Mr. MacNeil with her body. At least it would pass the time.

She heard Tom enter the room. He wore a peculiar expression. She listened again and heard light footsteps going into the MacNeils' room across the hall. She flashed her brightest smile at Tom, who smiled back. How easily reassured he was. As if she didn't know! Did they all think her stupid as well as mad, that she did not know?

⊰23⊱

Walking through the crooked streets of Parkertown hand in hand with Jeremy, Tom felt like the temporary custodian of a treasure. The sun shone down on the childish brown curls. He knew so little about children. Were they all so bright at this age? The boy asked so many questions, many of which Tom could not answer, not knowing the island well enough. Gwyn would know what they called that kind of knot or why those white flowers grew in a clump or how high the gulls could fly. Even more disconcerting than the questions was the way Jeremy would listen intently to the responses, trusting absolutely in the omniscience of his teacher. It took all of Tom's basic honesty to admit that he didn't have all the answers. He wanted to be God to this angel. Gwyn's boy. He saw Ethan's coordination and perhaps his gregariousness, but the boy was smaller in scale than Ethan, maybe even small for his age.

"How old are you, Jeremy?" asked Tom.

Ethan had said that his son was three. He and Gwyn had certainly not wasted any time. No, he mustn't think of her in Ethan's bed. Quickly, quickly, look at the pub ahead, take your mind away from it, he thought.

"I'm three and a half," said Jeremy proudly.

"I thought you were three," said Tom.

"Three and a half," insisted Jeremy. "I was three way last springtime. I've been three all summer." He skipped on ahead, hungry for the lunch Tom had promised him at the pub.

Tom refused to contradict him, so kept his silence. There was no way the child could be three and a half. Ethan and Gwyn hadn't married until September. He counted forward from October. June. He counted again. Perhaps June was springtime to a child. Only when he reached school age would June be summer. But what if Jeremy were right, if it had been April or even May? The realization hit him front on. He walked on. No, it was impossible. If she were pregnant, she would have told him. Or she would never have let him near the child. Still there was the memory of Ethan's face when Tom had run to their door. Could it have been fear he had failed to see there?

He was by now so excited at the possibility that he had difficulty carrying on a conversation with the still wildly attractive Colleen Murphy as she took their order of stew and milk for Jeremy, stew and ale for Tom. When Jeremy's head was safely bent over his bowl, Tom searched the small form, searching—for himself. The cowlick! He had one in the same place. The interest in painting; the small size—he

had been small as a boy. Ah, but there was the confidence
and the love of the sea. But couldn't these be acquired? He
wanted it to be true so much that he was sure it couldn't
be. And if it were? Jeremy was Ethan's child legally and
Gwyn loved Ethan. That was the last word.

"Tell me, Jeremy, can you count?"

"Up to twenty."

"Do you like books?"

"Yes, I have lots of them. Mummy gets special ones
from the liberry sometimes."

He must stop this. Questioning this innocent child
simply to discover a truth that would be unendurable if
discovered. He would find out Jeremy's birthday and that
would end it.

Dinnertime brought no relief to his consternation. He
found himself analyzing every feature of Ethan's face, trying to detect any resemblance to Jeremy. Damn the beard!

Gwyn was flushed with the day's sunshine and Olive
withdrawn.

Louise and Simeon were continuing a running battle
of anagrams, and whenever Simeon made a good word she
cursed him merrily in French and blamed her native
tongue for confounding her.

"Thomas? I'm very tired. Shall we go up to bed now?"
Olive had a lynxlike gleam under heavy lids.

"You go on ahead, dear," replied Tom. "I think I'll
challenge Dr. Rogers to a game of chess." Olive departed
without a goodnight, making Tom regret that he hadn't
acquiesced. The truth was that he could no longer make
love to her. It seemed perverted to use sexually this mentally unstable woman. In bed she had always devoured him,
used him up in a way that left him feeling both abused and
abusive at the same time. He would rather face her anger
now than her later contempt for his impotence.

"I'm afraid you'll have to count me out on the chess,"
said Dr. Rogers. "I'm taking Enid out for a breath of air and

then turning in myself. Ethan will take you on. He's a killer at chess."

That left Tom, Ethan, Gwyn and the Blanchards. Ethan looked tired but would not back down from a challenge from Tom. Gwyn was seated beside the inlaid chess table as the two men set up the pieces, Ethan taking the white, Tom the dark.

Gwyn sensed the absurdity of the situation, her husband and her former lover engaged in a mock war to the finish.

Tom was distracted, Ethan determined. The game was over in less than ten minutes. Ethan's smile of victory annoyed Gwyn, for she knew from experience that Tom was by far the better player and that Ethan's gloating expression was unwarranted. Until this moment she had not recognized the depth of his fear of Tom. Why else was it so necessary to win a simple game of chess?

Her husband was not unusually competitive in games; his popularity exempted him from the need to win every trivial contest. That was one secret of his success. Men knew that he was human and liked him the more for his occasional losses in social games. They respected the fact that in business he was as tough and determined as he had to be.

Gwyn resented his ferocity and felt her anger rising to her face. She excused herself and went out onto the veranda while Tom ordered a brandy for Ethan in an attempt to lighten the atmosphere.

In the darkness surrounding the almost empty hotel, Gwyn sat on a wicker chair and pulled her shawl tightly around her shoulders against the September chill.

It was not going to work.

When Tom first returned she had felt a weakening but had immediately stiffened her spine against the threat of his presence. She loved Ethan. She had had long conversa-

tions with herself in which she insisted on that fact. There
was a stability in her feeling for her husband which held
her fast against the fact that, love him as she might, she was
not in love with him. When Tom entered a room, he tam-
pered with her equilibrium, set her head and emotions into
a constantly accelerating spin. All this despite her knowledge of him. She knew his faults; she remembered his ways
as she would those of a dearest childhood friend. Surely
such familiarity should hve deadened some of the excitement by now?

Deep inside herself she believed that she was a good
woman. She trusted in her strength to resist this constant
temptation. After that first shattering meeting she had
gradually pulled herself together, set the strict rules of
conduct by which she would balance her life. It had been
an uneasy balance at best and tonight, watching in horror
as Ethan stalked Tom across the white and brown squares,
she knew that the scales had tipped in Tom's favor, had
always been tipped, held in false balance only by her will.
But what of it? Tom had said nothing untoward. He had
not made one overt move in her direction. Besides, he had
left her, abandoned her for Olive. To reveal the extent of
her distress would only serve to expose herself once again
to rejection and certain humiliation.

She was glad to be here on the island where the
strength and pride of her personality could be reinforced.
She heard Ethan call her.

"You go ahead, Ethan." Why could she not call him
"dear" in Tom's presence? "I'd like to sit here a few minutes longer."

"Fine," said Ethan. "I'll join you."

"No, really, it's all right. I'll be fine." Why was she
being stubborn? She knew he would not want to go up
while Tom remained downstairs. Still, there were Louise
and Simeon inside to chaperone. She sensed the reluctance
in his voice as he said through the open window, "All right,

but don't stay out long. These early fall nights get chilly."
He was tired of trying to keep up with the younger members of the party. How Enid managed it was no mystery;
she was obviously taken with Dr. Rogers, but Ethan was
not courting, had no need to fight his fatigue. He trusted
her. At least he trusted her in the company of the Blanchards. He knew he should never allow Tom and Gwyn to
be alone, but tonight he would risk it. The day had been
long and he was so very tired.

"May I join you?" Tom spoke easily, as though unaware of the significance of their being alone together for
the first time in four years.

"If you like." Her throat constricted unpleasantly. Behind them the window closed.

"Your Jeremy is a lovely boy. We had an extremely
pleasant day together. You should be proud of him."

"I am." To hear such praise of Jeremy from these lips
was heady stuff.

"He's very bright for such a young fellow. Full of
questions. I'm afraid I let him down with my ignorance of
the flora of Parker's Island."

You let him down, thought Gwyn, in more than that.
What a fool not to know his own son!

"He said he was three and a half, but of course all
children want to be older than they are. He is just three,
isn't he?" Tom's voice had taken on an inquisitional tone
which frightened Gwyn.

"Why should his age be of such grave concern?" she
asked, trying to keep her tone light.

"Stop it, Gwyn!" he said. She jumped to her feet. He
caught her elbows and spun her around to face him. His
eyes found hers in the light from the window.

"His age is of every concern! He is mine, Gwyn. I
knew it today." His voice was strong. She was afraid those
inside might hear.

"How dare you?" she whispered in fierce denial. "How dare you just sail away and then come back to claim Ethan's child? For he is Ethan's, make no mistake." She was terrified by the look in his eyes.

"Why did you marry him? Why? Could I have meant so little that you went to him almost before my ship was out of sight? Because in order for Jeremy to be Ethan's child, you must have been with him in the summer. What are you? How could you be so fickle? Answer me, dammit!" He had lowered his voice but it still seemed to fill the night.

"I'll answer you and then you will let me go and never speak of this again. Never!" This could not be happening. She had tried to prepare for such a scene, but now that it was taking place she was disarmed.

"In the first place, it was you who left me. You didn't even answer my letter. And now you think you can come and ruin all our lives. Well, Ethan is my husband and Jeremy is his child."

"What letter? You never sent a letter. I would have answered. I would have come. You are only saying this to hurt me, to excuse your own behavior. A letter indeed! To imagine for one minute that loving you as I did I would have left a letter unanswered." He was trembling with emotion.

She broke away from him at that instant. "If you ever say one word about Jeremy, I . . ." She could not finish but ran inside instead and, passing the startled Blanchards, flew up the stairs. Louise and Simeon waited for Tom to follow. When he did not, they put away their wooden letters and went to bed.

Tom heard the door slam behind Gwyn and stood silent a moment waiting to see if the Blanchards might not try to find out what had set off their friend. He recognized the friendship between Louise and Gwyn. Like Ethan, he was glad for it. Gwyn had always been such an introspective, solitary soul. Did Louise know?

He left the veranda and walked toward the lantern which hung on the farthest post of the pier. The other guests had left shortly after Labor Day and the air of desertion hinted at the barrenness of the winter to come. Her world was here; he would never know a winter here. There was so much he could never know about her previous life, but he was hungry for any scrap of insight into her complex personality.

Sitting on the pier, his knees drawn up to his body for warmth, he faced the fact of their having finally spoken. If she were telling the truth, what then? Had she sent a letter, a letter which never came? If it were true, then she had married in desperation. And what did that make him? Her seducer, the father of a son he could never claim, a son who could well be the only child he would ever father? "Jeremy MacNeil. Jeremy Warner." He spoke the names aloud. The sound carried over the water and echoed sonorously against the shadows of moored fishing boats. Most important, did she love him still? He must know. They could never be together as they'd been before, but if she loved him it would be something—no, everything. Ah, but if she loved him, then she was more trapped than he, surrounded by her children (yes, there was Ellen to consider) as well as by Ethan's possessive love. Over them all loomed the massive presence of Ethan MacNeil. The old enmity remained, augmented by the bizarre facts of their lives. What had happened? Had she gone to Ethan as a first option or as a last resort? Tom preferred to think that Ethan had taken advantage of the situation, had grasped at her youth and loveliness with the greed of the middle-aged. Had Ethan seen his life roaring past? How dare he use Gwyn as some consumable elixir of youth!

His anger was interrupted by the voices of Enid and Dr. Rogers returning to the Inn from the walk that had earlier removed them from the chess game. He moved nearer the edge of the pier, unwilling to reveal his presence.

"This has been a real pleasure, Enid. I wish it could go on a while, but my patients won't stand for my absence much longer."

"I suppose I should say that it's because you are such a marvelous doctor, but the truth is that being the only doctor in town, you have no competition." She laughed. "Except for me, of course."

"That's the truth! There's a law against practicing medicine without a license, you know."

"I just give good common sense advice, that's all. You've never caught me trying to set a broken bone have you?"

"No," he admitted, "but that's about all you haven't tried. To be fair I must admit that little Missy Palmer's scald did heal up fast after you rubbed it with the aloe."

"Of course it did! Everyone knows about aloe. Well, I'd best turn in. It's been a long day and at my age I just can't take it."

"Your age, indeed," said Dr. Rogers. "Why, there in the moonlight you don't look a day older than Gwyn."

"Oh, get on with you and get upstairs."

"Very well, but sooner or later you will have to learn how to accept a compliment, because I intend to go right on handing them out. Now don't forget to shut your window. The air's got a real chill in it tonight."

"Rubbish. I always sleep with a window open, even in winter. The fresh air's good for you."

"I give up!" said Dr. Rogers, and laughing they went inside.

Tom looked down to the black sea. How easy it would be to slide into that blackness and escape Olive and the frightened face of Gwyn. In a way, it would be a perfect solution. Olive might recover if she had the opportunity to marry someone who really cared for her, and he imagined that his death could be nothing but a

relief to Ethan and Gwyn. He thought of Gwyn. Never
to see that beautiful face again was unthinkable; and
now there was Jeremy, his son. He was sure of it. Why
else the terror on Gwyn's face? He had no right to put
her through this. If she had sent for him four years ago,
then she was the only true victim. He must go on and
try to make her see that he had not abandoned her.
How he would do that without making her more unhappy he did not know, but he would start by reassuring her of his silence about Jeremy. They would be
home in two days. She and Ethan would be coming to
his home for the gala celebrating the bank opening the
following week. He would speak to her then, after she
had had a chance to calm herself. He stood and turned
his back on the beckoning water.

❧24❧

Louise Blanchard was excited at the prospect of a
party. She had never been inside the Warners' house before. No one had. Olive Warner was invisible except for an
occasional evening out in the restaurant. As Ethan had
predicted, she had made no friends in Buckley. Louise had
invited her to tea and even once to dinner, but both times
she had refused. Gwyn had been negligent in her duties
also, a fact which convinced Louise that there was some
mystery surrounding the MacNeils and the Warners. Usually Gwyn was the first one to greet a newcomer or to bring

a pie when someone was ill, but toward Olive she had
maintained a stiff silence. The week on Parker's Island had
been overshadowed with strain whenever the two women
were in the same room. Louise had been able to see that
Olive was jealous of Gwyn's earlier friendship with Tom.
Ah, but it must have been more than friendship to elicit
such strong feelings in everyone involved unless, of course,
Olive was simply mad and the jealousy part of her madness.

The door sounded and Louise called out to Simeon to
hurry up or they should be late, the MacNeils were waiting
for them. The four were going together as much from a
need to reinforce each other as to make a good entrance.

"Gwyn, dear, you are lovely in yellow with your
pretty summer skin. You are very brave to expose yourself
to the sun the way you do, but it seems to do you no harm.
If I did it, I would surely be a mass of, oh, someone help
me, what's the word?"

"Freckles!" supplied Simeon.

"Ah, yes. Freckles. I should be covered, but not you.
That is unusual, is it not, for one of your coloring?"

"I suppose my skin has become accustomed to it. I
spent most of my childhood out of doors," replied Gwyn.
"You look wonderful, Louise. No one can wear violet as
well as you."

"It is a good color for me, yes? In this country it is
wasted on little old ladies." She pulled on lace gloves and
primped once more in the mirror, then took Gwyn's arm
as they left the house. "Ethan is looking very handsome this
evening," she said, knowing that he would overhear and be
pleased.

"Did I tell you what I have done to our dear Oakie?
Have you met Miss Ogilvie, the cousin of Mrs. Perth? No?
Well, my dear, she is a most frightful creature who wears
a red wig and pretends to be forty when she is sixty if she
is a day. The other afternoon I visited for tea, and she
inquired about the eligible men in town. She will be at the

party tonight. How could I resist? I told her that Mr. Williams was our town's most eligible bachelor and, do not be angry with me, that he was very partial to red-haired women who were of mature years, being a man of the world himself."

"Oh, Louise, you didn't!" Gwyn giggled despite herself.

"She talked of nothing else for the remainder of the afternoon. It will be very amusing to see our Oakie with this creature. I assure you, darling, that she is a dreadful person, always bearing down on her cousine with cruel remarks about the provinciality of Buckley and refusing to be introduced to anyone but the most prominent members of the community."

"But what about poor Oakie? You know how he is with women. He'll die, poor thing. You really shouldn't have, Louise."

"Nonsense. It will be good practice for him. If he can survive her, he need never be afraid of any woman again. We are doing him a great favor."

"Louise, you are impossible." Ethan spoke severely but his eyes were dancing. How typical of Louise to cook up some mischief to keep Gwyn's mind off other matters. Not that her scheme was completely altruistic. She had a wicked sense of humor and, although she loved him dearly, had always found Oakie's shyness with women to be a constant source of hilarity.

The foursome went to the Warner's door where they were announced by a butler in black. After the women were relieved of their shawls, and the men of their hats, they were ushered through a hall, barren except for an Oriental runner on the floor and a lovely Louis XV table on one wall, and into a formal room to the right. This room, too, was furnished in French antiques (provoking a sign of appreciation from Louise) but lacking in personal touches. The tabletops were bare except for the glasses of champagne which had been set down on them by guests and there was, overall, the Spartan look of the furnished hotel room. The large number of milling guests softened the look of the place and, of course, the Warners had been here only since July so perhaps, thought Louise, that accounted for the strange feeling that, should the other guests vanish, she would be left standing in a large, impersonal chamber where no memento gave a clue to the inhabitants' personalities. Her mood lightened once again as Tom Warner came to greet them. Louise noticed the special look he gave Gwyn, a look of such intensity that she would have been thrilled to receive it herself. Such an attractive man, she thought. Those blue eyes, they see into your soul. And what is he seeing in Gwyn's soul? she mused. Now he was shaking hands with the men and ushering them into the assemblage, and then Olive made her appearance. Tonight her blond hair was pulled back from her face and fashioned in a French knot, giving her thin face a gaunt, haunted look. She was vivacious, obviously enjoying one of her manic moods. She pranced from group to group, flirting with all the men, making them nervous, and tapping her toe in time to the music from the small group of musicians who, from behind a discreet arrangement of ferns, played light background melodies on a violin, a cello and a flute.

Ethan was delighted to see his old friend Maurice Darcy and his pretty wife Belle. He brought Gwyn to meet them, and Gwyn decided that she liked the Darcys very much. She discovered that they had a son, Tad, who was almost the exact same age as Jeremy. The two women compared notes on their sons' antics and before long had become so captivated with each other that they had made dinner plans for three weeks later. The men talked about their businesses, and Maurice Darcy was pleased to learn that his successful emporium in Salem had been the model for Ethan's growing establishment. The men had known each other in Ethan's sailing days when Maurice had been just a young fry learning the ropes about importing from the older Ethan.

Louise joined them and after greeting the Darcys gave Gwyn a nudge in the ribs and rolled her eyes toward a point across the room to where Miss Ogilvie had a firm grasp on Oakie William's arm.

"Please excuse us one moment, Mrs. Darcy. There is someone we must greet. We'll be right back," said Gwyn, anxious to help Oakie out of his bind.

"No, no!" said Louise. "Let us just watch a moment." She dragged Gwyn to a spot behind a large man who stood about three feet from Oakie. From here they could hear the piercing voice of Miss Ogilvie praising continental food and waxing euphoric about the virtues of tall men such as Mr. Williams. Louise had neglected to mention Oakie's wooden leg, so there was a terrible moment when she insisted upon knowing which of the current popular dances he preferred.

"Dear Mr. Williams," she finally said. "I feel as if I had known you all my life. Please call me Agatha. And what, may I ask, is your Christian name?"

"Oakie," he replied. His face was so scarlet that it seemed ready to burst above his black tie.

"Oakie? How charming, and how did you get such an unusual name?" she persisted.

"It's not my real name. My real name is," he gulped and looked around in desperation, "Obediah."

Louise and Gwyn burst into laughter and had to hold onto each other in a vain attempt to regain control.

"Ssh, they're still talking," whispered Louise.

"But how did you get your nickname, Obediah?"

More squeals from Louise and Gwyn.

Oakie had had enough of this damned ugly woman. Rising to his full height he looked her in the eye and said, "When I was seven years old I squished my leg on a float and they had to chop it off and give me an oak peg leg. Does that answer your question?" He stomped off and Gwyn and Louise followed him, leaving the ashen-faced Agatha Ogilvie standing with her jaw hanging open over her double chin.

Catching up with Oakie, Louise grabbed one arm and Gwyn the other. "Do let us get you a drink," said Louise. Then she paused and added pointedly, "Obediah, dear."

Oakie stared at her dumbfounded, then regained his tongue. "You tell anyone that's my real name, and next time you come to the restaurant I'll feed you poisoned mushroom soup!" Then all three fell into great peals of laughter attracting Ethan's attention. Gwyn was having a fine time. Good!

Ethan was not the only one who watched Gwyn. Tom, having decided that tonight he would speak with her and attempt to reassure her, was also following her progress around the room. He smiled when he saw the two women and guessed from Oakie's facial expression that Louise and Gwyn were sharing some joke at Oakie's expense. He was startled to hear Gwyn laughing so merrily. It was the first time she had opened up so completely in his presence since his arrival in Buckley. Her laughter made her look like a girl. Her skin, still brown from summer sun, complemented the yellow of her dress and turned her eyes into sapphires. She returned to the Darcys for a few minutes and introduced Oakie and Louise to her new friends from Marblehead.

Tom tore his eyes away and saw Olive watching him with the same intensity that he had been focusing on Gwyn. Angry with himself for having hurt her again and for his lack of self-control, he turned toward the wine table. When playing host he rarely drank, preferring to keep his full attention on the needs of his guests, but tonight he needed fortification. He detested this new feeling of shyness with Gwyn; before, they had always been so comforta-

ble together. The uncertainty mimicked their earliest days
when he had feared she would not love him as he did her.
Drinking his wine in two gulps, he sought Gwyn again but
she had left the room. Putting down his glass he left as
discreetly as possible and tried to find her.

After almost two hours of light conversation and
avoidance of Tom and Olive, Gwyn was feeling the strain.
Seeing Ethan safely surrounded by friends, she slipped
from the room. All evening she had felt Tom's eyes on her,
and it was only by the strongest effort that she forced her
eyes away from his. Here in his own house she was completely under his spell, and she discovered that once she
had left the sterility of the front room, she could begin to
discern his impeccable taste. Stepping into a narrow hall,
she saw a glow of light from the first room on her right.
Still acting on impulse, she entered what had to be Tom's
sanctuary. Feeling at first like an intruder, she soon began
to be engulfed by his personality, which was everywhere
in this room. There, in the left corner was his easel, and all
along the far wall from floor to ceiling were his books. She
crossed the room and ran a loving hand along the leather
bindings, touching with equal affection the strangers as
well as the old friends. The only jarring note came when
she discovered three books tucked away behind the others
and carrying titles dealing with insanity; strange books by
strange people, Kaulbaum and Bleuler and Hecker. She
averted her eyes and saw his deep blue woolen sweater
resting comfortably over the back of a desk chair. The desk
was old, Queen Anne she guessed, and the graceful curve
of the slipper feet on the faded Oriental carpet pleased her
eye. In the grate were the embers of an afternoon fire. He
had probably sat here this very day, reading and thinking
of what? Did he think of her? Did his mind, like hers,
return again and again to those days on the cliffs? She
reached out and stroked the soft wool of the sweater and

then held it to her face, inhaling his scent.

"Gwyn."

She turned around, caught like a thief, and there he stood. Flesh and blood and speaking her name.

"I'm sorry," he said. "I didn't mean to creep up on you like that, but we have to talk, Gwyn."

She could not speak. If she tried she would weep, wanting him so.

"I never got your letter, you must believe me."

She fell into the blue of his eyes and knew that he spoke the truth. "Yes," she whispered. "I believe you." Then the tears started and he took her in his arms and for a brief moment she let him murmur into her hair and feel her body next to his. Then she broke away.

"No, this is wrong. I will not do this to Ethan, and you mustn't do it to Olive. It's not their fault that we lost each other."

"But Jeremy, he is my child. Don't say anything; I know you can't admit it. I'll never tell him or anyone. You must know that I love you too much to hurt him that way. But what of us? What are we to do? There must be a way out of this."

"There is none, at least no honorable way. I will stay married to Ethan and you will stay with Olive. There's no other way."

"I can't do that. Do you know what it's been like for me, wanting you, loving you and not being able to tell you? Watching you go home with Ethan and knowing you would share his bed?" She blushed with the shame of having slept with her husband.

"Stop! You must stop saying those things," she cried. "We must never speak of this again." She ran past him and into the figure of Olive who had been listening just outside in the hall.

"Going so soon, you little slut?" said Olive, her face grey with rage and pain.

"Olive!" cried Tom. "Gwyn has done nothing. Be angry with me if you like, but leave her alone."

"Why? So you can meet again behind my back? Don't think I've been fooled. Don't you think I know you've been sleeping together ever since we moved here?"

"That's not true!" cried Gwyn.

"Shut up, shut up with your filthy lies! You've been a slut since you were a girl, and you've never left my Tom alone. You, with your innocent eyes." She began to rave hysterically, and rocking from side to side she lashed out until Tom said, "Go get Dr. Rogers, Gwyn. Quickly!"

Gwyn ran off, her heart pounding against the yellow silk. She found Dr. Rogers and whispered in his ear. He followed her without a word, and they returned to the room. Olive was crouched in a corner. Her hair had escaped from the chignon and stuck out crazily from her head. Tears streamed down her face, and she was shrieking obscenities so loudly that other guests came to the doorway and were horrified to see and hear her. Tom and Dr. Rogers each took her by an arm and half led, half carried her further down the hall to a back staircase which led to her room.

"Good God! What happened?" cried one man.

"She had a nervous upset, that's all. She'll be all right in the morning," said Enid, who had appeared from nowhere and taken charge. "Now everyone go back and act as if nothing happened. Go on, go on!"

Dutifully the frustrated guests returned to the main salon, but the party was destroyed. There could be only one interesting topic of conversation, and as they were too polite to mention it, the result was awkward. When Enid got Gwyn alone she whispered, "What did happen in there?"

"I was alone in Tom's study and he found me, and Olive thought we were having a lovers' meeting."

"Why were you in his study? That was a stupid place to be under the circumstances, wasn't it?"

"Yes, I suppose so. I honestly don't know how it happened. One minute I was leaving the room and the next I was in his study."

"I just hope Ethan doesn't get wind of it. He's jumpy enough these days," said Enid.

"No, Dr. Rogers was there before anyone else came, so no one but Olive saw me alone with Tom. You wouldn't tell him, would you?" There was fear on Gwyn's face.

"Of course not, child. I'm your mother. Don't you think I know what you're going through? I'll make it easier any way I can, but you must promise never to go near Tom again. I don't want to think what would have happened tonight if Jim and Tom hadn't got her upstairs before anyone had a chance to make sense out of her ravings."

"Jim?" asked Gwyn.

"James Rogers. He does have a first name, you know, besides 'Doctor.' Now smile. Here comes your husband."

❧25❧

Olive stole a glance around the bedroom and then shook her head in an effort to remember where she was. Recognizing her room, she flung back the covers and put first one, then two unsteady legs on the floor. Since the night of the bank-opening celebration she had been somewhere outside of herself while still in her own home. She had a vague recollection of unfamiliar faces hovering over her and of strange draughts being forced down her throat.

She tiptoed to the door and soundlessly gripped it in clawlike fingers, opening it less than half an inch. The sight of the emaciated fingers jolted her; she began to tremble with the effort of holding the door steady in her grasp.

In the hallway outside her bedroom door sat a woman dressed in white, knitting studiously as she rocked softly back and forth. So the faces had not been a dream! How long had she been here? It didn't matter. She would get away somehow. Her head throbbed painfully, and she carefully shut the door and returned to her bed, falling back into torpor for several moments before awakening for good.

After resting long enough to feel steady on her feet, she arose once more and went to the window. There was a curious iron grillwork over each window that had not been there before. Why was she locked up? She could vaguely recall seeing Gwyn MacNeil in Tom's arms and then nothing, nothing at all. Had that been a dream? Recently it was so difficult to distinguish between her dreams and actual events. Was it possible that she had done harm to Tom? The thought terrified her. Below her window the leaves on the oaks and maples were yellow and red. Raising her line of vision, she could see a mass of autumn color lining the yards and stretching almost to the sea; it was still fall. The leaves had begun to turn by the night of her party. She remembered thinking that she might soon be able to take walks without being trampled by vacationing school children. What had happened? Unable to bear the agony of not knowing a second longer, she ran to the door and called, "Nurse! Come here!" It was gratifying to see the white figure start and then drop her knitting in her haste to keep Olive from leaving the room.

"Oh, for heaven's sake, don't be an idiot! If I were going to run off, I'd have made sure you didn't see me. Come in here immediately."

"Let me call your husband," said the agitated nurse.

Her husband. Thank God he was here and alive! If she had not harmed him, then perhaps it was Gwyn she had somehow attacked. The thought was pleasant. She fell back against the door, her hands behind her back, and began to laugh. Her laughter filled the hall and brought the nurse to her side.

"You fool. Do you really find me dangerous?" said Olive, still shaking with groundless mirth. "What do you think I weigh? Ninety pounds? No, not even so much. Do you think perhaps I will strangle you with these powerful hands?" She held the ten bony extremities in a menacing posture and again began to laugh, first a giggle and then a series of ascending caws which ended abruptly, leaving the silence cracked and threatened in their wake.

"Well, where is he? You said you wanted to get him, so get him now before I get you first." Again amusement as she saw the woman vacillate between wanting to get away and fearing to leave her patient alone. In the end she decided to fetch her employer. She had seen cases like this before. First a gradual increase in excitement, then a violent outburst followed by a quiet phase of guilt and depression. She felt that Mrs. Warner was probably safe enough for the moment, but she began to run once she was out of sight of the wraith at the bedroom door. Despite her thirty pounds of overweight and her fifty-eight years, she could still move in an emergency.

When Tom came up the stairs, two at a time, he found Olive sitting tractably in a white chair, her hands folded in her lap.

"Do I get to hear the charges?" she asked, a smile threatening one corner of her mouth.

"What do you mean?" asked Tom. He couldn't decide which was worse, this sly Olive who looked so deceptively demure or the raging creature of ten days ago. She was like two different people and yet the same. Her madness seemed to be the mere ripping off of a veil. And he was all she had.

No parents, no sister or brother, just lawyers to administer
her money. Already they had come to Buckley, stern men
in dark suits insisting that Mrs. Warner be declared legally
incompetent so that they might prevent her from ruining
herself financially. Good God, thought Tom. Can't they see
that it doesn't matter now? She has been out of her mind
for years. The death of her parents and then her babies had
been only the final insults to her already troubled mind.

In the end he had accepted the decision of the lawyers
so that he could look after her at home. They felt that she
should be institutionalized immediately. At least, acting as
her legal guardian, he could keep her here. After all, they
had seen only the lunatic, not the seemingly normal
woman in the chair before him. Normal, that is, if you
could call a weight loss of thirty pounds in a year normal
or reconcile yourself to the fragmented thoughts which
found substance in her ravings. Somewhere trapped inside
her was the vivacious young woman with the blond hair
who had made him believe he could forget Gwyn and lay
down his weight of love at last. That Olive had failed was
more his fault than hers. His heart had been no longer his
to give. In retrospect he marvelled at his conceit in daring
to hope that he might love so deeply twice in a lifetime. No,
it was not her fault.

"Well, what have I done now?" she asked again. But
this time there was a humility in her voice which tore at
his heart.

"You became upset at the party and accused Gwyn
and me of having some sort of secret love affair. That's
about all, but we couldn't seem to calm you down. Dr.
Rogers called in your doctors from Boston and they
managed to quiet you with a tranquillizing medicine."

"Thank you for telling me the truth. Was it terrible?"

"You don't want me to answer that, do you?"

"It doesn't really require an answer. Please stop looking at me like that."

"I wasn't aware that I was looking at you in any particular way," said Tom.

"You were looking at me as if I were crazy."

Tom flinched.

"Yes, crazy. Crazy! Say it aloud, why don't you?"

He was silent.

"Perhaps I am. Wouldn't that be convenient for you? Just think. You could lock me up forever and then Gwyn could divorce Ethan and you two could live happily ever after. Think how nice it would be without crazy Olive to worry about. Maybe I'd even die. Yes, that would be even better for you. Of course that would still leave Ethan, but I'm sure Gwyn could find a way to get rid of him; he's so old and she's so young. Does that ever upset you to think of his hard old hands all over her body, touching her and making love to her?"

"Stop it!" cried Tom. "You're doing it again. Don't you see what you are doing to yourself? Oh, Olive, can't we try to be kind to each other?"

"It's a little too late for that, wouldn't you say? Don't fear, my love. I'll be a good little girl now. Why don't you get that horrible nurse to give me some more medicine. I want to sleep again."

"That would probably be a good idea." He went forward half intending to kiss her brow, but a peculiar look stopped him and he went out, calling to the nurse.

When the nurse came in she had a bottle in her hand. Carefully she measured out two large spoonfuls and then watched as Olive swallowed them.

"There now. See how cooperative I am? Now leave me alone. I have to use the toilet." After the nurse had gone she went into the adjoining bathroom and leaned over the toilet. Sticking a finger down her throat she gagged and brought up the medicine. She stood and pulled the chain of the water closet and then went to her room and rinsed her mouth. This accomplished, she sat back in her chair, looking out toward the MacNeil house and waiting.

At one o'clock in the afternoon she heard footsteps approaching. Feigning sleep, she listened as Tom and the nurse entered the room.

"I have to go to Salem, but I'll be back by four thirty. I'll stop in at the office until five and then come straight home. Do you think she's well enough to have dinner with me up here? We could dine early, maybe by five thirty." Tom was whispering, but Olive heard what she needed to know.

"I don't see why not, Mr. Warner. She seemed to be doing quite well this morning. I'll bring her a tea tray around three; she'll be hungry after sleeping through lunch. Look at her, poor thing. So thin. We'll have to build her up."

"I'll leave that part to you, Mrs. Wright. Just try to treat her as normally as possible. Now that she's herself again she's bound to be sensitive about what happened."

"Don't you fret now. Everything will be just fine. You've been home too much already. It's time for both of you to get back to normal. New banks don't run themselves!"

They shut the door and Olive waited until her husband left by the drive below her window. Thank heaven her window overlooked the street! Now she became impatient. First she went to her desk and penned a short note in what she hoped was a mannish hand. She grimaced when she noticed that her letter opener was missing. After the eternity of an hour a small boy appeared beneath her window, rolling a hoop.

"Boy!" she cried. The child paused and looked around uncertainly. "Up here," she called. "Would you deliver this to Mrs. MacNeil for me? She lives down at the end of Main Street in a big white house."

"I know her. She's the pretty lady with the dark hair."

"Yes," said Olive, not caring for the description. "But

don't give it to anyone else. If she's not at home, bring it back here right away. I'll be waiting here; don't go to my door. It's sort of a secret, so don't tell her who sent it. Promise? I'll pay you twenty-five cents."

"Two bits? Just for delivering a note? You bet, lady! Toss her down. I'm a good catch."

"Remember now, only give it to her and don't say who sent it. If she insists on knowing, just say it came from a man in the bank. And don't say anything about this to anyone." She wrapped the note around the money and tossed it down. The boy caught it and took off toward Gwyn's house at a run, leaving his hoop behind in his haste.

Ellen MacNeil licked jam from her fingers and reluctantly submitted to Mommy's demand that she come up for a nap. Jeremy didn't have to nap anymore. He could play outside in the garden with Grandma. Her lower lip trembled as she took her mother's outstretched hand and the tears began.

"Hush now, lovey," said Gwyn. "You're only sad because you're tired. If you don't have a nap, you won't be able to stay up and see Dr. Rogers when he comes for dinner tonight. You know how much he likes you. Think how sad he would be if he couldn't see you for a while." Poor little children, thought Gwyn. We do order them about so! Sweeping Ellen into her arms, she kissed the damp cheek and felt the curly head droop onto her shoulder. After tucking her into her bed, she pulled the curtains and gave her daughter one last kiss before leaving the room. She knew she should let the nurse put Ellen down for her nap, but she disliked having someone else do for her children. Ethan and she had had words on the subject of nursemaids many times, but she had been forced to admit that it was not fair to expect Enid to babysit when they went out, especially now that Dr. Rogers was taking her out more and more frequently. He would always be Dr. Rogers to Gwyn, but he was Jim to Enid. There was certainly something going on there, but Gwyn didn't dare mention it for fear that she would annoy her mother. Enid always acted annoyed when anyone queried her about Dr. Rogers, but that didn't stop her from going out with him. Gwyn chuckled at the thought of poor James Rogers trying to court her mother. She hoped he persevered. Enid deserved some happiness and the good doctor was obviously smitten.

She had descended the front stairs, intending to check on the flower arrangements to see if they needed replacement when she heard a knock on the door. "I'll get it," she said as the housemaid emerged from the kitchen. That was another thing she couldn't get used to, having someone come all the way from some other part of the house to answer the door when she was standing right there. She opened the door and was surprised to see a dirty-faced little boy standing there with a note in his hand.

"This is for you," he said.

"Are you sure?" asked Gwyn.

"You're Mrs. MacNeil, right?" asked the boy in return.

"Yes," said Gwyn.

"Then this is for you," he insisted.

She took the note and read it. "Who sent this?" she demanded.

"I'm not supposed to say," responded the boy, beginning to suspect that this was no mere joke.

"Who sent this? I insist that you tell me!" Her tone frightened the lad, who cried, "A man at the bank!" and ran down the steps and up Main Street before she could question him further. She read the note. It was a request to meet Tom at the bank at four thirty. Why did Tom want to see her? She hid the note in the bodice of her dress, realizing suddenly that this was the first time he had ever written to her. His handwriting was different from what she would

have expected, uneven and messier than his artistic nature
would indicate. It could be nothing indiscreet if he wanted
to meet her at his office. Perhaps he wanted to apologize for
Olive? No, that was ridiculous. Olive had caught them in
each other's arms; they were the offenders. She had neither
seen nor spoken with him since that night. There was
nothing more to say. Any faint hope she might have had
that they could ever be together had vanished at the first
sound of Olive's accusatory voice. To inflict such horror
and humiliation on her children and Ethan as she had endured that night was impermissible. She would have to be
totally without conscience to subject them all to such pain.
No Karenina she, to abandon a child for a lover's embrace.
Life was not a romantic novel which existed for the selfish-
ness of lovers. Still, she had wept for Anna and Vronsky
and had despised the pious Karenin even while sympathiz-
ing with him.

She decided to consult Enid about the note but turned
back before she had taken two steps toward the back door.
The note burned her chest. She knew she must not go to
the bank as he requested, but her desire to see him waged
formidable arguments. "After all," said her common sense,
"imagine how foolish you will look if he only wishes to
discuss a business matter and you refuse to go." "Imagine,"
mocked her heart "if you do not go and he never tries to
see you again?"

During the last four years her already private nature
had taken a further turn inward, had convoluted upon
itself in the necessity of shielding herself and Ethan from
the realities of her feelings for Tom. It was as simple and
yet as complex as the unclenching of a fist, yet she felt
liberated even to be able to consider following her heart in
this matter. If his intent in sending the note was innocent,
then perhaps it didn't matter if her acceptance of his polite
summons was motivated by something darker.

It was only two o'clock. She would let the whole thing

rest for an hour or two and then reexamine it. Already she had decided not to tell Ethan, and with this decision she accepted her guilt. It baffled her that this stubborn love for Tom could survive, cradled as it was in such monstrous cushions of guilt; yet there it was, shining out as straight and tenacious as ever.

She rejoined Enid and Jeremy in the garden. Jeremy and Ethan had planted a small vegetable garden behind Gwyn's flower beds, and now Jeremy took her hand to show off his pumpkins. Their circumference was impressive, and it required no effort of maternal pride to praise them.

"Are you sure they are the best you ever saw?" asked Jeremy.

"Oh yes, dear. Quite the best. See how turning them has kept away the flat spots?"

"That's so." Jeremy sighed in satisfaction.

He and his father had enjoyed their garden. Ethan's seafaring and island runs had precluded any former horticultural activity, and he was as surprised as the rest of them to discover the joy of growing food from seeds. Every evening when he returned from work, he took a child in each hand and together they toured their rows of beans and tomatoes. Many of the vegetables had gone by, but there was still corn and of course the pumpkins. These peaceful moments had become his treasure, a time of communion with his children and the earth below his feet. He knew that something was wrong with Gwyn, and he knew that Tom was behind the faraway look in her eyes. She did not shun him in bed, but there was a haste recently in her lovemaking that left him emotionally unsatisfied. He wanted all of her, but he knew he could have only her loyalty and affection, not her passion; and recently he had begun to have doubts about her loyalty. That scene with Olive Warner a few weeks back had unsettled everyone. He had wanted to question Gwyn about it but had been advised by Enid to leave it alone. Now it rose like a hedge between them. They should have talked about it before Gwyn had had a chance to lock it away. She kept too much inside, always had. He had been so sure that he could let the air sweep through her locked-up thoughts, but the key was not in his possession.

The conviction was growing that the only man who had ever been allowed into her heart was Thomas Warner. He should hate Tom for it but he was weary of fear and hate. His age was beginning to torment him. He was as alert as ever, but physically he was slowing down to the point where fatigue often overcame lust and plans were more enticing than their execution.

In the garden, Gwyn sat back in a wicker lawn chair and turned her face to the descending sun. The days were growing shorter and the heat felt good on her face. Louise would be horrified to see her ruining her skin thus, probably more horrified than if Gwyn were to start seeing Tom. Under the heat of the sun she felt an underlying chill. Could she face another winter in this house with Ethan? His proud eyes had become sad. She knew she was the cause of it and she loved him in every way she could, but he seemed frail to her. He, who had been such a mountain of strength, seemed to be losing his self-confidence. When he walked in the garden with Jeremy and Ellen he looked like a doting grandfather. There was grey in the beard now. When had it come? More important, had she put it there?

At twenty minutes past four she told Enid that she had an errand downtown.

"When will Ethan be home?" asked Enid. "Jim is taking me for a drive as soon as his office hours are over. He says we'd better enjoy what time we have before the winter colds begin."

"He should be home soon. Just tell him that I'll be back by five o'clock."

"Where will you be if Jim comes before Ethan gets home?" asked Enid, curiosity overwhelming her wish not to pry.

"Don't worry. He'll be here anytime now. You know he's been coming home earlier recently."

"Jim is a bit concerned about him. He asked him to come into the office for a looking over, but you know Ethan. He just laughed and said he was working too hard." Enid's brow furrowed.

"Do you think he's ill? I've also noticed that he was not quite himself." Now Gwyn had one more worry on her mind.

"It's probably nothing, but maybe you could talk him into seeing a doctor one of these days. It would please Jim, at least."

"You want to please Jim, don't you?" teased Gwyn and darted off before her mother could protest. Upstairs she put on a businesslike doe-colored bonnet and wrapped a beige shawl around her shoulders. As she went down Main Street she heard Ethan's voice inside the store but hastened past before he could see her and then marvelled at her duplicity. She was treating this appointment like an assignation but was too excited at the thought of seeing Tom to stop herself.

❧ 26 ❧

Olive picked dutifully at her tea cake and swallowed, without tasting it, the dark Oolong tea. Earlier she had seen the boy return to retrieve his hoop, and she had ascertained that he had delivered the note. Now she threw the last bit of cake out to the birds and started to call to the nurse. Just in time she checked herself. There was still the problem of escape. She would wait until she saw Gwyn en route to the bank. Olive had no doubt whatever that Gwyn would answer the summons. She had deliberately made the note ambiguous so that Gwyn's curiosity would get the better of her. Besides, they were lovers and what lover could resist a secret note? The only problem was the handwriting. Would Gwyn detect the forgery? No, even if it did not appear to be Tom's writing, it was worded innocently enough to have been written by a bank employee on Tom's behalf.

She waited and at twenty-five minutes after four she saw Gwyn walking down Main Street. As she passed her husband's emporium Gwyn increased her pace. Good. That confirmed all of Olive's suspicions, as if they needed tangible confirmation.

She called to the nurse and waited impatiently for the footsteps to reach her door.

"Come in. The tea cake was too sweet; I threw it to the birds. Could you possibly fix me an egg? I'm so terribly hungry."

Mrs. Wright looked gratified to hear such evidence of her patient's rapid recuperation. "Of course, dear. I'll have Cook do it right now."

"Oh, please don't let Cook do it. She ruins everything! I want it poached for exactly three minutes. And on toast, please, not too dark. Would you do it yourself? I swear that half the reason I've lost so much weight is that woman's cooking."

"Of course, if you wish it, and may I say that it's a real pleasure to see you taking an interest in your food again." Mrs. Wright bustled out and down the stairs, secretly relishing the opportunity to insult the cook, whom she found to be overbearing and rude. It was a pity to see what became of some servants when they had no mistress to keep them in hand.

In less than a minute Olive had thrown her dress over her chemise and pulled on her shoes. The laces were bothersome so in the end she just fastened every other hook and grabbed a cape. Peering into the hall she then gingerly stepped out and went as noiselessly down the stairs as possible. She went out the unattended front door and darted down Main Street towards MacNeil and Son. Reaching the near wall she had to lean against it. Her legs were weak and it took the strongest effort to keep from falling onto the street. She was perspiring profusely and had to remain still for more than a minute before she could gather the strength to enter the store. She walked toward Ethan's office and went in without knocking. She had not gone through such labors to be turned back by some ignorant store clerk.

Ethan was huddled over a page of almost undecipherable order forms when he was burst in upon by Olive Warner. She was hatless and her hair had a dull, oily, unwashed look. The laces of her shoes were dragging on the floor, and the buttons of her sleeves were undone, causing the sleeves to flap like the wings of some ungainly bird. Ethan instantly envisioned the pristine orderliness of his own wife and shuddered inwardly at the unkempt creature before him.

"They are together," said Olive, a look of purest malice in her eyes.

"Who is together? Sit down and tell me what this is all about," replied Ethan, trying to focus on what she was saying.

"Who? Tom and Gwyn, of course, or are you so blind as to not know that they are still lovers? You men, all taken in by her! She's had the both of you all along in her bed."

Ethan rose to his feet. "I will not have you speaking that way about Gwyn." Then, in an effort to calm her: "Olive, I know they were close once years ago, but you must see that it is over now."

"Over is it? Is that why I found them in each other's arms the night of my party? Ah, so she neglected to tell you what had upset me, set off 'my little outburst,' I believe they called it. They were there, in each other's arms and in my own house. It's true, I swear it." She rocked back and grabbed onto a chair for support, waiting to see the effect of her words.

She had shaken him at last, this dull infatuated fool was finally beginning to recognize the depravity of his dear little wife.

"Oh yes," she continued. " 'Poor mad Olive,' they said. 'She imagines things,' they said. And all the time they were meeting and slaking their nasty lust while we stood helpless. Don't you see what fools they have made of us? Why who knows if those dear little children are even yours?"

This hit too near the mark. Trembling with doubt and hating himself for it, he grabbed her by the arm, then quickly released her when he discovered that his rage was great enough to snap her frailty like a twig.

"You must go on home now. It is not true, none of it," he cried.

"But they are together this minute at the bank. I saw them. Together in his office. Perhaps this very minute they are embracing. Come! See for yourself if you too think I am mad." She clutched at his arm and began to pull at him like a child dragging a procrastinating parent to a circus. He followed her out the door, unable to resist the raw force of her madness any longer.

"Yes, I shall come and deliver you to your husband, and he may take you home and calm you. Gwyn is at home today with her mother and the children." Please, dear God in heaven, let it be so, he prayed.

When Gwyn reached the bank she hesitated, then walked through the marble pillars which gave permanence and dignity to the entrance hall. Seeing the familiar face of one of the clerks, she stifled her conscience and gave him her sunniest smile. The twenty steps to the office marked a marathon as she carefully placed one foot in front of the other, trying unsuccessfully to muffle the sound of her heels on the granite floor. Her footsteps echoed in the open space. Other than the bank guard who had let her in and two clerks, she was alone. The bank was closed for the day. Only her position in the community had gained her such easy access. She wanted to turn back, to rush home and pen a polite answer requesting further explanation. Now she was at his door and the gulf behind her was a burning bridge. She rapped lightly on the door with her fist, disregarding the shining brass door knocker. An elderly gentleman admitted her to an antechamber. The man was vaguely familiar. Had she met him somewhere? Yes, of course, at the party. He was Tom's secretary.

"Good afternoon, Mrs. MacNeil." Once again the slight hint of notoriety or was it just respect? "I'm here to see Mr. Warner," said Gwyn. She declined to mention the note—no need to bare one's private life to a stranger.

"Certainly. I'll tell him you're here, if you'll just have a chair." Within seconds Tom had emerged and had taken her into into his office.

"This is a real pleasure, Gwyn. You've never been in here before, have you?"

"No," she answered.

"Do you like it? I tried to make it as comfortable as possible. Most bank offices are so forbidding, at least I used to think so when I was young." Why was he making conversation? Couldn't he see how curious she was and how totally miserable?

"I came about your note."

"My note?"

"The note you sent, asking to see me."

"I'm afraid I don't know what you're talking about. I didn't send a note."

Gwyn's self-control was at the breaking point.

"I received a note, signed by you, asking me to come here today."

"Let me see it. Perhaps one of the department heads sent it out under my name. Damned irregular, but it could have happened. Maybe it says Mr. MacNeil."

"No, the boy who delivered it said it was for me."

"Was he in uniform?"

"No, why?" Her hands were damp with embarrassment.

"We have only one messenger, a young man in a green uniform."

"This was just an ordinary boy."

"I'm afraid, dear, that someone has been playing a trick on us."

"Olive." The truth was obvious. Who else would attempt to humiliate them like this?

"I agree," said Tom, taking her arm and seating her on a gold brocade settee. He sat down beside her. "Why do you think she would throw us together like this? Also, she is under close supervision, one could almost say under guard. I don't see how she managed it."

"Easily enough, I'll wager. Olive has never been accused of stupidity."

"Let me see the note," he repeated. How devastating for Gwyn to have to reach into the bosom of her dress and bring forth the loathesome document for his inspection. It's very hiding place betrayed her completely. She extended her hand and dropped the note into his palm, avoiding contact with his flesh. He looked at the folded paper as if it were contaminated, as indeed it was, thought Gwyn, contaminated by Olive's hate and suspicion. He unfolded it and read it carefully. "It's Olive's writing. She's tried to disguise it but the *m*'s and capital letters give it away. Didn't she realize that I would know her writing, and in God's name why did she do this?"

"Perhaps she thought I would throw it away before coming," said Gwyn. Her face was flushed and her dark hair gleamed ebony as she bent over her hands. She could not meet his eyes.

"But you didn't, Gwyn. You saved it."

She nodded and with the motion her tears overflowed their bounds and spilled onto her lap. She buried her face in her hands.

"Don't, darling," said Tom. "Don't let her hurt you. She's insane with jealousy and she's just hurting herself. A sane person wouldn't do this sort of thing."

"I know, I know, but it is dreadful to be so hated. She makes me feel guilty, as if I deserved her hatred." Tom put his arm around her shoulder and with one finger lifted her face up to look at him.

"You have done nothing to deserve this. Olive is my problem and I shall deal with her as best I can." Gwyn was, as usual, too lost in his eyes to gain any reassurance from his words.

When Olive opened the office door, she and Ethan were presented with this tableau: Tom and Gwyn were seated side by side, his arm was around her and his hand supported her chin. Gwyn was visibly overcome with emotion, her face was still wet with tears, and the look she fixed on Tom was unmistakable.

They all remained frozen for a moment and then everyone began to talk at once. Tom's voice prevailed and spoke earnestly to Ethan, trying to make him see the reality of the situation yet knowing in his heart that the illusion was nearer the truth.

"Gwyn received a note telling her to come here. She thought it was a business matter, but I swear it wasn't sent by me. Someone has deliberately tried to throw us together, and I think we all know who it is." He looked at Olive, whose voice had risen to rival his steady pitch.

"Lies!" She cried. "Can't you see it's all lies again?" She turned beseechingly to Ethan, frightened by the contemptuous looks which were coming her way from all sides.

"Tell them, Gwyn. Tell them about you and Tom!" She advanced toward Gwyn, who had risen to her feet. She grabbed her shoulders and began to shake Gwyn until the dark hair escaped the pins and fell recklessly around the young woman's face. "Tell them, tell them what you have done! Ethan doesn't believe me, he thinks I'm mad."

Tom tore her away from Gwyn and held her wrists, but he could not still her tongue. "They think I'm insane but they're the ones who are out of their minds. "Look at them!" she cried. "Both driven wild with wanting you. Two dogs and a bone. And they call me crazy! Even now, catching you in my husband's arms, your idiot husband is trying to pretend he doesn't know, can't see. Listen to me, all of you." Her voice dropped ominously, "She shall never have Tom. I would kill her first and with not a scrap of remorse. She has destroyed us all with her lust."

"No!" cried Gwyn. "I have done nothing! It is your madness speaking. I have not been unfaithful, Ethan. Please! You must know it, know that I could never do that." She ran to Ethan, who had turned the color of rain.

"Let us go home now, lass." His use of the affectionate term reassured her. With what seemed to be a considerable effort, he spoke to Tom. "I don't know what brought you two together, no doubt it is Olive's work, but it must never happen again. If Gwyn hasn't the judgment to avoid seeing you, then, by God, you'd better exercise a little more brains yourself." He took the scarlet Gwyn by the elbow and led her to the door. He opened it and turned once more to Tom. "Another thing. Get that bitch you're married to under control and away from me and my family or I'll have the law on you both. Why the hell you ever came here in the first place is beyond me."

"But Ethan! It's not his fault! He knew nothing of my visit until I arrived," said Gwyn, in a last attempt to soothe the two men.

"Be still, Gwyn. We're going home," said Ethan. He led her across the granite floor, leaving Olive and Tom together.

Olive was silent and fearful. What had gone wrong? She had seen many things on his face but never before naked rage. He said nothing, but put on his hat and stuffed some papers into a briefcase. "Tom?" she said.

"Don't say another word, Olive. You've said enough today." There was resignation in his voice and a note of resolve which forebode the worst. She fell to weeping, determined to have at least his pity if not his love. He looked at her coldly, as if she were beneath his sympathy. Her head was spinning with confusion. What had happened? The room was out of focus, and when he finally took her home she had left the last shred of her reason somewhere in his icy eyes.

❧27❧

On the street Gwyn almost had to run to keep up with Ethan's rapid strides. Before they reached the house, he was panting and once inside the door he threw off his coat and headed for the stairs. On the third step he stumbled and lurched forward. She ran to him in alarm when he fell and tried to support his bulk, but he lay across the stairs like a felled giant. His breath came in huge shuddering gasps and his color was terrifyingly pale. She loosened his collar and saw the panic in his eyes. Then she began to scream.

Within seconds the hall was filled. First the maid and then the cook and finally the children and Enid ran to the sound of Gwyn's voice.

"Take them away!" she called to the maid. "Take them to Louise and someone call Dr. Rogers." They stood paralyzed. "Quickly! Can't you see he's ill! Get help. Oh please, get some help!" The door opened and Dr. Rogers came in. In her confusion Gwyn forgot that he was due here to see Enid. "Help him!" He fell on the stairs and can't get his breath."

"Come here, Enid. You, Gwyn, hold him under one arm and Enid, you the other. I'll take his legs. Get him onto his bed." With great difficulty they carried him up the stairs and onto Gwyn's bed, which was the nearest. "Leave us now," said Dr. Rogers. "Bring up some brandy; I think it's his heart."

Gwyn ran down the stairs to fetch the decanter. The children were gone, thank God. She grabbed a crystal glass from the tray and raced up the stairs. She was aware of no emotion except fear.

"Here!" She cried when she reentered the bedroom. Ethan was stretched out on the bed, his great chest exposed and heaving. Dr. Rogers poured the brandy—Gwyn's hands were shaking too much to do more than hold onto the decanter. Holding the wine to Ethan's lips, Dr. Rogers held his head up and seemed relieved when Ethan sipped hungrily at the wine. Gradually his breathing slowed and a faint blush of color returned to his face.

"Will he be all right?" whispered Gwyn, automatically covering her ears in a childlike gesture of unwillingness to hear the response.

"I'll talk to you later. Let's just get him comfortable now. Send for some clean bedding. He's soiled himself."

When Enid ran back with the linen moments later, Gwyn had found some measure of control. "Let me do it," she said firmly. "I want to take care of him myself."

"The best thing we can do now is let him rest and wait. I've given him an injection. We'll know better in a while how he's doing," said Dr. Rogers.

"Shouldn't he be in a hospital?" asked Enid, who had not spoken since she saw Ethan on the stairs. "Probably," said Dr. Rogers. "But we can't move him now. Perhaps later on when his heart settles down. Call up the maid to watch him for a moment; I'd like to talk to you two women in the next room."

"You're sure it's his heart?" asked Enid when the maid had returned and was seated anxiously in the rose-colored chair beside the bed.

"I want to be with him," said Gwyn.

"In a while," responded Dr. Rogers. "First I want you to tell me exactly what happened." Painfully Gwyn recounted the events of the afternoon, forgetting her shame in her concern for Ethan. As the story unfolded, Dr. Rogers sadly shook his head. "Has he ever had anything like this before?" he asked.

"Not like this," said Gwyn. "Oh, he's had spells of shortness of breath before, but we always thought it was just overexcitement. God knows what filth Olive must have filled him with even before they got to the bank. To think it was me she wanted to hurt and now this."

Dr. Rogers had been witness to many such scenes before. He recognized the guilt which always accompanies the illness of a dearly loved spouse, and he was confident that despite everything else, Ethan was dearly loved. Gwyn looked so very young sitting across from him. She was still a child herself, too young for the emotional burdens placed upon her. She must have inherited her mother's strength, he thought, to have endured it all. He put an arm around her shoulder and knelt before her. "Now I want you to listen to me, Gwyn, and you must accept what I say. In the first place, you did not do this to Ethan. It was his heart all along. Those episodes of shortness of breath, that was his heart too. He could have helped himself but was too stubborn or maybe afraid to come to me."

"If it hadn't happened today, it would have happened tomorrow or the next day. That's the way it is with an untreated heart condition. A man can go for years ignoring it, and then one day it's too late. Just thank your stars that he was not alone on his boat or in his old house on the island when this happened! Try to see that you did all you could."

"You sound as if you thought he was going to die," said Gwyn, her eyes begging him to deny it.

"He's not young, Gwyn, and he's been pushing himself too hard all of his life. He might make it this time, but if he does, he'll have to change his ways. No more long hours at the store and no more lifting Ellen and Jeremy over his head. And no more liquor for a while. Brandy helps in an emergency but over the course it's dangerous. It makes a man forget his limitations."

"May I go to him now?" asked Gwyn, silent tears covering her face with a silken shine.

"Of course, go to him but don't exhaust yourself. He's going to need you if he pulls through. Have some brandy yourself; you could use it. I'll stay here the night so you can get some rest. Don't give up, child. He's a determined man and that always counts for something." Gwyn gave one choking sob then wiped her face with the back of her hand and went to her husband.

"I must go to the children. What shall I tell them?" asked Enid.

"The truth would probably be best. They should be prepared. Try not to alarm them but they do have to know. If he survives, they'll need to know how to treat him."

"You don't think he's going to make it, do you?" asked Enid.

"I honestly don't know. Believe it or not, the earlier episodes are a good sign. Sometimes the ones who survive the earlier attacks have a better chance. But truthfully, I'm not too hopeful. Could Louise keep the children for a day or two? It's best they not be here for a while until we know what's what. Gwyn shouldn't have any more cares than are absolutely necessary."

"I'll explain to Louise. She can keep folks away. News spreads fast in this town."

At eleven o'clock that evening Ethan had still not awakened. Gwyn sat beside him on the chair trying to see behind the closed lids. She had neither moved nor spoken since eight o'clock when Enid had tried unsuccessfully to tear her from her vigil. Outside was blackness, while in the room one solitary lamp sent a small circle of light around husband and wife. From time to time Ethan stirred in his slumber and then settled down again into his silent struggle for life. His breathing was steady but shallow, and Gwyn tried to match each breath with her own in an attempt to secure for him precious minutes of rest. The flesh seemed to have fallen away from his face, leaving the angular bones revealed in the lamplight.

Gwyn's mind was in turmoil under her pale calm. To think she had brought him to this, had perhaps taken his final measure of strength.

How they had all leaned on him, depended on him! It was as if the foundations were eroding away from under them all. What a false mansion she had built for her soul! She had been draining away his vigor for years; she could see clearly now how much he had given up to have her. What a poor prize she had turned out to be, a woman torn in two, able to give only scraps and fragments when he needed whole cloth. Must love always give with one hand while taking away with the other? she thought. She never stopped to see it from the other point of view, that she had given him her youth and as much love as she was capable of giving, and it is to her credit that she never once considered that his death could remove one barrier between herself and Tom. Indeed, it was too dear a price to pay.

She had always thought that more love was better than less, but it was obvious now that her surfeit of love had overwhelmed her life, forcing her to be forever at its mercy.

She had tried to separate the two loves into neat compartments, calling one "love" and one "in love." Now she knew that she had been simplistic, that it was only her conscience that had demanded definitions and divisions. To deny her passion for Ethan was as dishonest as denying her affection for Tom.

Ethan's voice broke the silence. "Gwyn?" His voice was faint.

"Don't try to speak, darling," she said. "It's all right. You've had a spell with your heart, Dr. Rogers says, but you'll be fine if you just rest awhile."

"Did I ever tell you about the first time I saw you? I mean the first time I truly saw you?" He continued on despite her warning. "I had been at sea for two years. I had known you before, but you were just a baby. We had just pulled up alongside the island. You'll never know how good it was to be home again. Just as we passed the cliffs I looked up and saw a little dark-haired girl playing in the flowers on the hill. You were so wrapped up in those flowers that you never even noticed the boat passing. I've never forgotten it. The wind was blowing your curls all around and you looked so wild and free that it brought tears to my eyes. It was as if everything I had ever loved about Parker's Island was right there in that little girl. So you see, lass, I've loved you a long, long while."

"That's a lovely story, Ethan. Did you know who I was?"

"I had no idea until I went to see your mother and father. We were having a homecoming drink when you came in the door all flushed and tangled. You were the most beautiful thing I had ever seen. And, Gwyn? You still are, lass."

"Oh, Ethan." Gwyn fought down a sob and was still. Ethan's eyes closed once more, but now there was a peaceful expression on his face.

Not more than ten minutes later he woke again and searched the room frantically with his eyes. "Gwyn? Where are you?" he cried, trying to raise himself up on one elbow.

"I'm still here. Please don't move! The doctor said you must rest now."

"I have to tell you something else. No, don't stop me. Just let me tell you this, then I'll sleep."

"Very well," said Gwyn.

"I've done you a terrible wrong, child. No, hear me out. Do you remember the letter you sent to Tom when you realized you were carrying his child? Well, I lost it in the water and never told you."

"Lost it?" Gwyn's mind had trouble focusing on what he was saying. "You threw it away?" she asked, astonished.

"I honestly don't know. Please believe me. I had it in my hand one minute and the next thing I remember it was floating on the water."

There was a long silence while he struggled for words. Gwyn was afraid to speak, afraid of what she might say.

"Can you forgive me? It would mean so much to me if you could forgive me. I should have told you before, but I was afraid you would leave me. Gwyn? I can't see you very well. Say something, please!"

She heard the agitation in his voice and hastened to speak. "There's nothing to say. What's done is done. There's no point in looking back." She measured each word scrupulously, afraid her emotion would overwhelm him.

"But will you forgive me?"

"Forgive you? Yes, Ethan, I forgive you." Her voice was emotionless.

"Ah, lass, you are so good. I had to have you, do you understand? I thought he'd never love you right. Was I wrong Gwyn? Have I spoiled your life?"

"Oh, Ethan! How could you ever spoil my life? I belong with you. We island people are different somehow. I don't suppose anyone else could ever understand our odd ways."

"So you do know what I'm saying; that's a relief to me. It's been like an anchor on my heart, Gwyn, to see what Olive has been doing to you and knowing that it was all of my making."

"Don't think of it anymore, dearest. It's all gone away now. You can rest easy."

"Ah, my sweet, sweet Gwyn." He sighed so deeply that she was alarmed, but then he spoke again.

"Kiss me, lass, and then I'll go to sleep for a while."

She bent over and held the bearded face between her two small hands. Softly she kissed his lips and then she laid her cheek against his and felt the life flowing out of him.

She was not sure that he was gone until she put her hand on his chest. After she was certain he was dead she sat down once again in the chair and let the tears cleanse away her sorrow. When all was washed away except for the love, she rose and called her mother.

❧ 28 ❧

Ethan MacNeil was laid to rest in style. Half of Parker's Island came over to say goodbye to one of their own. One by one the dear old faces passed by Gwyn and the children, and each face carried a memory of happy times.

Jeremy stood straight and tall in his dark suit and bravely took the hands that reached down to him. His father must have been a very great man, he thought, to have so many friends. He had done his crying and was now determined not to upset his mother with his tears. Mummy had been so strong and comforting, explaining about Daddy's heart and how it became too weak to beat anymore. She had been with him and Ellen every minute since Daddy died, even bringing a cot into the nursery so that she would be there when he woke up afraid in the night. He had heard her crying when she thought he was asleep, but he had not known what to do to help her. He had lain awake in the dark wondering. Grandma had told him to try to be as brave as he could for Mummy's sake.

Ellen didn't understand what had happened. She kept asking when Daddy would wake up again. Today she was sitting on Grandma's lap, accepting the sympathy of all these people while a look of stubborn pride furrowed her pale eyebrows.

Gwyn was able to control her grief until from a spot not far from the cemetery there came the wail of a bagpipe. As the sound swelled and flowed over them all, Gwyn recognized the sad coranach of the island and she knew without looking that Oakie Williams, inarticulate with words, was paying the most eloquent tribute of all to his dearest friend. One by one the islanders joined in the melody, and soon the hum of fifty voices filled the churchyard with the solemn tune. The Buckley folk were uneasy at the sound, but Gwyn's heart was bursting with pride for her islanders and for the heritage that had now passed on to her children. She stood in silent homage to them all and remained standing until the final note faded away. Then she took her children by the hand and left her husband to find his peace.

If she had turned back she might have seen the slender figure of a man standing apart from the crowd, hat in hand, watching her as she made her way back to her house.

The rest of the day passed in a blur. Later she would remember Louise by her side almost constantly, leaving her only intermittently in order to keep the sympathizers well supplied with food and wine.

Gwyn had been surprised when the minister told her that Ethan had bought a burial plot in the Buckley church. She had always assumed that Ethan would want to return at the end to the island, but knowing now what anguish his secret had cost him, she realized that Buckley had become his chosen home. He had helped to build it into what it was, and it would have been inappropriate to abandon it in death. She began to see that there had always been another Ethan, a man of ambition and accomplishment whom she had overlooked in her recent domesticity. As the weeks passed, this man became an obsession. She wanted to know all about him now that he was no longer here to fill her ears with tales of his youth.

One November afternoon when the leaves had dissolved into the frost-hardened ground she left the children playing and went to the attic in search of his ghost. Here, in two water-stained trunks, she found the person she was seeking. Carefully she opened the leather straps which bound her treasure chest. She cleared the dust away from a circle on the attic floor and sat down. One by one she examined the letters from his mother which bore the odors of foreign ports. She saw through his mother's eyes the young lad out on huge adventures whose parents reminded him to dress warmly at sea and had he received the sweater? She was impressed by a letter of thanks from the government praising the work of his ship during the great war between the states. What was history to Gwyn came alive as she realized with a start that he had participated in running Southern blockades and in bringing back escaped Union prisoners.

She counted back. He could have been only in his early twenties then. Did he have a beard then? she wondered. Strange, she had never seen his unshaven face. What she would give now to see him as he was then, the same age that she was now. Had he been in love with some exotic girl? Pressed between the pages of a ship's log she found a faded crumbling flower. It must have been very bright to have retained such a rose shade over the years. She did not recognize the variety. Into her mind sprang the image of a smooth-cheeked sailor with his arm around some dark island beauty. She hoped it was true. She hoped that somewhere in this world there had been a girl who thought that he was the moon and the stars and whose heart had quickened at the sight of his sail in her native harbor. What had he been searching for that he had never married until late in life? Why were alien lips not enough? She remembered the feeling she used to have when she sat looking out to sea trying to visualize the rest of the world. As the old longings filled her she felt close to the young sailor. Perhaps if she had been born thirty years sooner, he would have taken her off with him and they could have sailed the world together.

Her mother's voice called her downstairs.

Heavens! She had been four hours in the attic; dinner was ready. After dinner she could scarcely contain her desire to get back to the attic, but it was dark and the children needed her. She was trying to spend as much time as she could with them, trying to make life as normal as possible. Jeremy was too quiet, accepting her caresses eagerly but holding inside him a mountainous burden of confusion and loss. Oakie came by frequently and took him for long walks and an occasional trip to Salem. The two were good for each other. Oakie lost his shyness with children and it was one of her few remaining joys to hear their quiet laughter when they were returning from an excursion. Ellen was Ellen. She had bounced back almost immediately. Gwyn was torn between relief that her daughter was doing so well and fear that she would forget her father. The next morning Gwyn brought down the portrait that Ethan had given her at her special request the past Christmas. It was an oil painting showing Ethan in work clothes and holding his pipe. He had wanted to pose in his business clothes, but Gwyn had insisted that he be painted as she knew him best. She hung it in the front room, and when Ellen came down and said "You bringed Daddy down here. Good!" Gwyn was satisfied. Then she returned to the attic and continued her thorough examination of letters and souvenirs. It became her daily work, to see the children settled and then to go to the attic.

Just before Christmas, Enid took her in hand and firmly informed her that she must begin to let go. Gwyn was at first angry and then saw that her mother was right, that she had been living out another life, trying to bring back what was gone. The next day she went Christmas shopping and could tell by the relieved faces in Ethan's emporium that she had indeed been away too long.

The business had gone on. She had early decided that the store must remain intact for the children. Ethan had an assistant, an earnest young man named William Maxwell who seemed to have everything under control. Gwyn started to take an interest in the store. What she lacked in experience she made up for in common sense. The first thing she did was to increase Mr. Maxwell's salary. She accepted the fact that the store could not survive without him. She examined the books until she was completely convinced that he had done his job well and appointed him general manager. When she told him of her decisions he was pleased.

"I didn't know just what to expect, Mrs. MacNeil" he said. "My wife and I have been wondering what you'd want to do with the store. It's a fine business and growing every day. I'd be proud to run it for you, ma'am. Also," he blushed, "I just want to say this once that your husband was the finest man I ever met, and you can trust me not to let his memory down. You hear so much talk these days about businessmen and their shady deals, but your husband was as honest and fair as a man can be, and I'll do my best to be the same."

"Thank you, Mr. Maxwell. I don't doubt it for a second," said Gwyn. How old she felt suddenly, looking at the earnest young face before her. She had thoughtlessly kept him in suspense all this time and still he didn't seem to mind. She felt lucky to have him and resolved to invite him and his wife to dinner soon.

"Have you been married long, Mr. Maxwell?" she asked.

"Please ma'am, you can call me Bill if you like. Yes, my missus and I have been married four years now. We just had a fine baby girl this fall, perhaps you heard?"

"No, I'm sorry I didn't." Gwyn was aware of how self-centered she had become in her grief. "Bill?" she asked. "Would you and your wife like to come to dinner this Friday? I know it's a busy time of year, but I'd like to get to know you and your family better. What did you say the baby's name was?"

"Barbara, and yes, we'd love to come." Mr. Maxwell was a happy man.

"Good. Bring Barbara if you like. I know new mothers don't like to be away from their babies for long. We have a very reliable nurse who would be delighted to have a baby to look after again for a few hours. Our children are beginning to grow up."

She began to tremble inwardly from this great social exertion, so she set a time and quickly went out into the cold air. She took a few deep breaths and went home to tell Enid what she had done. Enid would be pleased. The house had been still too long, with Dr. Rogers creating Enid's only social life. Oh, there had been friends for quiet teas but no real entertainment. Ethan would have detested the shroud of mourning which had darkened his beautiful home. Christmas was a time for new beginnings. What better time to try her shaking hands than at a small dinner party? Her pace quickened as she began to plan the menu.

❧ 29 ❧

In the next three days Gwyn became a dervish. She soon gave up on the cook and decided to prepare her dinner herself. Although she and Enid were both competent cooks, she was rusty in the kitchen. The dinner party seemed huge and overwhelming to her frail mourning disposition, and it took considerable effort to keep on reminding herself that there she would only have to contend with herself, Dr. Rogers and Enid, the Blanchards, Oakie and, of course, the Maxwells. Almost a family party she would think, but then her hand would hold the cookbook and tremble. There was too much trembling these days and a persistent fatigue from the sleepless nights.

There was still another problem, this one not as easily solved as a dinner menu. During the two months following Ethan's death, Gwyn had become a totally mind-centered person. Her thoughts had been the core of her entire personality, dominating her life so completely that she would find herself with her children and be astonished to perceive that although she was dressed, with her hair arranged, she had no memory whatever of the act of dressing. Her bodily sensations had been submerged in her grief and it had been a welcome amnesia. Somewhere in late November she had awakened from the dark escapist sleep which followed the long hours of wakefulness to find her body in painful need. With no outlet for her passion, she became increasingly humiliated by her desires. They began to rise up during the day. The turning of a coverlet would evoke such a shuddering of physical want that she would be filled with self-disgust. The inappropriateness of her feelings angered her. From this anger came a wish to come to grips with herself. Going to the store for the first time had been in many ways a revolt against this internal animal whose hunger was increasing day by day.

As she turned the pages of the cookbook, she felt some measure of authority. She decided that a soup was in order. Too bad the garden had gone by, but never mind, she would make barley soup island-style. The entrée was easier, perhaps a hunter's ragout with tiny whole carrots, mushrooms and onions laced with red wine. She had learned to appreciate the continental use of wines in cooking from Oakie, who had transformed many of the old Scottish and French recipes from the island into gourmet delights. Dame Nellie Melba the opera singer had inspired a delicious dessert with peaches and raspberry sauce which Gwyn was sure she could manage. She added a watercress salad, a vegetable purée, a chicken in aspic, assorted pastries (à la Pierre) and three good wines and decided that it would do for a small party. She made a mental note to provide a sherbet to clear the palate between courses and sat back, satisfied.

When Friday evening arrived she felt the same nervous pangs which she had felt at her first Christmas party with Ethan.

"How do I look?" she asked Enid.

"Lovely, dear. This isn't the Queen of England, you know. It's just your manager and his wife. She'll probably be a nervous wreck, meeting the boss and all! Does she know anyone else who's coming?"

"I don't know. Louise hasn't met her, but perhaps she knows Oakie from the restaurant. But you're right, there's no need to worry. I'll just try to make her as comfortable as possible and forget about my jitters."

"Your jitters are understandable, Gwyn. After all, its your first social plunge by yourself." Enid paused. "Have you ever stopped to think of how far we've all come in just a few years? Why, when you were younger I scarcely dared to leave the island and now look at us, giving dinner parties and living in this beautiful house. It makes me realize how selfish I was not to get you out into the world sooner. This seems so natural, to see you here all dressed up. I was wrong not to be more ambitious for your sake."

"People are pretty much the same here as on the island I think," replied Gwyn. "It was a good solid beginning and you mustn't regret it. If I behaved badly back then, it was my own nature, not your fault." Remembering those weeks of turmoil after Tom left the island still made her stomach tighten, and she was relieved to hear a knock at the door.

"Hello, dear one!" called Louise. She and Simeon had come exactly on time. Louise knew Gwyn's state of mind and was determined to make the evening merry for her friend's sake.

"Tell me about Mrs. Maxwell. Is she very young?" she asked after they had surrendered their outer wraps and settled around the fire in the front room.

"She has a baby, Barbara, and they've only been married a few years, so I suppose she's my age or thereabouts."

"Let's guess what she will look like. Describe Mr. Maxwell and then I can tell what she's like. Opposites are attracted."

"He's not short or tall, medium height and brownish hair and a moustache," said Gwyn. "I especially like the moustache. His face is so young-looking otherwise that he looks like Jeremy when he sticks a lock of Ellen's hair under his nose." She laughed and rose to greet Dr. Rogers, who had come into the room with Enid.

"You two look like a nice married couple. What do you

say to this, Gwyn?" asked Louise, a lively gleam in her eyes as Enid blushed.

"I'm not sure," said Gwyn. "They look too happy to be an old married couple. Mama? Do you remember the couple who used to sit in the wicker rocking chairs at the inn and argue all day, summer after summer?"

"Ah yes. They enjoyed it so!" said Enid. "It was their only form of recreation. You used to think it was dreadful. I remember once how you wanted me to put candles and roses on their dinner table so that they'd feel more romantic. It was a kind thought, but I imagine it would have spoiled all their fun. They had forgotten how to talk sweetly to each other."

The door knocker pounded out its message once again, and Gwyn went to greet the Maxwells, who had arrived with Oakie.

"How do you do?" said Gwyn, and before she could say more Mrs. Maxwell broke into speech.

"It's so nice to meet you at last, Mrs. MacNeil, and what a perfectly beautiful house you have. Why I was just saying to Mr. Williams here, whom we met coming in, that this is the house I've always liked the best here in town. Some of them are so gloomy and dark, but yours has such nice tall windows that I knew it would be cheerful inside. What did I tell you, William? Isn't this just as I said it would be?"

"Why yes . . ." began Mr. Maxwell.

"And this is Barbara, Mrs. MacNeil," continued Mrs. Maxwell without acknowledging her husband's reply. "She's a bit fussy, I fear, but perhaps I can just put her in the nursery. My husband said you had a girl who's good with children. Such a relief to have good help. Babies are so worrisome, don't you agree? And Barbara is so sensitive." She went on and on about the worries of motherhood as Gwyn led her upstairs to the nursery.

"Good grief," said Louise to Enid after the doctor had

taken Mr. Maxwell in for a before-dinner sherry. "Do you
suppose she is ever still?"

Enid smiled and whispered in Louise's ear. "I told
Gwyn that she'd be shy and intimidated. Do you see what
a good judge of character I am?" They laughed and went
in to join the men. Enid gave a look up the stairs as she
turned into the front room, wondering how Gwyn was
holding up under this fusillade of words.

With his wife out of the room, Mr. Maxwell proved to
be a competent conversationalist, and before long the men
were first-naming each other. One reason that the Mac-
Neils had always been so popular was their lack of formal-
ity in speech even while entertaining lavishly. Someone
had once remarked to Gwyn that their gatherings always
seemed like a family party, and Gwyn had replied that it
was because they didn't know any better. "If you grow up
with too many rules of proper conduct it's very difficult to
get rid of them later on. We islanders have never had much
use for titles. Perhaps others find us a bit raw, but we do
seem to have a good time of it!"

By now Mrs. Maxwell, who would be "Mary" within
the hour, had come back downstairs, and Gwyn had seen
her introduced all around. She's probably a nervous talker,
thought Gwyn. Interesting how some folks can't find their
tongues and others can't turn theirs off. Sherry lubricated
the proceedings, but rather than relaxing Mary Maxwell,
it seemed to fuel her loquaciousness. She interjected her
comments everywhere until they finally gave her her head
and let her run. When she paused for breath, they would
change the subject and in that way they insured a variety
in topics if not in speakers. There was no subject too un-
known to her to prevent her opinion from dominating and
no subject on which she was not tenaciously conversant.
Louise began to get the giggles and Gwyn feared to meet
her eyes, knowing that she would dissolve at the slightest
recognition of Louise's condition. Oakie sat dumbfounded,

beginning to take a purely scientific interest in how long this woman could go on. All of his apprehensions about the opposite sex found embodiment in the pretty red-haired woman who sat yapping on her chair like a dog in a rabbit trap. Enid decided that she could forgive Mrs. Maxwell her noise if she could only have been interesting or at least have some sense of humor.

Alas, all of Dr. Rogers's dry wit was wasted as were Simeon's attempts at lightheartedness.

To the relief of all, dinner was announced. Dr. Rogers presided over the table. Gwyn had seated Mary Maxwell next to Oakie while reserving Mr. Maxwell for her own right side. The soup was served and eaten in relative silence, broken only by Mrs. Maxwell, who commented favorably on it's quality and began to recite her own favorite soup recipes. Annoyance flooded over Gwyn finally, and she was on the verge of rudeness when a delightful thing occurred. Mrs. Maxwell was leaning over her soup plate chattering about her own spinach soup recipe when, without looking down, she thrust her spoon into the near edge of her plate and overturned the hot soup onto her lap.

Shrieking with surprise and a not inconsiderable amount of pain she stood, and the entire group watched in morbid fascination as the contents of her plate trickled down the front of her cream-colored dress like a vegetarian waterfall. Louise, always the first to see the humor in a situation, lost control and brought her napkin to her mouth to conceal her laughter while Gwyn rose and, putting her arm around her disheveled guest, led her to the kitchen where the mopping up of her ruined frock could be more privately begun. Mr. Maxwell quickly followed and left the remaining guests at the mercy of Louise, whose merriment soon infected them all.

When Gwyn and the Maxwells returned, it was a subdued Mary who took her place once again. Relieved of the burden of her chatter, the party took on a balance and soon they were all having a fine time and enjoying the food immensely. Gwyn, pitying her guest, found that she could like her, and in her efforts to make all well again she forgot her own fears and rose magnificently to the occasion. By the time the Peach Melba was served even Oakie was talking and Mary Maxwell was sufficiently recovered to be adding a discreet amount to the conversation.

The Maxwells were the first to leave. Mary's dress was brittle with barley soup despite her efforts to cleanse it. Baby Barbara was a good excuse for an early departure and so, once again, Gwyn accompanied her female guest up to the nursery.

"Mrs. MacNeil, I'm so terribly sorry about the soup! I hope I didn't spoil your lovely dinner party with my clumsiness." She looked genuinely abashed. Your clumsiness, thought Gwyn, is exactly what saved my dinner party. "Of course not, dear," she said aloud. "Once I spilled a whole pot of tea on Louise's lap, before I knew her well. You can imagine how I felt! New to town and Simeon soon to be mayor! We've all had a similar experience, and you and I will laugh about this someday the same way Louise and I do now."

"It's been a trying week for me," explained Mary. "First Barbara caught a cold, and then there was that awful business with our neighbors, the Warners. Of course, you heard about that, it's all over town."

"No, I hadn't heard a thing," said Gwyn, trying to hide her curiosity.

"Well, Mrs. Warner has never been quite right. She never speaks to anyone and at night, especially in the summer, we've heard her weeping and even screaming once or twice. There's a nurse there all the time. They said it was her nerves, but we all knew it was worse than that."

I should stop her now, thought Gwyn, I shouldn't be hearing this, it's disloyal to Tom. But she wanted to hear, needed to hear. She had blocked Tom from her mind, but now he was here again, as vital to her as air.

"Two days ago she went after her husband with a kitchen knife. No one knows how she got it. Between you and me, she's been under guard all fall. It seems that she pushed the nurse down the stairs, she has her arm all bound up—the nurse, that is; and then went after Mr. Warner. Poor man! He's been so patient and loyal, protecting her reputation all the way. Everyone adores him, he's so funny and kind, and my William says he's doing wonderfully at the bank."

No more, no more, you silly ass, thought Gwyn. "Was he hurt?" she asked, fearing the worst.

"She cut his face. They say he'll have a scar, but the servants got her, and now she's been sent away. William heard that her doctors have said she's a hopeless case, she'll have to be locked away forever. She's physically ill, too. All skin and bones. . . ."

"How terrible!" broke in Gwyn, who could not hear more without breaking down herself. "We shall talk no more of such sad events. Look at your Barbara. See how she sleeps like an angel. I hate to disturb her."

"Oh, that's all right. She'll go right back to sleep as soon as we get her home. Thank you again for having us all; I hate to leave. I hope you will come to see us very soon. Now that you've become so involved with the store, we should all get to know each other."

"Yes, of course. We'll get together soon," said Gwyn. Not too soon, she promised herself.

Once downstairs she saw that the others were preparing to leave.

"I'll visit you tomorrow," said Louise with a knowing look in her eyes. "Sleep well, ma chérie."

Dr. Rogers remained behind, sitting with Enid by the dying embers of the fire. They must marry, thought Gwyn. Once again she realized that she had unknowingly stood in someone's way.

In her lonely bed she thought of Tom wounded by Olive, scarred. But had she not scarred him too in a more profound way? Olive was gone but still there, a vengeful spirit hovering over a troubled conscience and provoking Gwyn's brooding nature into one of its black unfathomable moods.

❦ *30* ❦

Christmas came and went. There were the usual festivities and an unusual amount of activity in Buckley. The town was larger. It had extended its borders to encompass the outlying farms, and buildings which were once isolated became urban almost overnight. Folks in the countryside acquired a taste for town living, and many gladly surrendered their agrarian heritage for the benefits of bourgeois comfort. Men who had never owned a suit became dandified, and their women avidly compared notes on the latest New York fashions. Louise's dress shop, now under the management of a stout Boston retailer, did landslide business, and Oakie's restaurant, while maintaining its supremacy, had several lesser competitors. The boats which were stout enough to survive the winter seas began to turn from the fishing trade and filled their holds with goods from Boston and Salem. The old salts were appalled at these defections but eventually became reconciled as fish prices crept up.

January was a hard month. The snow, which had peevishly avoided the holidays, set in after the New Year and, once it had made its debut, overstayed its welcome. There were three heavy snowfalls within two weeks, and the horse-drawn plows were kept busy clearing the main roads for commerce. The cold kept the boats in the harbor; the sailors were stalwart but not foolhardy. People stayed home unless work drew them out, and the area around the town prospered as more and more firewood was required.

By early February there was so much snow on the new library roof that the volunteers had to get out the shovels and clear it off. Winter, as always, had become a way of life. No longer did the weather dominate the conversation, people were reconciled to the cold and the ungainly paraphernalia of cold weather clothing. Someone cleared the pond behind Oakie's restaurant, and little skaters trampled a path from the main street to the glassy paradise in the woods.

Tom Warner looked out his window at the snow-covered street. The snow had fallen again during the night leaving inverted cones of white on the trash barrels. They reminded him of the frosting on the little chocolate cakes he had gobbled up with his childhood nurse at teatime.

He went to the sink in the bathroom and slowly stropped his razor. Shaving was more difficult with the scar tissue to avoid. He remembered how at Harvard College he and his friends had talked of Heidelberg students and their magnificent dueling scars. Tom had thought the whole notion of maiming oneself for effect obscene, but one of his friends had deliberately carved a line down his cheek in order to impress the girls with his mysterious past. Tom had laughed at the absurdity of a proper fellow from Maine brandishing an ersatz dueling scar, but it had turned out to be a most effective ploy when accompanied by a grim reluctance to describe the details of the terrible occurrence. To see the fellow scowling during a questioning by some nubile debutante was a source of hilarity to Tom and his friends, but they kept the secret; friends were friends.

Tom fingered his three-inch scar and felt the sense of absurdity again. To be a twenty-eight year-old-banker of slender build, and with what his mother had always described as dirty blond hair, sporting a perfectly straight scar on his left cheek was incongruous.

The scar had made him see himself in a mirror for the first time. As a child he had examined his nose to count freckles, and as a young man he had carefully combed his hair and scrutinized his face before attending parties, but he had not really looked at himself for years. What he saw was not encouraging. Despite his trim build he might have been a man of forty. There were deep lines around his eyes, and the skin of his face had coarsened. He was taking on the aspect of the town, looking more weatherbeaten than city-bred. Only the eyes remained his own. They were as blue and vulnerable as those of the child eating cakes.

He remembered only vignettes of his childhood, outings on the Charles, a long bout with mumps which recalled his mother's scent as she read tirelessly to the uncomfortable boy, conversations in the kitchen with the servants, and wonderful trips to the museums and children's theatricals. There were bitter memories too, of his father's face when he was caught reading a book which was considered too mature for his tender eyes, and memories of being alone without siblings in the large house while his mother was at her endless committee meetings. Only in preparatory school and in college had he developed a sense of comradeship, and his recollections of those times marked the first continuity in his memories. He clearly remembered the shock of learning from his roommate's sister that he was considered "a good catch," and the way this information had subtly influenced his opinion of the opposite sex. Not until Gwyn had he felt totally comfortable with a woman. There had been a trip to a brothel during his college years, a trip bolstered by alcohol and the knowledge that his virginity had become an embarrassment. The girl who took him to her bed that night had been his own age; the proprietress had sensed his discomfort. The girl had been not at all as he had expected; he had supposed that prostitutes were all older and less attractive. The red-haired girl was surprisingly sympathetic, and he had accomplished what he had set out to do; but later he had felt little elation, only a sense of relief that it was done. Still later he would feel shame.

Gwyn dominated his thoughts as she had since the first time he had seen her. His sight of her at Ethan's funeral had left a deeper scar than the one on his face. He had always believed that he knew her best, that he alone had penetrated her heart, but the face she had turned toward her islanders had shattered his confidence.

If he had not married Olive, he could go to her now, but Olive was always there. Her madness had permeated his life, had poisoned his youth, and the ugliness of his own guilt in marrying her weighed on him. Two women, one loved to excess and the other unloved to insanity, and still the blue eyes stared back at him in the mirror, mocking him with their stare of innocence. He was twenty-eight years old, and already his soul seemed burned out. Only in dreams did he come alive, dreams from which he awakened in a sweat, the room redolent of his spent sex. Then he would wash and shave and go off to his bank, where his desire to escape his thoughts had caused him to create another entity. The success of his bank was due, in part, to his misery.

He pulled on his galoshes and buttoned his coat to the neck. Then he wrapped a scarf around his collar, put on his hat, and trudged off down the street. As always, he glanced at Gwyn's house, and as always, his heart leaped, and he hoped for a glimpse of her. He knew he could not endure too many more days without seeing her, but he was unwilling to intrude on her mourning. Let her get done with her grief; let her work her way beyond Ethan before they talked. He was convinced that Gwyn would eventually let go of her husband's memory. Then he would feel the hideous gnawing of jealousy for the dead man and wondered if she would ever be free again. He did not want her to have changed. He wanted "his" Gwyn, and he knew that he would always want her. No matter that he had a mad wife, no matter that Gwyn had two children and the weight of her memories of Ethan. His heart railed against the malice of fate which had separated them.

Walking through the snow-filled street he was less than a block from her house, but he could not touch her. Time, he thought, time; but he was growing old with time and he mistrusted it. Time sometimes healed but more often created vast unbreachable chasms between the past and the future. Happiness yesterday, happiness tomorrow, but never happiness today.

A boy passed then, trudging through the deep snow with a bag of schoolbooks. He toppled slightly and Tom caught him. The boy was hatless and his cheeks and nose were crimson. Tom righted the boy and ruffled his hair as the boy smiled his thanks. A lad like Jeremy. The unspoken name pierced his heart. The unbidden tears froze on his lashes as he continued down the street.

In his office he glanced at his appointment calendar and noticed a reception at the Blanchard's written in for the next Saturday evening. He had refused all social engagements since Olive's abrupt departure. It was too painful now to see the curiosity and, worse, the undeserved sympathy in the eyes of his Buckley friends. It called up visions of the hospital where Olive now sat, trancelike, accepting her food like a baby and smiling witlessly at the staff. Gone now was the rage and the sharp retort. Her childlike acceptance was harder to bear than her wrath. He visited her every week, taking an afternoon off to make the long trip in a day. Their visits were always the same. She looked up at him as if he were a pleasant stranger who had come to see her. The long robes in which they dressed her for his visits covered her gaunt body. It elicited his last drop of pity to see the flatness across her chest where the breasts she had been so proud of had wasted away until she had physically as well as mentally lapsed into childhood.

After these visits he would return home and retreat into his library. Here by the fire he could conjure up the best things of his short lifetime, the books, the easel and the aura of Gwyn all intermingled in this cozy room to bring him a measure of peace. The room reminded him of the Connell sitting room on Parker's Island. It had the same atmosphere of ease and the same feeling of accomodation to the human condition. He wondered what the island looked like in winter as he pulled his private stationery from the bank office drawer and penned a personal acceptance to Louise and Simeon Blanchard. Would she be there? It had been just a week short of five months since Ethan's death; surely it was too soon to hope for her reemergence into society. Still, Gwyn had never been one for meaningless ritual, and Louise was her best friend.

When he arrived at the Blanchard home on Saturday evening he was disappointed not to find her there. Indeed, disappointed was too mild a word for the crushed feeling in his chest when he finally accepted the fact that she was absent. He spoke of her to Louise when the opportunity arose for them to be alone for a few minutes.

"I had hoped to see Gwyn here tonight," he said.

"Oh?" replied Louise, her dark eyes searching his own.

"Is she well? I have heard nothing of her for weeks." He knew he was betraying himself, but he was unable to keep still.

"If you ask 'Is she well physically?' I would have to say yes," answered Louise. "Oh, she is a bit thinner, a bit paler, but, yes, she is well. If you inquire about the Gwyn who lives inside the body, I must say that I truthfully do not know. She is sweet-tempered and good to the children and has begun to see a few friends for dinner at her home, but she sometimes leaves us, if you understand. She is there beside us, but her eyes say that her thoughts are far away, perhaps back on her island. Of course, this is very natural, I think, for one who has suffered such a loss." Louise must have seen something of the truth in Tom's eyes, for she continued. "You must come for coffee this week. I will invite Gwyn. It will be good, I think, for her to see you." She spoke lightly, but there was a kindness in her voice which made Tom's spirits soar.

"When? When shall I come?" he asked, afraid to let the invitation float.

"Would Tuesday be convenient? Your bank closes in the midafternoon. I know this because I came there ten minutes too late one day last year and was very annoyed by my wasted trip. Can you come at four o'clock?"

"Yes, four o'clock is fine, just fine." Now that the date was made, he could scarcely see how he would survive until four on Tuesday. While Gwyn was remote from him he had managed to go about his business for months, but now that he had allowed the demon hope to tantalize him once again, the span of three short days was unendurable. Would she come, knowing that he would be there? He knew that she would consider carefully any move in his direction. She had become more self-protective in recent years, and with good reason, thought Tom. He hoped that there was still enough left of the defiant island girl to take one more risk in her life. He knew he had no right to expect it; having hurt her so he could never again demand her trust. He accepted that any decision must be made by her and he must abide by it.

That night he saw again the tangled mass of her hair and the blaze of passion in the sea-blue eyes as she reached out hungrily for him in the cave on the West Cliffs. He still felt the desire that, once satisfied, came back tenfold when next he saw her smile or heard her throaty voice speaking his name. The freedom of her! The sense of absolute balance within himself when he was with her! He had thrived on her acceptance of him and she on his. Had he told her often enough? He would not be so apprehensive now if he could believe that she knew absolutely how it had been, the way he knew it, carried the knowledge around within him like a miser's treasure. It was indeed his most sacred possession, the knowledge that she had loved him and he her.

❦ *31* ❦

"How can I have coffee with Tom Warner? It wouldn't look right," insisted Gwyn.

"You insult me, my friend. Can there be anything that is not perfectly respectable in the house of Louise Blanchard? I think, perhaps, that it is your own feelings for this man that make you fear this innocent meeting."

"You have no right to say that even if you are my friend," said Gwyn, flushing a deep rose in her confusion.

"It is because you are my dearest friend that I have every right to say what I think," said Louise.

"But you don't understand about Tom and me!" said Gwyn.

"Perhaps I do not understand it all; perhaps there is much I should not know and will never understand, but I can see certain things very clearly."

"What things do you see, then?" demanded Gwyn.

"I see that you once meant much to each other, and I see that there is still feeling there. His face changes when he speaks of you and you, yes this very minute, color and pale like a sunset when I speak of him. Do you deny it?"

Gwyn was silent. "You cannot deny it for it is all the truth. So. Will you see him and let yourself begin to live again or will you sit here forever, the widow with her children to protect her? I warn you, it is a ridiculous picture, a woman of twenty-four years masquerading as a doting old woman."

"You are cruel, Louise," said Gwyn.

"No, chérie, it is you who are cruel to yourself."

They were silent for several minutes. It was Sunday afternoon and Louise and Gwyn were sitting in Gwyn's parlor while a fire crackled in the marble fireplace and the freezing rain of early March mercilessly eroded the honeycombed snow piles outside.

Gwyn broke the silence. "You forgot that Tom Warner is a married man."

"Mrs. Warner might as well be dead. There is no more life for her, now. I agree that he is, how do you say, 'technically' married, but no one with an ounce of sense would expect him to sacrifice his entire life for a mad wife. But I fear you miss what I am trying to say. I do not want to encourage a liaison between you and Mr. Warner. I merely want you to stop hiding from your true feelings. Our Ethan was a big man in many ways. Big enough to hide behind, I think. It is time to step out of that comforting shadow. Perhaps Tom Warner will play no role in your future, but you must find out."

"You seem to think it's easy, finding out," said Gwyn, a half-smile on her face.

"Easy? Naturally not! Most people I would not even encourage to try, but you and I know what you are made of. A friend sometimes can see what even a mother or husband cannot. You will do more than endure, my friend. You will be happy again."

Gwyn laughed. "If I had half your confidence I would be afraid of nothing."

"You have confidence but you have not used it or called it up. Now, promise me that you will be here before four o'clock. I shall give you a bit of brandy maybe to release all that wonderful confidence!"

"Courage from a bottle, is that it?" asked Gwyn, her eyes dancing.

"Why not? You are no drunkard!"

"Louise, have I ever told you how good you are for me?"

"Yes," answered Louise. Gwyn felt as if a dark winter cloak had fallen from her shoulders.

Not since before Ethan's death had Gwyn felt so alive. Her excitement was unlike the apprehension she had felt prior to her first encounter with Tom and Olive at the bank reception. Then, she had been afraid and angry. Her fear had been for Jeremy and Ethan, and her anger was the result of Tom's apparent rejection of her love.

She knew now that Tom had not abandoned her, that he also was a victim of the lost letter. She tried not to think about the letter; it raised ugly possibilities about Ethan that she preferred to leave alone. Her widowhood was too recent for her to allow Ethan's memory the relief of descending from near-sainthood.

Despite having carried around for five years the conviction that Tom was faithless, she nevertheless had been completely restored to faith by Ethan's confession. She even trusted Tom's word that the secret of Jeremy's parentage was safe. The nightmare that was Olive was, if not eliminated, at least set off at a distance. Already the virago who had screamed at them all was receding from the real world. In her heart Gwyn would always blame Olive for Ethan's death, even while knowing that she herself had sown the fruitful seeds of his destruction. Thinking of the four of them, she was reminded of the wild island reels where one dancer whirled another around and then suddenly let go to spin yet another partner until senses became disjointed and equilibrium was shattered. She and Tom had had their wild fling while Olive and Ethan waited alongside to grab their arms for the next turn. Now, it seemed, the dance continued on. Not knowing who or what would claim her next exhilarated her and infuriated her at the same time. Louise was right, she must take some control over her own life. Her passivity since first discovering that she was pregnant with Jeremy disgusted her. In retrospect, she could scarcely believe that she had allowed so much to happen to her at the hands of others. It would be nice to blame it on the others, but she had sat back like a bisque doll while they arranged her into postures that pleased them. Her lack of resistance was a complicity of its own.

Gwyn put on a dark brown dress and in an act of bravado fastened a white lace fichu at her throat even though it was too soon in her mourning for white lace. Her hair was parted in the middle, exposing her brow, and pulled back into a loose chignon at her nape. She looked older than her twenty-four years and was glad for it. Today she would be in control; no more girlish flutterings at the sight of Tom Warner. She steeled herself against his still-potent attraction and vainly attempted to subdue the roses in her cheeks. Then she kissed the children and stepped out alone into the brisk March air.

She had not reckoned on her sympathetic nature. The first sight of Tom's scarred face evoked a terrible flood of pity which undermined her resolve. It was not so much that his face had forever lost its youth (actually he was more attractive than ever to her), but the sudden comprehension of what the scar represented in terms of life endured was painful in the extreme to one who knew at that moment that whatever she had planned was irrelevant; she loved him still. She wanted to hold the dear face to her own, to kiss the scarred cheek. Instead, she stretched out a gloved hand and through the fabric felt the heat of his hand holding hers. Louise intervened with coffee in transluscent Limoges cups. How steady my hand remains, thought Gwyn, finding it extraordinary that she could dissemble so successfully.

"Did I tell you two that I think our Oakie might have met his match?" asked Louise, with the look of one who is about to impart a great secret.

"No! Why, I thought that he was the most confirmed of bachelors," said Tom. He was grateful even for gossip if it helped him to find his usually fluent tongue.

"Tell us, Louise!" said Gwyn, in similar relief.

"Well, my dears, it all happened last week when Mr. Patterson brought his daughter, Agnes, to the restaurant. She needed gainful employment and Mr. Patterson felt that our Oakie's reputation for propriety made him a suitable employer. Oakie engaged her to help with his bookkeeping. She had handled Mr. Patterson's farm accounts for years. She's a pretty girl and very quiet. Oakie seems to be displaying an unusual interest in her welfare. What dunces we have been, Gwyn! All of this time we have believed that he might succumb to someone who was more outgoing, but in truth it is her very shyness which seems to have disarmed him!"

"Do you truly think it will work out?" asked Gwyn.

"Heaven knows, but it is a beginning."

Louise continued to chatter about this and that until she remembered the time. "I forgot to tell you that Simeon is planning to join us as soon as he finished his meeting

with the finance committee. I hope you can stay until he
arrives. Like most of you men"—she nodded to Tom—"he
takes his work far too seriously and refuses to see that he
is going to become very dull if he won't enjoy himself more.
I assume you are the same, Thomas."

"I suppose so," said Tom. "But I have decided to turn
over a new leaf starting today."

"And I have decided to spend less time at leisure and
more time at work," said Gwyn.

"Ah, so it is balance you both lack. Take care. Balance
can make us all feel safe, but safety is not necessarily the
key to happiness."

"Listen to the Gallic philosopher!" teased Tom. "Do
you recommend that we all throw caution to the winds? It
is tempting, I confess."

"But of course, you must pay no attention to me. My
own life is hardly reckless. You must do as you think best,
but remember that Napoleon had a very full life and he
never chose safety."

"Yes and look how he died," said Tom, laughing.

"Pooh! We all must die at the end. Think rather of how
he lived!" said Louise.

"I can see that it is impossible to debate with a Bona-
partist. I must confess, however, that he was a fascinating
man," said Gwyn. "If I could be Napoleon, perhaps I
would accept the risks, but never would I be Josephine!"

"Well said, Gwyn," said Tom. His eyes met hers, and
she felt once again the blissful communion of thought that
had marked their earlier relationship.

"But you two are even more advanced than this Bona-
partist here if you think our world is ready for a female
Napoleon!" Louise rolled her eyes in mock horror.

"We have succeeded in shocking you, how grand!" said
Gwyn.

"I don't believe it," said Simeon, who had come in the
door. "Nothing shocks Louise."

"You make me sound like a depraved person!" protested Louise.

"She really is too wicked for words, right, Simeon?" said Tom.

"Of course. That's why I married her." He planted a kiss on his wife's upturned cheek and then sat down. "I'm sorry to be so late, but these finance committee meetings have a way of dragging on and on. We miss you there, Tom. You seemed to do much better at getting some sort of consensus out of that stubborn crew."

"Perhaps I shall rejoin you again. Those meetings were always fun for me. It never ceases to amaze me that people can be so impassioned about money. Once again it supports my old theory that there is a mystical quality about large amounts of money; even the most level-headed fellow becomes dizzy with the thought of the power of hard cash."

"Only too true, I fear!" said Simeon. "Say! Why don't you two stay for dinner. I've had no chance whatever to see my friends recently. What do you say, Louise?"

"I say," replied Louise, "that it is a marvelous idea. Let me go tell the cook."

"Oh, no. Really, I couldn't stay," said Gwyn. "The children are expecting me."

"Nonsense! They can survive a few hours without you. I'll send a message to your mother. By the way, how is Enid these days?"

"It's not public knowledge yet, but I believe it's all right to tell you. There's to be a wedding in May. Mother wanted to wait a year, with the house still in mourning (here she lowered her eyes away from Tom's), but she and Dr. Rogers have already waited too long on my account, so they will marry on Jeremy's birthday. He's quite overcome with the prospect; he adores Dr. Rogers and has never had a grandfather."

"That's wonderful news, Gwyn, but don't you think

you will have to call him James now that he is to be your
stepfather?" asked Tom. The talk of marriage and romance
had titillated him but not as much as the prospect of spend-
ing an evening with Gwyn. She was so lovely, so eerily
composed. He searched her face for traces of the old fire
and fancied he saw it lurking behind the dark lashes. Now
and again her hands would move on her lap, and he
watched the delicate fingers as he would an exotic wood-
land creature. The turn of her slender waist as she rose to
take a glass of sherry in the drawing room, the indentation
at the back of her neck that he had kissed repeatedly, the
mild scent of flowers as she passed by, and the cameo per-
fection of her profile all intoxicated him until he felt the
last years slip away. During dinner he surprised them with
his wit and charm; Gwyn had not seen him thus since the
early days, and the Blanchards who had seen only his con-
tained sobriety were dazzled by this new Tom. Louise
watched Gwyn's face when it was turned to Tom and
began to fear that she had opened Pandora's box. These two
were creating a mysterious alchemy that had transformed
them both. Believing intensely in passion, Louise was,
nevertheless, alarmed to see her dearest friend unmasked
by desire. It was as private side of Gwyn seen heretofore
only by Tom.

The dinner passed quickly, too quickly, and it grew
dark and then darker still. At ten o'clock Gwyn forced
herself to speak of returning home.

"I'll bring you home if you really must go," said
Simeon. They were all flushed with wine and heated by
stimulating conversation. If Gwyn had not broken the
spell, it seemed to her that it could have gone on and on into
blissful exhaustion.

"No. I'll walk Gwyn home; it's foolish for you to go
out, and besides I want to." Tom's open smile at Gwyn
revealed how far the two had come in the space of a few
short hours. They said goodnight, and they praised the

dinner, and Gwyn gave Simeon a kiss and Louise an embrace and finally, finally they were alone.

"Let's walk down to the harbor before we go home," said Tom, terrified that she might refuse.

"All right. I'm glad I dressed warmly."

"You look so different to me in your beautiful city clothes."

"Do you disapprove?" asked Gwyn. The March air felt cold against her face as they approached the water.

"Disapprove? No. Not at all. It does seem strange to me that you can be so lovely now and yet you were already perfect before."

"Perfect? With my torn hems and bare feet? Perhaps to you, but I hated those clothes!"

"And do you now feel like Cinderella?" They were on the dock, and the sound of the waves lapping the pilings emphasized the underlying stillness of the night.

"Cinderella lived happily ever after." She looked out to sea, seeing only the blackness of night before her.

"It certainly hasn't worked out well for us, has it? I keep asking myself what we could have done to prevent it all."

"I suppose that the moralists would tell us to look to what we should not have done. We have paid a terrible price, you more than me. I had Ethan and the children."

"And I had Olive."

"No. Don't speak of her. I feel the responsibility for what happened to her too much already."

There was momentary silence, then Tom took her hands and said "I must hold you. Just once I have to feel you in my arms again." He gently enfolded her, and she let her head rest on his shoulder.

"I love you, Gwyn." He took her chin in his hand and turned her face to him. This time there was no hesitation. She found his mouth and gave herself up to the blind sensations of his kisses. All the pain of the years dissolved in the

mutual feelings of solace and the goodness of their love.
When she finally broke away, she took his hand and together they sat on the rough bench above the walkway
which led down to the float.

"What shall we do? What can we do?" she whispered.
"There are still Olive and the children. I would be your
mistress if I thought we could be happy, but the others
would hate us for it."

"Would you be able to live that way?" he asked.

"At this moment I could say yes and mean it, but there
is tomorrow and the next day to face."

"And there is Jeremy. Our child. You don't have to
confirm it; I understand your loyalty to Ethan, but I know.
He must never be hurt. Do you know what it means to me
to know that he is ours? There have been moments when
I would not have cared to go on living if it were not for you
and Jeremy."

"And there is something I must tell you if we are to
be honest with each other." She paused. "I loved Ethan. I
know it must be painful for you to hear it, but I grew to
love him, and no matter what he may have done, I must
acknowledge that."

"Exactly what happened? I have to know."

"He lost the letter I sent you overboard or perhaps he
threw it away. In any case, it seemed to him to have just
happened. He told me just before he died."

"A simple letter and it has cost us all these years."

"Perhaps we would not have been happy. There were
your parents, don't forget."

"My parents are so devastated by what has happened
that I truly believe they would do anything to see me
happy," said Tom, still holding her hand.

"Now, perhaps. But not then. Oh, we would have
managed, but it would have hurt you, I know."

"Nothing could have hurt me if I had had you," said
Tom. "Do you think me so weak?"

"No, and yet it is only since Olive's illness that I know how very strong you are."

"I don't think I can be strong much longer. Look at me! An old man at twenty-eight."

"Your poor dear face. Tonight at dinner you were no old man. There's plenty of life left, but what to do with it." She was quiet as she hunted for words. When she spoke next, the matter was clear to her.

"There is no answer, so we must go on as before and see what happens. I can't be your mistress; you can't divorce Olive, and you are no murderer, so that's that."

"At least you haven't lost the island touch for plain speaking." Tom smiled ruefully.

"I meant it when I said I would work harder. There's enough to do at the store to keep me busy. Don't forget that MacNeil and Son is Jeremy's birthright and Ellen's too. You and I mustn't see each other except in social company. Can you do it?"

"If it's what you want, I'll have to. Tell me you love me, Gwyn."

"I love you. I've always loved you, even while I loved Ethan too. Maybe something will change."

"You mean Olive. Yes, she'll not live long. Now it's my turn for plain speaking. Can you wait for me?"

"I have waited all this time and you for me. Kiss me again, and then I must go home."

They walked to her house in silence, afraid that a single word would destroy the bond.

At her door she turned and gave him a twisted smile. Then, giving his hand a squeeze, she raced up the steps and into the house.

Tom went back to the harbor and sat alone for another hour, and then wearily got to his feet and went to the empty shell called home.

❧ *32* ❧

The knowledge that she and Tom still loved each other carried Gwyn through the next few weeks. She laughed frequently and joined the children in games of hide-and-go-seek. One day she organized a treasure hunt for Jeremy, Ellen, Aimée and two neighborhood lads. She drew picture clues and sent the children hunting high and low around the big house until every room echoed with their squeals of discovery.

Spring was manifesting itself in the gardens along Main Street, but more so in the MacNeil house. Enid and James Rogers were behaving like perfect sweethearts. They had decided to be married on the island in a simple ceremony. Gwyn and Dr. Rogers's best old friend, a retired surgeon from Manchester, were to stand up for them.

"Where will you honeymoon?" asked Gwyn early in April.

"We are going to New York for a week. Can you imagine me in New York City?" asked Enid. "Do you know that I have always dreamed of going to New York? After your father died, I gave up the notion. Strange, isn't it, the turns life takes. I used to imagine myself going to the theatre. I would be young and pretty and wear a pink dress. Guess I'm too old now for pink."

"But still pretty!" said Gwyn. "Oh, Mum, I'm so happy for you. Just think! A doctor in the family."

"A retired doctor," corrected Enid.

"Just as well," said Gwyn. "If he still had his practice, you two would be arguing all the time about the best way to treat his patients."

"Go on, laugh at me, but Jim finally admitted that he had learned a thing or two from my home remedies. He even said I'd be a good nurse."

"Not a doctor? Why I'm disappointed in him!" Gwyn laughed and picked up the pillowslip she was embroidering for her mother's trousseau.

Romance was everywhere that spring. Louise had been correct in guessing that Oakie had met his Waterloo. Agnes Patterson didn't seem to mind that Oakie was eighteen years older than her thirty years. She came to dinner with him one evening, and Oakie shyly announced their engagement. Once the words were our of his mouth he seemed to relax. Gwyn had been a bit afraid that Agnes might be marrying him for security, but it was apparent that she worshipped him. How good it was to see him properly loved at last! He had always been the trusted friend, the extra man at dinner. Now, at last, he was the most important person in the world to another human being. Enid knew how he felt, having lived on the periphery of others' lives for too long herself. Everyone was content, but Gwyn was unable to sustain the mood. By May she was chafing at her own decision not to see Tom. She wanted him more than ever, and the happiness of her family and friends threw her loneliness into sharp relief. Several times she barely restrained herself from going to him. Once she walked by the bank an hour after closing time hoping that he would come out and share, at least, a few words, but he did not appear and she felt the old insecurities rising up in her. How could he so easily avoid her? Did he suffer as she did? At night in his bed did he ache for her, did his dreams carry him to the cliffs? She felt full of her own sexuality. She imagined that her desire showed clearly

on her face and that every person who passed her by must
see her naked need. The men in town began to approach
her obliquely, testing the waters for future fishing. She was
beautiful and well-to-do. She was also alone and, worse,
alone by her own edict. All she had to do was reach out and
he would be there. Olive would live for years, perhaps.

On the dark days Gwyn began to have the feeling of
being trapped, with her best years slipping away. Had she
really come so far from the longing girl on Parker's Island?

On the good days she watched her children and almost
cried aloud in shame for her ingratitude. They were at an
enchanting age. Jeremy would be four next week on Enid's
wedding day and Ellen would be two soon after. Jeremy
was still mature for his years, carefully considering his
actions. His astounding sense of humor saved his personality from stuffiness. He would worry over the decision of
whether to side with the Indians or the Cavalry and then
do a droll imitation of himself worrying. His ability to
laugh at himself was a good lesson for Gwyn.

Ellen was cocky and determined. She loved physical
activity and organized the neighborhood children into cha-
otic races and competitions (all on a two-year-old level, but
hotly contested nonetheless). Ellen was a lover of animals;
she cried over every wounded creature and brought home
more than Gwyn could be expected to deal with. If a patient died, she wanted it buried with full ceremony in the
back yard under the elm tree. At first her insistence on
funerals worried Gwyn, she sensed a preoccupation with
death; but Enid felt it was good to let the child come to
terms with her father's loss in her own way.

Gwyn and the children were going to the island with
Enid a day early to prepare Enid's house for the ceremony.
Dr. Rogers would come over the next day with the minister. On an impulse Gwyn asked William Maxwell if he
could manage the store alone for a while. He looked
offended and answered in the affirmative. Hastily Gwyn

packed a trunk and announced to the startled children that they would be going to Parker's Island for a month. This news was greeted with great whoops of joy by Jeremy and Ellen and tears from Aimée, who was visiting at the time and could not imagine life without her friends for a whole month. "Don't be sad Aimée," said Gwyn cradling the tearful child in her arms. "I'll make sure that your mummy and daddy will bring you over for a visit in a few weeks. It will be June then, and the wildflowers will be out. We'll take you exploring in all the places I used to love when I was your age."

In the stern of the stout catboat which carried the four of them out to Parker's Island, the two children of Ethan MacNeil sat huddled in anticipation. Despite his insistance to the contrary, Jeremy couldn't remember much about his last visit. "There were horses!" he said. "Was there horses, Mummy? Jeremy says there was horses," asked Ellen, her eyes begging Gwyn to refute it.

"Perhaps on the other side, in the pastures, there might have been one or two, but I think Jeremy is thinking of another visit we made that summer out to Mr. Patterson's farm," replied Gwyn.

"Liar!" said Ellen. "There was no horses at all, so there." She stuck out her tongue.

"How do you know? You were just a baby. You're still a baby!" He said this last word with all the contempt he could muster.

"No horsies, no horsies," chanted Ellen happily.

"Make her be still, Mummy!" cried Jeremy. "You be still, Ellen, or Mummy will throw you overboard!"

"Will not!" screamed Ellen, alarmed at last.

"Hush now!" said Gwyn, "No one is going overboard, and I certainly hope you two aren't going to quarrel all the way over. I would hate for my island friends to think that Ethan's children were not as nice as Daddy said they were."

This mention of Ethan had the desired effect, and before long the children were busy pretending to see amazing fish and monsters beside and under the boat.

Gwyn searched the waves for an answer. Was it here that Ethan had released the letter? She refused to believe that he had tossed away her happiness on purpose. The sea gave no clue in response.

Shortly after noon, when the remains of the picnic lunch had been thrown to the fish, Enid spotted land. "Almost there, children!" she called to the stern. "See those green patches? Those are the fields behind the Inn, and over there to the left, that's Parkertown." The children scrambled forward to get a better look, and Gwyn sat down in the stern. The island grew in her sight, filling her heart with memory. The past spoke to her in golden tones of summer. She slipped under the enchanted spell of the island as the Parkertown dock loomed into sight. Through a mist of emotion she saw the ghosts of lovers on the West Cliffs, and again a longing for what had been swelled in her chest and left her drained of the present. She gave way to this sensation until voices from the dock called her back.

Who was that waving so madly? Could it possibly be Colleen Murphy's oldest boy? Yes, it was, although to call him a boy now would be inaccurate. He resembled his mother with his laughing eyes.

"Halloo!" he cried. He ran along the pier and tied up the boat fore and aft with effortless dexterity. "Mum says you're to stop in at the pub before you start to open the house. She'll send some of the kids to help out."

"That's very kind of her, Jim," said Enid, taking his hand as she stepped out of the boat. So it was Jim Murphy! How he had grown. Gwyn felt excitement overtake her as she wondered what other changes she would find. The island seemed to be in good shape. The railings on the pier were of new wood, not yet weathered down to grey. The hard winter must have taken its toll of Parkertown. The

Curran sisters had all planted gardens. Good. That meant they were still in reasonable health, thought Gwyn. She grasped each child by a hand and let the Murphy boy set the trunk in a wheelbarrow and bring it up behind. In her excitement she almost forgot to pay the boatman and had to run back to where he was waiting, too shy to demand his due from so fine a lady as Mrs. MacNeil.

The first big surprise was Colleen Murphy herself. Where before she had been a blousy blond with unkempt curls trailing down her back, she was now as neat and clean as the deck of Ethan's boat. Her impressive bosom was safely tucked into a square-necked blouse and further camouflaged with a red neckerchief. The blond hair was brushed and sleekly caught into a knot at the back of her neck. Behind her was a diminutive man, who looked shyly at the newcomers. Colleen came out to meet them with outstretched arms.

"Good to have you back, Mrs. Connell, although I hear it won't be 'Connell' for much longer. And, Gwyn! Oh, such a fine lady you've become. And these are yours?" She gazed at the children as if pixie-struck. "Oh my, doesn't the wee one look like Ethan!" Her eyes filled. "Such a dear sweet man he was, and now here are his very children!" Wiping her blue eyes with the corner of her immaculate white apron, she took control of herself. "I'm so sorry. I always go on about things too much. Oh, and I almost forgot to introduce you to my Henry. Would you credit that after all these years of living on the mainland I finally talked him into moving out here with his wife and children? Say how d'ya do, Henry."

"How do ya do," said Henry obediently. So this was the fantastic Mr. Murphy, come to life at last; or was he merely the latest Mr. Murphy? mused Gwyn. In any case, good for Colleen to have found a father for her brood, even if he might not be the original!

The restaurant was spotless with red homespun cloths

on all the tables and shining brass lamps on the walls. There were fresh rushes on the floor, and the mugs that lined the bar glowed from frequent washing.

"Well, Colleen, you've certainly done a wonderful job with this place," said Gwyn. "Oakie will be downright jealous when he sees how pretty you've made it."

"Oh he's seen it already. He was over just last week with a young woman. He was showing her the sights." Enid and Gwyn exchanged looks and smiled.

"So that's how it is!" said Colleen. "Who would've thought it? I tried to pump him about her, but you know Oakie." The women all laughed, and the children joined in just for the joy of it. After everyone had taken tea and milk, Colleen gathered up five of her children. "This here's Jim, you already saw him, and this one's Tom, and the twins here are Mary and Ann. This dark-haired one's Lizzie. There's more, but these are the best workers. I've told 'em to get over with you and put the house to rights and then to bring you all back for supper. Likely you'll be too tired to cook. Get along now, and don't let me hear that you left so much as a speck of dust."

The Murphy children had somehow learned obedience as well as clean habits, and before the sun went down the Connell cottage looked as if Enid had never left. Mattresses were aired and dishes were washed. Cupboards were cleaned and closets were swept. Curtains blew on the line and windows sparkled.

As a last touch Gwyn took the children out to gather flowers. The Murphy children had gone to fetch up the food supplies, and Enid was resting on the grass in front of her house, her legs stretched out before her.

The fields were green with early summer, and bees buzzed in the clumps of wildflowers that were just coming into bloom. Gwyn knew where there was an abandoned garden and led the children there. Many years ago a quiet Englishwoman with lavender skirts and a frightened look had come to the island as a summer renter. With her, she had brought cuttings of her favorite perennial flowers, which continued to bloom long after her departure. This garden was rarely touched except for special occasions. The islanders had taken their own cuttings, and now peonies, coralbells and primrose were fairly commonplace. Gwyn smiled as she saw the white peonies that swayed and nodded in the late afternoon air. She gathered an armful of the white blooms and, foreswearing the long-desired walk, returned to the house. The children were dirty and tired. Gwyn washed their hands and faces at the pump, and they all went to Colleen's for supper. Word of their arrival must have spread, for the place was crowded. They were warmly greeted and the children made much of, to their delight. The men expressed their grief at Ethan's passing by telling funny stories of the old days. Gwyn drank three mugs of ale and felt alive again. She could have stayed up all night, but tomorrow was the wedding and the children were nodding in their chairs.

❧ 33 ❧

Enid awoke early on her wedding day and broke tradition by going to the dock to meet James Rogers and his friend Dr. Upton at eleven o'clock. When she was satisfied that they were safely ensconced at the Inn, she kissed the cheek of her intended and went home. Gwyn was horrified by her mother's foolhardiness in defying the old supersti-

tion. "Don't be ridiculous, Gwyn. How you can be so intelligent and still cling to these old wives' tales is beyond me.
Do you want me to be a wreck all day wondering whether
he got here safely or not? I'm too old for such nonsense."

Gwyn was not assuaged. Being back on the island had
awakened her old mythology. Fortunately the sun was
shining, a good omen, so she resisted her apprehension, but
it was not until two o'clock when the bridegroom and his
best man presented themselves at the door that she relaxed.

This was no hurried ceremony. Oakie had come over
with Dr. Rogers, and it seemed as if the entire island had
gathered on the newly scythed front lawn to watch the
nuptials which were taking place on the stone doorstep.
There were even elegant guests from the Spraycliffe Inn
who remembered Enid with affection from summers past.
Enid had spread the word that all were welcome, and it
appeared that an old-fashioned island party was brewing.
Gwyn thought of her wedding to Ethan, of the haste and
the grey clouds over head. She looked out past the crowd
to the sea until her composure was restored. Her mother
was stately in palest blue. She was radiant with the bril-
liance of unexpected joy. Dr. Rogers was solemn, and as the
minister referred to their happiness with previous spouses,
his eyes filled. Enid looked at him, moved with similar
emotion, and then the bond was tied and they were man
and wife and the crowd erupted with laughter and excitement.

The reception was held at the meeting house. Once
again the trestles groaned with homemade food and once
again Gwyn was thrown back to the night of Jeremy's
conception. With effort, she held onto the present. The
fiddler had arrived, and Enid and Dr. Rogers dutifully took
the floor and enjoyed a dignified waltz. After that, dignity
was abandoned as whiskey flowed and the pipers struck up
a reel. Gwyn did not think she should dance but then
decided that in light of her recently expressed feelings for

Tom any further display of mourning was the purest hypocrisy. She accepted an invitation for a sedate country dance with Oakie, which was convenient to both her mood and his leg. After that she had many partners. Even Jeremy decided to join in, whirling Ellen around until she staggered with dizziness and sat down flat on the floor. The day was warm and folks drifted in and out of the shingled building until almost eleven o'clock that night. Then the bride and groom departed to spend their wedding night at the Spraycliffe Inn.

Gwyn stayed on to clean up. The children were sleeping nestled against each other in a corner.

"You run along, now," said Colleen. "The young 'uns are done in, and we'll clean up here just fine. Go along, now."

Gwyn obediently roused Jeremy and Ellen, and taking the two somnambulists by the hands she returned to the cottage. After tucking the children into their beds, she went outside to sit awhile in the yard. For the first time in her life she felt a measure of resentment for the hold the island still had on her. Like a mother, it was enveloping its child in a buxom embrace. Before, she had succumbed willingly to its protection, but now she felt the belated pangs of the adolescent who desires freedom while still loving the jailor.

The midnight breeze tugged at her upswept curls and she reached up and loosened the coils of hair until the dark cascade covered her shoulders. She sat thus in the moonlight, struggling with some embryonic thought, until the chill of night overtook her and drove her to an empty bed.

The days blended into a melody of solace and satisfaction. Gwyn's starved senses fed upon the roar of the waves and the gentle whispers of wind through the heather which grew around the rain ponds at the eastern point of the island. The morning air was cool and exhilarating while the evening mists fell heavy and fragrant with the mingled scents of flowers.

Gwyn was sleek and brown with sun, and the children ran about bare-legged and constantly hungry. Jeremy's pallor turned into rosy warmth, and Ellen's hair bleached to a golden white. They would pack picnic lunches and set out to pick blueberries or find shells. There was usually a Murphy child in tow, often two, as the islanders threw away the last vestige of reserve and accepted the MacNeils as their own. Gwyn bore little resemblance to the controlled matron who had arrived less than a month before. Her hair, released from bondage, curled around and caressed the brown cheeks, while her teeth and eyes shone bright from her face. She laughed frequently and tried to recapture her youth for her children as a present.

After the Fourth of July bonfire she finally admitted that the island seemed smaller than she remembered. Her thoughts began to steal away to Buckley. A visit from Louise and Aimée left her missing them more than before they had arrived. The children, however, remained under the enchanted spell, and Gwyn, relieved to see them happy again, agreed to extend the stay for another two weeks.

Thoughts began to insist on recognition. She took walks alone, leaving the oldest Murphy girl, Lizzie, to watch over the children at naptime. For the first time, Parker's Island began to loosen its hold on her. She caught herself thinking 'when we go home' and realized with a start that Buckley had become home to her; and if Buckley were home, then what was Parker's Island? She came to accept that she had ceased to be a part of the island when she had married Ethan. With this acceptance came a sympathy for all those writers of children's tales who told of idyllic lands of childhood where adults must not, indeed cannot, ever venture. The final knowledge that childhood was forever gone caused her intense regret. She could not remember growing up. It had been a condition imposed upon her by circumstance. But in her youth, a youth which she recalled now with tender nostalgia, had she not been often angry and more often desperate to put it all, childhood and Parker's Island, behind?

These daily delvings into a part of herself which she had never understood left her emotionally exhausted. Then she would seek out company and spend an evening laughing with her children and the islanders at Colleen's restaurant.

"You look like yourself again," said Colleen one such evening.

"It's been a wonderful vacation. I've already promised the children that we'll come back again next year."

"Good for children to be outdoors! I don't suppose they do much of that in the city." Buckley was "the city" to Colleen.

"We have a big yard and a vegetable garden, but you're right, it's not the same."

She thought about the children that night. Yes, they were healthy and happy, but would she be content to see them living in bare feet forever? She found in herself a new ambition for her children, the desire for a better life, opportunity to learn, even travel. Just as Enid had dreamed of New York, so Gwyn now dreamed of Paris, of London, of the ports of the East described by Ethan in his letters home. The careless language of the Murphy children fell like a jarring foreign tongue on her ears. She tried to deny these feelings but knew that she wanted her children to know, at least, the difference. As long as she lived, she would not forget the feeling of inadequacy she had had when the white-skirted girls from the Inn had passed her by. Her children would not ever feel diminished by water-stained shoes, but wanting the best for them also meant to Gwyn that they must never, never look with disdain at children such as she had been.

They were to leave the island in three days. Already there were bags packed with seashells and assorted island treasure. July had been hot and this day was no exception.

Gwyn had avoided the West Cliffs. Despite her acceptance of things the way they were, she had been unwilling to expose herself to the force of those particular memories. This morning she resolved to exorcise her last demon. Leaving the children with Lizzie, she packed an apple and a jar of lemonade and set off alone. Arriving at the meadow which hid behind the crest of the first hill, she saw no trace of the path they had used that summer. She crossed through the marguerites and found her own special spot on the cliff. Sitting down with her knees drawn up, she let the memories swell up in chorus with the waves below.

Overhead, a gull shrieked "might have been!" at the small figure huddled below and then he caught a puff of wind and soared higher still. As his black eyes scanned the waves for food, he saw another figure approach the cliff. The seated woman remained still as the fair-haired man crossed the meadow and came up behind her. Sensing someone near, she suddenly turned and rose as the man spoke her name. With a cry, she fell into his arms. They stood thus, silently embracing, until the gull lost interest in them and flew off toward the Inn.